The Desolation of Hunters

JACK FINN

ANUCI PRESS

First paperback edition 2025

Anuci Press edition 2025

www.anuci-press.com

Cover Design by Ruth Anna Evans

ruthannaevans.com (google.com)

ISBN 979-8-9989778-2-4 (paperback)

ISBN 979-8-9989778-3-1(eBook)

The Desolation of Hunters

The Wolves of Kalinin

Book 2

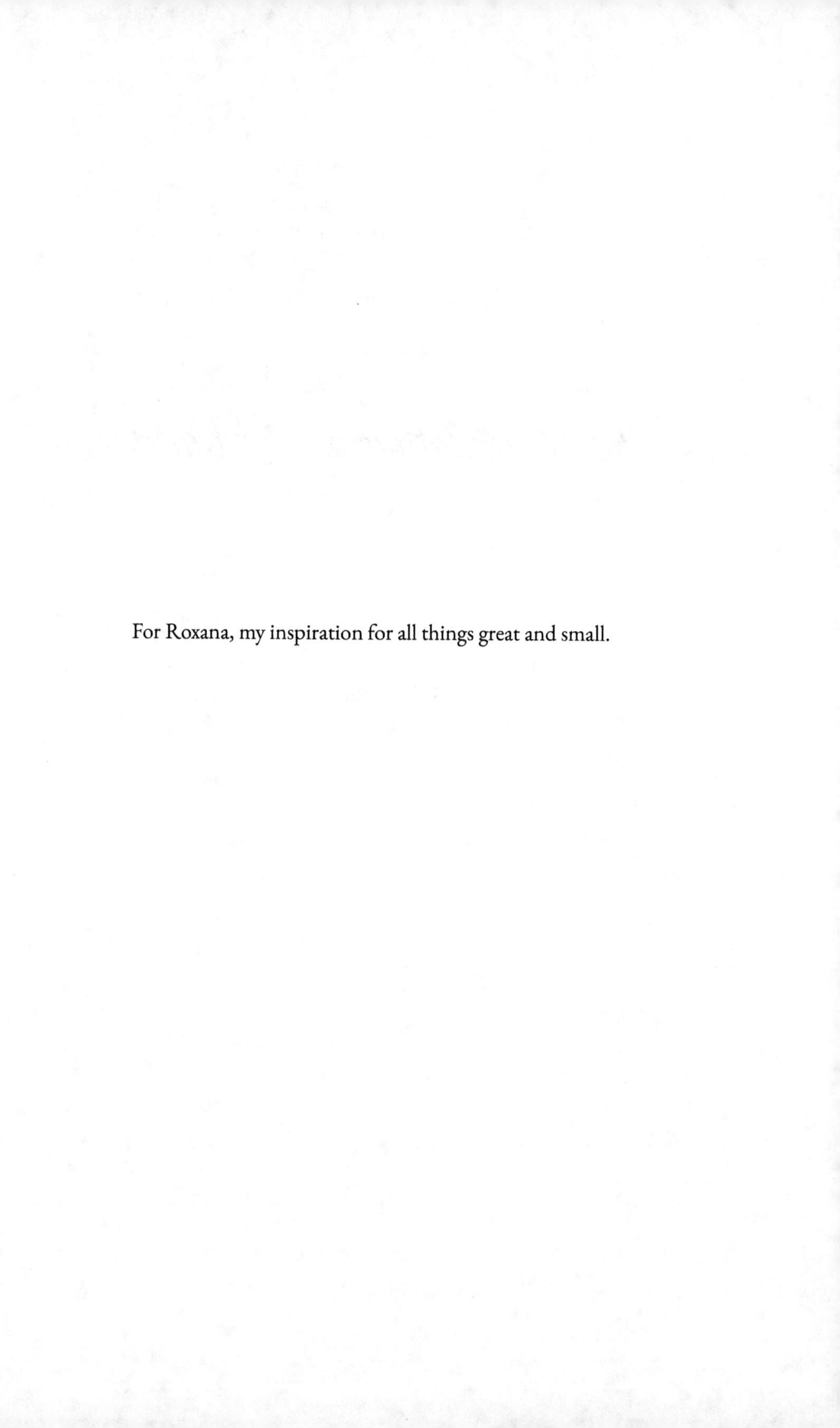

For Roxana, my inspiration for all things great and small.

"All stories are about wolves. All worth repeating, that is. Anything else is sentimental drivel....Think about it. There's escaping from the wolves, fighting the wolves, capturing the wolves, taming the wolves. Being thrown to the wolves, or throwing others to the wolves so the wolves will eat them instead of you. Running with the wolf pack. Turning into a wolf. Best of all, turning into the head wolf. No other decent stories exist."

   • *Margaret Atwood*

Chapter 1

Petro adjusted his black fur hat, a gift from his mother the first time he went to war. The hat bore the red and black eye, a symbol the Cossacks believe warded off bullets from striking the wearer. As his dark eyes scanned the forest, he wondered if the ward protected him from wolves, too.

He stood guard over the camp's three horses as the other men slept. They doubted that even the fools in Obrechen would try to steal a horse from a camp of armed Cossacks, however, Rostov was concerned the horses would make too tempting a target for the wolves plaguing the village.

The snores of his comrades filled the night, sounding like a chorus of malfunctioning crickets. Petro adjusted his rifle to stretch his fingers and work the kinks out of his joints. He felt disquieted tonight.

Damn, Yermak. Petro cursed his fellow Cossack for the half-dozenth time that night.

The Cossacks slept two in a tent; only Rostov had a tent to himself; but he was their leader, so that was to be expected. Petro shared his tent with Yermak, the cook, a Cossack from Belarus who joined with them in Kalinin. The man liked to start the day off by opening a fresh bottle of vodka as he sat up in his bed, claiming it kept illness away. Yermak worked through the bottle during the day and finished it right before bed. Petro was Okay with the man's drinking, which had little impact on his ability to perform his duties during the day. However, he sternly warned Yermak that he needed to put the empty bottle on the floor when he finished it at night. Anything else was bad luck. This trip had already had its share of ill-fortune with that crazy dog taking out Ilia's eye; Petro did not need any more of it.

"If I find that empty bottle in your bed, I'll shove it up your ass," Petro had threatened him.

Yermak would grumble and curse, but every night, the man's arm would reach out from his bed and drop the empty on the floor, except tonight. When Yemelyan roused Petro for his turn on watch, he rubbed the sleep from his eye and caught the glint of firelight from outside, shining off Yermak's empty vodka bottle as it sat on the table beside the snoring man's bed. Petro flew into a rage; grabbing the bottle by the neck, he swung it down onto Yermak's head three times before throwing it to the ground in disgust.

"This is where it belongs," Petro yelled as a dazed Yermak rubbed a spot just over his right eye that was already swelling.

"Fucking idiot," Petro swore as he stormed out of the tent and pushed past a grinning Yemelyan.

Damn, Yermak.

Petro glared at his tent, certain Yermak had returned to blissful slumber. His eyes glanced at the steel cage as the moonlight showed through the thick bars as it sat in the shadows on its wagon bed.

I should lock the fucking idiot in there until we catch the wolf. Hell, I should lock him in there with the wolf. He's a shitty cook anyway, and then we wouldn't need to feed the wolf until we delivered it to the circus man.

Movement in the camp caught Petro's eye, and he watched as a figure groggily slipped from one of the tents and shuffled toward him. The man's head was down, but Petro caught a glimpse of the bandage on the man's head in the moonlight.

"I thought you were supposed to be sleeping," Petro called to Ilia as the man approached.

"Have to piss," Ilia grumbled without looking up. "My eye is killing me. I can't sleep."

"You sure you can find that tiny dick with just one eye?" Petro laughed at his joke.

"Your wife seems to find it just fine," Ilia gave a wry smile, wincing as his cheek movement sent a fresh wave of pain through his injured eye socket. "Ahhh, that fucking dog."

"Relax, Ilia. The scars will give you character," Petro clapped the man on the shoulder, grinning. "You were too pretty before, anyway."

"My mother said I had my grandfather's eyes," Ilia shook his head. "They were the icy gray of frozen water in the Urals."

"Now you have his eye," Petro closed one eye and stared at the man.

Ilia's good eye narrowed in annoyance at the man's lack of sympathy, however, Petro only shrugged in response.

"I'll come with you; I need to take a shit," Petro shouldered his rifle and rubbed his belly. "We should never let Yermak cook; that man's food sits in my stomach like lead."

"I heard you yelling at him tonight," Ilia glanced at Petro with his one good eye, slipping a *papirosa* into his mouth as they walked into the forest. He offered Petro one of the tissue-paper-wrapped tobacco cartridges affixed to a slim, hollow cardboard tube mouthpiece.

"No," Petro shook his head. "They smell like shit and make your dick limp."

Ilia gave another wincing laugh as he struck the wooden matchstick and lit the *papirosa*, "I'd rather smell this than your shit. You stink up the whole forest."

"Blame Yermak," Petro rubbed his belly again, then pointed toward a nearby tree. "I'm shitting here; go piss where you want."

Ilia nodded, heading further upwind in the forest, as Petro unslung his rifle and leaned it against the tree. Dropping his trousers, Petro squatted with his back against the tree and let out a loud burst of flatulence punctuated by a groan.

"Ugh, that fucking cook," Petro shifted his back against the tree as he defecated.

When Petro finished, he looked around and frowned, seeing no leaves within easy reach to wipe his backside.

"Hey Ilia, I need one of your bandages to wipe my ass," Petro heard Ilia walking toward him and smiled at the gest, sliding some leaves closer with his foot.

Something warm and wet landed on the back of Petro's neck, landing heavily and startling him. He jumped as it struck the back of his neck, causing him to lose his balance and land in his waste.

"Goddamn it," Petro leaned over and looked at the feces smeared on the back of his thigh. "Ilia, you fucking idiot."

"God help me, Ilia, if you threw shit at me, I'll make you eat it," He reached up and grabbed the moist wad that had slid down his neck onto his shoulder. "What the fuck?"

Petro ran his thumb over the soft, slick surface of the wad as the iron-tinged smell of blood mixed with the odor of his excrement in his nostrils. He held his hand up into the moonlight to get a better look at the object and recoiled in disgust as the celestial light glinted off the blood-slick eyeball in his hand. Dropping the eye onto the ground, Petro shook his head angrily as he stood and yanked his pants over his soiled legs.

"Think it's funny to toss deer eyes at a man taking a shit, do you?" Petro angrily reached for his rifle and then caught another glimpse of the eyeball in the moonlight.

It looked wrong. Kneeling, Petro picked the eye up again, his brow furrowing in confusion as he looked at it. He rolled it between his fingers, trying to catch the moonlight just the right way. Squinting, Petro studied it closely, then, his eyes opened wide in shock when he realized what he was seeing. The color was all wrong. It was not the dark brown eye of a deer or dog; it was gray—the icy gray of frozen water in the Urals.

Petro reached for his rifle, but a hand covered in thick gray fur grabbed his wrist. A figure, towering in the shadows, stepped from behind the tree and struck him in the mouth before he could sound the alarm. The immense fur-covered fist thrust into his mouth, tearing the corners and ripping his front teeth free of his gums as the figure forced the clenched hand deep into the back of his throat. Gagging as the fist tore his tongue from the lingual frenulum, the thin strip of tissue connecting it to the floor of his mouth, Petro flailed his arms and legs against his attacker. The figure drove its knee into his chest, driving the breath from his lungs through his nose in a stream of blood, air, and mucus.

Petro collapsed back onto the ground, the fist twisting and turning in his mouth, ravaging the soft tissue as it forced its way deeper into his mouth and throat, pinning him down. The figure moved into the moonlight as it advanced, the immense gray head and shoulders of a wolf standing inexplicably upright like a man becoming visible. The beast snarled, its eyes radiating malice as it opened its maw to show teeth tinged with blood. Small curtains of skin and flesh dangled from the pointed canines where it had torn flesh from Ilia's body.

The Cossack reached for the dagger at his waist, but the wolf slammed its knee down onto his chest, snapping bone and cartilage as it drove the dislodged ribs into his lungs. Petro's limbs went limp, and his eyes began to roll back in his head as consciousness began to slip from him. The beast swung its fist, buried deep within Petro's mouth, against the tree. The man's head struck the tree with a thud, and a section of the Cossack's ear and scalp split open and slid away from his skull to reveal a sliver of white bone.

The wolf struck Petro's head repeatedly against the tree, shattering bone, tearing skin, and dislodging the man's eyes. With its chest heaving from exertion, the wolf tore its fist from Petro's mouth, the jaw dislodged and hanging agape. The man's face was in utter ruin. The left side of Petro's head was crushed inward like a damaged melon; white shards of bone dotted the gray matter that hung from the shattered skull. His left eye was dangling by a long muscle tendril from a misshapen socket. Teeth, cracked and broken, lay in the dirt, dark with blood, alongside the torn flap of skin that had been a cheek.

The wolf loomed over the corpse of the man who had slain his best friend, his dog, and then Alexei fed.

✳✳✳

Even though the sun shone brightly in the sky, Oksana felt the day dark and oppressive as she walked the forest path. Losing Alexei broke her heart and then hearing her dreams of living with Galina in Kalinin were over crushed her soul. She would still leave this wretched place and travel with Galina, but the future felt uncertain.

She looked down at the handful of herbs she clutched, a bouquet of mint, sage, and other local plants. It was too late in the season for flowers, and she did not want to visit Alexei's grave empty-handed. However, she figured he would appreciate the earthy-smelling herbs more than flowers anyway. Oksana sighed heavily; so much had changed and been lost so quickly. How many times had she walked this path with Alexei? A hundred times? A thousand? How many laughs had they shared on this path? Now, all she heard was her shoes crunching upon the path; even the birds seemed too sad to sing.

As Oksana stepped into the little clearing where Alexei's family had lived, her breath caught in her chest. Alexei's home was a smoldering ruin of charred wood. Only the old cast iron stove, leaning heavily on the house's scorched bones, stood. The air felt thick with the smell of burned wood, and thin tendrils of smoke continued to rise from the ruins of the house.

She walked a wide circle around the blackened remains, the places where she had sat with Alexei on the porch barely identifiable. Oksana felt the urge to cry welling up deep within her. The destroyed house added finality to Alexei's death; even his home was gone now. She forced the feeling down; Oksana had already cried so much for Alexei, Ivan, and the loss of her future in Kalinin that she had promised herself would not shed any more tears. Then Oksana's eyes fell upon Alexei's grave.

"No," the word was barely audible as it slipped past her lips, and her eyes welled with tears.

A gaping hole lay next to the smaller grave of Ivan, surrounded by unearthed dirt and shreds of fabric. Oksana picked up a scrap of the cloth and rubbed it through her fingers. She felt sure this was the sheet Bogdan had enclosed around Alexei's body. Someone or something had defiled his grave and removed his body. A wild animal or worse?

She would not put it past her uncle to dig up Alexei's body and parade it around the *Kanti Gans*.

It was all too much for her to bear. Oksana let the bouquet fall from her hands and began running. Brambles and branches smacked against her face and limbs, but she did not care; she welcomed the pain as the tears flowed freely down her cheeks.

When she reached the road, Oksana stopped and sank to her knees, panting with exertion. Her face felt red and sore, but her tears were gone. She felt like she had no more tears to cry as she laid back on the ground beside the road. Oksana stared up at the sky. A single white cloud floated slowly across the pale blue canopy. She watched it, eyes fixed on the pure white of the cloud; it looked so soft and welcoming, and she hoped Alexei was in heaven lying on a cloud just like it, free of all the sadness and pain of the world. The sky seemed so vast and the cloud so distant that it made Oksana feel very small and insignificant. To the cloud, she was just a speck upon the earth.

A whimpering sound followed by laughter shattered the calm of the moment. Oksana sat up and cocked her head to listen. Again, the whimpering sound, a high-pitched sound of pain and fear, followed by cruel, mocking laughter. She knew that laugh and recognized the mean-spirited sound of it: Petr Morozov, the Land Captain's son.

Not a boy or girl in Obrechen did not fear running afoul of Petr Morozov; only Alexei had proven to be a match for the boy. At fifteen, Petr was only two years older than Oksana, but he was at least a full head taller with adolescent muscles buoyed by long days of work out in the wheat fields. Petr once tried to force Oksana to kiss him behind the blacksmith's shop, and Alexei laid him out with one punch, giving Petr a black eye that swelled shut for days. But Alexei was gone now; he would not arrive to rescue her again.

Petr was the meanest and cruelest person Oksana had ever encountered in her brief life, and being the focus of his anger was no trivial matter. Only a year ago, Petr had beaten an older boy, Alexandru Popov, so severely that the Popov boy had permanently lost sight in his left eye. All for the infraction of laughing at a joke made about Morozov's red hair.

Oksana slowly got to her feet and crossed the road, skirting along the forest's edge to avoid being seen. She glimpsed something red in the forest, Petr's head moving amongst the trees amidst a chorus of fresh whimpering and laughter. Careful not to give herself away by stepping on any dried branches, Oksana crept closer to where she spotted the boy.

She peered around a large oak tree and spotted Petr and two older boys, Vadim Shishimarin and Mikhail Khodaryonok. Petr clutched a small gray puppy by the scruff of its neck. The puppy whimpered as it wriggled in Petr's grip, its small legs flailing as it sought purchase. Oksana was taken by how much the puppy looked like Ivan when she had found him years ago and wondered if the dog could be a distant relative. The puppy could be the offspring of one of Ivan's siblings.

As Oksana watched from behind the tree, a cold feeling clutched her stomach. She watched Petr place the puppy on a low-hanging branch; the poor animal looked terrified and whimpered as it stood on uncertain legs. To Oksana's horror, Petr and the others began throwing rocks and sticks at the puppy. It whined and flinched as rocks sailed over its head and bounced off the branch, inches below its paws, until one well-placed stone sent the terrified puppy tumbling to the ground. The boys laughed uproariously as the hapless puppy seemed to try to run in the air before hitting the ground with a loud yelp.

Oksana darted from her hiding place behind the tree and ran toward the boys, their backs to her as they laughed. She dipped her head and drove her shoulder into Vadim Shishimarin's back. The boy cried out in surprise and tumbled forward into Petr, sending the larger boy tumbling to the ground.

"What the fuck?" Petr shouted and punched Vadim hard in the ear as they lay in a tangle on the ground.

"Hey!" Mikhail Khodaryonok shouted as Oksana scooped up the puppy and ran for the village. "Nostrova took the dog!"

Oksana clutched the puppy to her chest as the older boys gave furious chase, but she was much faster. She quickly distanced herself from her pursuers as the smoke from Obrechen's wood burning stoves poked above the treetops before her.

When Oksana reached the church barn and collapsed behind the hay bales, she was nearly breathless. She desperately tried to get her breathing under control before Petr and the other boys heard her panting. Father Grigori's gray-brown mule stared at them dispassionately as it chewed a mouthful of hay. She tried to make herself as small as possible as she hid behind the hay bale, the whimpering gray puppy held close against her chest. Oksana could hear the boys searching for her outside the church stable.

"Where are you hiding, Oksana Nostrova?" called Petr Morozov.

"Are you hiding in here, little thief?" Mikhail Khodaryonok called as he kicked a wooden bucket at the entrance to the barn, sending it tumbling.

The noise of the heavy wooden bucket banging about spooked the terrified puppy. It squirmed desperately in Oksana's arms and let out a loud whimper.

"She's in here!" Mikhail yelled, and Oksana felt her heart thudding in her chest as she heard the other two boys come rushing into the barn.

Like a cornered animal, Oksana's eyes darted around, looking for a way to escape. Her eyes settled on the small window behind the mule. She was sure she could reach it, but she would have to pull herself up to get through. Hoping the donkey would mask her flight, Oksana sprinted for the window.

"There she is!" Vadim Shishimarin pointed at the small figure darting across the barn.

"Get her!" Petr commanded.

Oksana's feet carried her as fast as she could past the mule and up towards the window opening, the puppy howling in terror the whole way. Her left hand caught the lip of the window, and she had to jump slightly to get her right hand, the one holding the squealing pup, up on the window. Needing both hands to pull herself up, she dangled the puppy out the window and let him drop. She winced as she heard the pup yelp as it landed. With free hands, she pulled herself up and halfway out the window. Oksana smiled as she saw the puppy darting away toward the woods and safety. She was not as fortunate.

Rough hands grabbed her about the waist and legs as blows rained down on her back. Oksana cried in pain as they pulled her back through the window and threw her onto the floor. She cried out as the older boys shouted insults and kicked her. Not hard kicks meant to injure; they were taunting kicks of cats toying with a trapped mouse. Kicks that moved her back and forth on the dirt floor. Kicks that promised violence to come once the tormentors tired of the game. Kicks that would become ferocious and bone breaking once they grew bored of the mouse's terror and would be satiated only by inflicting pain.

Vadim grabbed her by the hair, twisting it in his fist as he dragged Oksana across the floor and pushed her face into a pile of mule manure. The scent of dung filled her nostrils as the older boy pressed her face hard before lifting her head and repeatedly slamming it down into the animal's waste.

"What is going on here?!" Shouted a man's voice.

All three boys quickly moved away from the gasping girl. Oksana peered her manure-smeared face up at the man, a dark-haired man with a short, cropped beard dressed in an orthodox priest's long black frock—Father Grigori.

"What is the meaning of this?" Father Grigori looked sternly at the three older boys before turning a disgusted gaze upon himself. "Your face is covered with filth, Oksana Nostrova."

"Father Grigori, Oksana Nostrova is a thief!" Petr stepped forward and pointed an incriminating finger at Oksana. "She stole the puppy my father gave me."

"It's true, Father," agreed the ruddy-faced Vadim.

Father Grigori raised a hand to silence the boys and looked down at Oksana as she tried to wipe the manure from her face.

"Is this true, Oksana? Did you steal the puppy?" Father Grigori's voice was stern, and his tone bore no sympathy.

"I... I..." Oksana's mind raced with where to start.

"Does the Devil have your tongue, girl? Answer me!" the priest shouted and loomed over her, a tower of menace.

"I only took it because..." started Oksana.

"There is no excuse for thievery, Oksana Nostrova!" growled Grigori. "It is a sin against God!"

Oksana could see the smug grins on Petr's and the other boys' faces as Father Grigori reached down, grabbed Oksana roughly by the collar of her homespun shirt, and pulled her to her feet.

"I am not surprised that you are ignorant of God's laws," Grigori shook his head. "Your family did not attend church; they kept to their peasant ways, and God punished them. But you must ask God for his forgiveness."

Father Grigori stared down at her, his left hand gripping Oksana so hard she visibly winced. Without warning, the priest swung his free hand and slapped Oksana. She let out a cry that was a mixture of pain and surprise as her head jerked sideways at the blow. When Oksana faced the priest again, her cheek quickly reddened, her eyes watering as she fought back the tears.

"You will come to the church and beg forgiveness for your sins," said the priest, dragging Oksana out of the barn.

"Thank you for saving us from this sinner!" Petr's voice filled with mean-spirited mirth, and Oksana could hear the three boys snickering as the priest led her to the old wooden church.

***

Kirill Romanov stepped off the train onto the grassy field and looked around with utter dismay and disappointment at the rolling hills. His blue eyes scanned the small camp of men, tents, and horses in the clearing. The men had taken notice of the halted train and were watching the small group exiting with mild interest.

"This can't be right; where's Obrechen?" Kirill turned to Volkov, who was disembarking with Batu and Sergeant Razin close behind. "There's nothing here but some gypsy camp."

"The village is a short ride west," Volkov answered as he eyed the men in the camp, noting they were all armed. "That's no, gypsy camp. Batu, what do you make of that?"

"Whoever they are won't trouble us," Batu shrugged. "I am going to assist Herzen and Tyutchev with the horses. Arkady, the key?"

"I'll be along in a moment," Volkov said, slipping the key from his pocket and handing it to Batu.

"Maybe they are circus performers; look, they have some kind of cage," Kirill pointed to a steel animal cage on a wagon set back among the tents.

"They're Cossacks," Sergeant Razin observed. "I can tell by their clothing; see the *chokhas*."

"Why would they be here?" Kirill asked the sergeant, but the man just shrugged.

"It looks like we're about to find out," Volkov said as a stocky bald man approached from the camp.

As he neared, the man stroked his short, pointed beard thoughtfully and visibly assessed Kirill and the others. His faded green Imperial Army coat fluttered open in the breeze, revealing a pistol holstered on one hip and what appeared to be a hammer on the other.

"I don't like this," Sergeant Razin unslung his rifle and whistled to Herzen and Tyutchev, waving for the men to halt unloading the horses and join him.

"Easy now," Volkov looked sidelong at Razin and then back to the man. He noted that back in the camp, four Cossacks watched stoically, their rifles in their hands.

The man waved in greeting; Kirill waved back and then glanced back at Razin, "A friend of yours, Sergeant Razin?"

"No, this one is not a Cossack," Razin shook his head and narrowed his eyes at the approaching man. Herzen and Tyutchev, their young faces red from running, gripped their rifles as they joined him. "Stand ready, men."

"What brings such a serious-looking group of passengers to our quiet meadow?" the man called to them as he approached.

"We're here to hunt," Volkov's voice was gruff and impatient. He wanted the man to understand they were not interested in idol chit-chat.

"Ah, you've come for the wolf?" the man stopped a few feet before them. "I'm afraid to disappoint you, but I am already here for the wolf."

"And who, may I ask, the fuck are you?" Volkov folded his arms across his chest. They stood on higher ground than the man, allowing Volkov to look down at him.

"I am Valerian Rostov," the man dipped his head in greeting. "I am the personal representative of Albert Salamonsky. He has commissioned me to capture the Beast of Obrechen and frankly, I intend to do just that."

"Is that so?" Volkov narrowed his eyes at the man.

"Is that the reason for the cage?" Kirill gestured toward the camp.

"Indeed," Rostov nodded.

"Excuse me, Sir," the conductor called from the steps of the train car. "If you could finish disembarking your horses, we have a schedule to keep."

Sergeant Razin motioned toward Tyutchev with his head, and the young soldier turned back toward the train.

"Get back on the train," Tyutchev prodded at the man with the barrel of his rifle. "We're on Imperial business, and we'll finish when we finish."

The conductor stumbled back aghast and scrambled into the train car as a grinning Tyutchev turned back to see an approving nod from Sergeant Razin.

"Imperial business?" Rostov raised an eyebrow.

"I am Kirill Vladimirovich Romanov, second cousin to the Grand Duke," Kirill accentuated his speech in the cultured manner of the aristocracy. "My companion is Arkady Volkov, the Tsar's Imperial Huntsman."

Volkov grimaced at Kirill's introduction.

"Your Highness," Rostov bowed his head in deference to Kirill, however, the man's mocking tone bespoke of someone familiar with dealing with the many distant and irrelevant members of the Romanov imperial dynasty.

"Rostov, this hunt is of a personal interest," Kirill began, but Rostov cut him off.

"It's personal to me as well," Rostov sneered as he tapped his hand against his chest. "The beast killed two of my best men."

"I don't give a fuck about you or your men," Volkov took a step toward Rostov. "The wolf is mine. It is not a matter for debate; it is an imperial decree."

"Is that so?" Rostov's eyes flared. "Well then, you better watch yourself in the woods, huntsman; I would hate for one of my men to mistake you for a wolf."

"Just be sure you don't find yourself as prey," Volkov said, his eyes narrowing and his voice filling with menace.

"As delightful as this chat has been, you two will have to sword fight with your pricks at another time. I believe the horses are ready," Kirill said, stepping between the two men and gesturing toward the approaching horses.

Batu rode up on Sar, gripping the tethered reigns of Nar and the other horses. The short, black warhorse snorted as it approached, drawing Rostov's attention.

"You're hunting this wolf with a Chinaman and some fat ponies?" Rostov spoke loud enough for his men in the camp to hear and punctuated the words with a mocking laugh.

Volkov's temper flared, and the huntsman lunged past Kirill, slipping free a small knife secreted in his belt. As his pulse thundered in his ears, Volkov heard Batu yell for him to stop, but the voice sounded distant. Rostov's eyes opened wide in surprise as the smile slipped from his face. Kirill's hands reached for the knife as Batu surged forward with the horses to separate the two men. Volkov sliced the tip of the knife across Rostov's cheek, opening a thin half-moon-shaped cut under his eye.

Hooves beating against the ground filled the air as Batu drove the horses between the two combatants. Rostov stumbled backward, one hand reaching for his pistol as the other hand pressed against the wounded cheek. A cry rang out in the camp as the Cossacks shouldered their rifles, and Herzen and Tyutchev dropped to a knee and aimed theirs. Sergeant Razin leaped forward, shielding Kirill with his body as he pointed his rifle at Rostov. A cruel smile crossed Rostov's lips, and the man laughed.

"It's Okay, boys," Rostov raised his bloody hand and waved to his men. Blood dripped from his wound like the red curtain of a play unfurling onstage. "Our friend was just overcompensating for the inadequate size of his... pony."

"Arkady, we are here for the wolf," Batu leaned down in his saddle and spoke quietly to Volkov.

Volkov looked from the smirking Rostov to the serene almond-shaped eyes of Batu and felt the tension ease from his body. He nodded to the tracker and accepted Nar's reigns.

Rostov continued his mocking laughter as he walked back to his camp and as they mounted their horses.

"Welcome to Obrechen and happy hunting," Rostov called as he walked away.

"I already hate this fucking place," Razin grumbled as he climbed atop his horse.

***

Pavel guided his horse through the crowd of onlookers crowded around the front of the *Kanti Gans*. Villagers reluctantly made way for the horse and rider as the mare's chest pushed against their backs, grumbling and casting angry glances at Pavel.

"Our brave gendarme, always late to the action," Yulia shouted, her ample bosom barely contained by her dark dress as she leaned against the bar's open door.

As several villagers snickered, Pavel restrained himself from acknowledging her taunt with a sharp retort. The crowd centered around the watering trough, where something dark bobbed and floated in the murky water. A grim-faced Igor Balkov stood beside the trough and looked at Pavel as he approached; the man appeared utterly bereft of his usual mockery.

"What are you going to do about this?" Balkov pointed toward the trough.

Pavel looked toward the trough, trying to discern what was in the water when one of the villagers poked at the water with a stick. The dark mass bobbed in the water and turned to reveal Gleb Andreev's bloated face. One of Andreev's eyes bobbed alongside the head, attached to the socket by a short length of muscle; his other eye was so bloodshot you could see no white. Andreev's mouth was agape in a silent scream as the severed head rotated in the water and disappeared from view.

"Who is responsible for this?" Pavel grimaced and looked away from the grotesque sight. "Where is the rest of his body?"

"I don't know," Balkov shrugged and looked down into the water, dark amber from Andreev's blood. "The Chernyshevskys are missing, too. No one has seen them for days."

"The neck's torn," the villager with the stick, an old man with a greasy, white beard, spoke in a low voice.

"What's that?" Pavel eyed the old man. "Speak up."

"Andreev's neck is torn, not cut," the man gestured toward the bobbing head with the stick.

"So what?" Pavel hated dealing with these ignorant villagers, and he let annoyance drip from his words.

"He means Gleb had his head torn off, not cut off," Balkov looked at Pavel with eyes filled with scorn.

Pavel shook his head in irritation; none of this made sense. "Who is capable of doing a thing like that?"

"No one," Balkov shook his head. "Something took Gleb's head off, not someone."

Pavel could see the fear in the villagers' eyes as they spoke in hushed tones. He heard the words "wolf" and "Vseslav" mentioned several times and more than one made the sign of the cross.

"Nonsense," Pavel guided his horse backward, away from the press of villagers. "You're saying some animal decapitated Andreev and left his head in the trough? Ridiculous, we need to search the area for his body."

"We're not going in those woods with that wolf out there," one of the villagers shouted to a chorus of agreement.

"You're the gendarme; you find his body," shouted another to even louder agreement.

"Looks like something is chasing the Englishman," Yulia called out and pointed down the road.

Pavel turned in his saddle to see McMurrough galloping down the road into town. Despite the barmaid's claim, nothing pursued the rider; however, the man did appear to be riding urgently. McMurrough spotted the crowd and guided his horse in their direction. Several villagers had to scamper out of his way to avoid getting trampled as he reined his horse to a halt before the crowd. Pavel could see McMurrough's horse was panting heavily, its nostrils flaring, as if they had ridden very quickly for a long distance.

"Where's the Land Captain?" McMurrough called to Balkov.

"He's in the church," Balkov replied, pointing toward the church in the center of town.

"McMurrough, what is it?" Pavel edged his horse forward.

"I just came from Galina Sekova's cottage. It's a charnel house. It looks like the wolf killed Sekova, Olga Putina, and her brothers." McMurrough shook his head. "It's a fucking mess."

A ripple of shock and fear spread through the crowd as word of the deaths spread among the villagers. Knots of people began to break off, wives pulling at their husband's arms, urging them toward their homes while there was still the safety of numbers. Pavel suspected people would begin barricading themselves in their homes after this until the threat of the wolf passed. By nightfall, Obrechen would be a ghost town, with its doors barred and windows shuttered. Villagers would dip into their winter food stores instead of venturing out to the market or to hunt. Morozov would not be pleased if life in Obrechen shut down as the villagers huddled in their homes in fear. No workers in the fields or merchants in the markets meant no money in Morozov's purse; that would drop Pavel quickly out of the Land Captain's favor.

Pavel knew the wolf must die, and Obrechen expediently returned to normal, or he would see his upturn in fortunes quickly upended.

McMurrough griped his reins and urged his horse back into a trot toward the church. "I need to tell Morozov."

"I'll come with you," Pavel followed after McMurrough.

***

Despite the chill in the air, sweat ran from Oksana's dark brown hair down the nape of her neck to make her back feel wet and clammy. Her body hurt in at least a dozen places from the beating she had received, but nothing seemed broken. She knelt before the church's large wooden cross fashioned in the Russian Orthodox style of three horizontal crossbeams with the lowest one slanted downwards.

The church was constructed of rough-hewn logs and topped by an aspen-shingled roof that bore the wood-framed onion-shaped dome. Inside was the space where the villagers of Obrechen would come to stand, pray, and worship. Three evenly spaced beeswax candles burned on each wall, illuminating the dark church and casting ominous shadows on the faces of the Russian saints hand-painted on the wall. The only other illumination came from a small seam between two logs along the bottom of one wall. The seam let a narrow sheath of light break through the gloom of the church to light a small spot on the floor.

For those seeking penance, Father Grigori had a wooden beam affixed to the floor where one would place their knees when they knelt, seeking forgiveness for their sins. It made the act extremely uncomfortable, to which Father Grigori always remarked that the suffering was but a mere fraction of what Christ Jesus had suffered upon the cross to wash them of their sins. That is where Oksana knelt now, head bowed, fingers interlaced in prayer. The priest instructed her to stay that way until he returned and released her from her act of contrition, then departed through the door leading to his private quarters.

Father Grigori should have listened to me. Oksana quietly shifted her knees to alleviate the wooden beam's pain, if only for a moment.

She knew Grigori did not need to listen; he knew what had happened. Half of the people in Obrechen worked in the grain fields of the Morozovs or forested in their woods. Even the trees that made this church were a gift from Petr's father, Andrei. Nobody would ever speak against the Morozovs. Her father used to say, "The Tsar told us we're all free, but the Morozovs showed us we're all still serfs."

A look of sadness came over Oksana's face at the thought of her parents. Her father had been a great bear of a man and always had a wide grin on his thick bearded face. He possessed a booming laugh and would put thick hands on his belly and laugh at the easiest provocation. Oksana's mother had been a beautiful woman, and Oksana always loved it when Alexei would say how much of her mother's features were in his friend's face. The small woman had fallen gravely ill one winter, and Oksana suspected that when she succumbed to the sickness, Oksana's father had died as much from a broken heart as from his illness.

Light streamed into the dimly lit church as the front door opened, and Oksana heard heavy footfalls enter. She turned her head just enough to see the silhouette of a large man standing in the doorway.

"Priest!" bellowed the man in a deep voice, a voice Oksana knew well—Andrei Morozov.

The door to the private chamber opened, and an angry-looking Father Grigori stormed in, eyes ablaze; his black frock flapped as he stalked past Oksana, and she caught the man's expression changing from agitation to a feigned smile.

"Andrei, so good to see you," the village priest rushed to meet the newcomer.

"It is always good to be in the house of the Lord," Morozov said, closing the door and clapping his hands together.

"How can I help you today?" Father Grigori failed to keep the eagerness from his voice.

"I wanted to see if you obtained a bottle of that perfume that my wife desired—the one that smells of lavender and lilac," the Land Captain said, giving Grigori a leering smile. "I know she will be very appreciative that I acquired some. She thinks it makes her smell like the Tsarina."

"Yes, of course, Andrei. The merchant appreciated my blessing his wares so thoroughly that he gifted me a bottle this morning," Grigori dipped his head in acknowledgment. "Please, come into my chambers."

Oksana saw the two men walking toward Father Grigori's chamber in her periphery. Andrei Morozov was a large man, taller and broader than Father Grigori, with a long red-brown beard. His wide midsection bespoke him to be a man of means in the small village, the rare man with more than enough food to get by. Before Tsar Alexander II freed the serfs from servitude to landowners, the Morozovs owned the most sizeable swath of farmland and forest north of Kalinin. The Tsar's reforms had seen portions of that land given to the peasantry, but Morozov's father and grandfather took advantage of poor crop yields and rough winters to repurchase much of that land back from the peasants. They allowed the peasant farmers to work the land still and keep some of what they grew for themselves while giving a larger share to the Morozovs. The villagers of Obrechen had become serfs once again in all but name. Some peasants, like Oksana's parents, had held on to their lands, but there were fewer every year.

Morozov stopped and turned toward the kneeling girl; how he looked at her made her jaw tighten.

"Father Grigori, what do we have here?" He gestured towards Oksana with a hand adorned with a thick gold ring.

"A sinner is asking God's forgiveness," Grigori looked at Oksana and did not attempt to hide his disapproval.

"You are Elena Nostrova's daughter, yes?" Morozov studied Oksana's face.

"Yes." Her voice was quiet in the empty church.

"Elena was a beautiful woman, taken from us too soon." He looked her up and down appraisingly. "What manner of sin have you committed?"

The way Morozov looked at her gave Oksana the impression that his mind was imagining all kinds of sins she may have committed.

"She lied before God." Grigori's face showed evident distaste. "In a matter concerning your son, in fact."

"My son! It is a wonder you do not have that boy kneeling alongside her," laughed Morozov before turning back to Oksana. "You should come by the house, girl; I can find work for you for good wages, especially with Galina Sekova leaving Obrechen soon. I will speak to your uncle about this. Though I judge from your bruises that you are as pigheaded as your father was and learn your lessons the hard way."

Oksana just looked down, not wanting to meet his gaze; a wave of self-consciousness washed over her at the thought of her bruised, manure-streaked face.

Father Grigori smiled cruelly at Morozov's jest, and the two turned to head into the personal chambers when a sharp knock came on the church door. The two men looked at each other, and Grigori shrugged as something wooden knocking against the door rang out again.

"Andrei, one moment while I send them away." Grigori started toward the door.

Before Grigori could reach the door, it flew open wide, filling the candlelit room with bright sunlight. Oksana heard several pairs of feet enter the church and saw Morozov's eyes open wide in surprise. Turning, Oksana caught sight of six men standing in the church doorway.

Three of the men were Russian soldiers dressed in long green coats, with rifles slung over their shoulders. Two soldiers were young, barely out of their teens, clean-shaven, and wiry. They reminded Oksana of what Alexei would have looked like if he had survived his teenage years. The third soldier was broad-shouldered and thick-chested with a full dark beard and the stern gaze of a seasoned veteran. He stood on the opposite side of the open door from the younger ones.

A young blonde-haired, blue-eyed man, tall, clean-shaven and dressed in the finery of the Russian aristocracy, stood between the soldiers looking over the inside of the rustic church with the look of a man appraising a lame horse. Alongside him stood a man dressed in black boots and trousers with a leather coat lined with a tiger's orange and black striped fur. Despite the finery of the man's clothes, he had a rough look about his tanned face. The man had dark, piercing eyes that quickly studied the small church.

However, the fifth man drew Oksana's attention. He was a short, thickly built man with Asiatic eyes and a long, thin beard like that of the men of the Mongolian steppe. He wore a long, dark coat that crossed in front to attach at the side and shoulder with white buttons made from polished animal bone. Two large knives sat in leather sheaths at his waist, and a small hunting bow lay across his back.

"Who is in charge here?" the blonde man looked around the sparse church.

"I am Father Grigori; this is my church." Grigori said as he made an awkward bow.

"No priest, who is in charge of this village?" the man in the leather coat spoke with more than a hint of impatience.

Father Grigori did not answer the man and looked awkwardly at Morozov, who grimaced slightly before fixing a smile and stepping forward.

"Gentlemen, I am Andrei Morozov, the Land Captain, and I speak for Obrechen." He straightened his back to rise to his full height. "How may I help you?"

"There is a matter of a hunter killed in these parts," the blonde man began.

The man in the leather coat pointed at Oksana, "Send her away."

"Yes. Yes, of course," Father Grigori quickly turned to Oksana. "Child, get yourself home."

Oksana quickly rose to her feet, wincing from knees bruised by the wooden beam, and hurried past Father Grigori and between the men in the doorway. In her haste, Oksana ran straight into the Mongolian. The man was as solid as a tree trunk, and Oksana gave a small shout of surprise at the sudden impact. She looked at the man to apologize, but the Mongolian stared down at her with cold, dark eyes. Oksana hurried out as one of the soldiers closed the door behind her.

Oksana, intrigued about the newcomers, searched the side of the church for the seam between the logs. She ran her fingers along where the logs met, trying to find the gap.

Here it is. Oksana smiled as her fingers found the seam and leaned down, pressing her ear against the small opening. She looked around nervously for any villager that should see her. The wood was coarse and dry against her ear and chafed her cheek, but she could hear the conversation inside.

***

"I am Kirill Vladimirovich Romanov, second cousin to the Grand Duke," Kirill recited his well-rehearsed greeting. "My companion is Arkady Volkov, the Tsar's Imperial Huntsman."

Morozov's face registered surprise, but he quickly recovered and dipped his head in greeting, "I am humbled at such auspicious guests; welcome to Obrechen."

Volkov knew men like Morozov; his family did as they pleased in their little villages and answered to no higher authority. He suspected the man relished the arrival of such well-connected visitors to Obrechen and would make it widely known that he associated with Romanovs and members of the Tsar's court.

"Perhaps you could be of some assistance to us," Kirill gave the man his most disarming smile.

"Well, of course," Morozov's smile widened. "I am at your service, Kirill Romanov."

"Excellent! A wolf hunter was killed not far from here," Kirill glanced at Volkov as he spoke.

"Yes, we have had some issues with a wolf lately and lost several village hunters to the beast. However, I assume you are referring to Dimitri Volkov; some woodsmen found his body," Morozov turned toward Volkov. "Was he a relative of yours?"

"Yes, he was my brother," Volkov's voice was cold and emotionless.

"I am sorry for your loss. I performed the last rites myself," Father Grigori made the sign of the cross. "His wounds were quite grievous."

"Who found the hunter's body?" Volkov asked.

"Two woodsmen, brothers." Morozov hooked his thumbs into his belt and shook his head. "No one has seen them for several days. We fear they may have become the beast's latest victims."

"I understand a gendarme examined the body as well?" Volkov narrowed his eyes, studying Morozov.

"That would be Pavel Verenich," Father Grigori nodded. "He instructed the Chernyshevsky brothers to bring me your brother's body for consecration and burial."

"I would like to speak with this Pavel Verenich," the tone of Volkov's voice made it clear that it was a demand, not a request. He noticed his hand absently running over the pocket where he carried the note recovered from his brother's body, the paper making a slight crinkling noise, and he moved his hand back to his side.

"Yes. Yes, of course," Morozov nodded.

The doors of the church flew upon, flooding the interior with daylight. Morozov and Father Grigori reflexively brought their hands up to shield their eyes from the unexpected sunlight, but it was the commotion that accompanied the daylight that drew Kirill and Volkov's attention. Two men had thrown open the doors and strolled in, one calling for the Land Captain, before Sergeant Razin and his men intercepted them.

One of the men, in the light blue uniform of a gendarme, lay sprawled on the floor with Sergeant Razin's knee pressed against the back of his neck. Razin held a small single-shot Derringer, the barrel pushed against the base of the gendarme's skull. The pistol looked tiny in Razin's beefy hand, with only the short barrel and a hint of its brass frame visible.

The gendarme's companion, a blonde man finely dressed in a military-styled red coat adorned with a gold-colored braid that circled his shoulder, stood with his hands held away from the sword and pistol he wore on his belt. Batu stood beside the man; his outstretched arm held a blade pressed against the man's throat.

"My, what a small gun you have there," the man said, moving only his eyes to look down at Razin, a faint smile on his face.

"It was a gift from my mother," Razin growled, not taking his eyes from the gendarme.

The blonde man looked at Kirill and cocked a questioning eyebrow. Kirill shrugged, "Cossacks."

"Can we all put our toys away for a moment?" the blonde man glanced from Kirill to Batu, carefully not to do anything that would result in the blade pressing deeper into his neck.

"Gentleman, please. This is the house of the Lord," Father Grigori said, raising his hands to implore the men to refrain from further violence.

"Do you know these men?" Volkov turned to Morozov.

The Land Captain smiled and pointed to the gendarme, "That would be Pavel Verenich; the other man is McMurrough, Count Guriev's man."

Sergeant Razin looked to Kirill, who nodded, "Let him up."

Batu lowered his knife, and McMurrough released an overly dramatic sigh of relief as Sergeant Razin helped Pavel to his feet. The gendarme was visibly displeased with his treatment but said nothing.

"Do I know you? You look very familiar," McMurrough studied Kirill and extended his hand in greeting.

"I am Kirill Vladimirovich Romanov, second cousin to the Grand Duke," Kirill said as he shook the man's hand.

McMurrough beamed with recognition and pointed at Kirill. "The Imperial luncheon for the Feast of the Epiphany at the Winter Palace. You danced the night away with Margaret Eager."

"You have quite the memory," Kirill laughed and nodded.

"I will never forget the man who kept Margaret Eager away from the rest of us for a whole evening," McMurrough bowed slightly.

"Verenich," Volkov slipped the note from his pocket and held it up. "You found this note on my brother's body?"

Pavel was noticeably surprised to see the note but managed a slight nod, "I did. I found it thrust between his lips."

"Between his lips?" it was Volkov's turn to be surprised. "I was led to believe a wolf killed my brother."

"A wolf ravaged the body. That much is clear," Pavel nodded. "No man could tear a body up like that. However, when I discovered the note in his mouth, I raised the concern with my superiors in Kalinin that anarchists may have killed your brother and his body attacked by wolves afterward."

"Is there trouble with anarchists in Obrechen?" Kirill asked Morozov.

The Land Captain shook his head, "No, we have not had trouble of any sort except the wolf."

"A wolf could have caught him unawares and gotten the better of him," Volkov looked at the folded-up note. "My brother was cunning; Dimitri would have slipped the note into his mouth to ensure they knew the body was his. He knew I would avenge him upon the beast."

The room fell silent as if they were standing vigil for a man few knew and even fewer liked. Pavel looked sour as he realized his grand investigation had been thwarted; in the end, they still believed it had been the wolf.

"Pavel Verenich, thank you for getting this note to me," Volkov slipped the note back into his pocket. "Now, I have a wolf to kill."

"The wolf has killed again," McMurrough said, turning to Morozov. "That's why I was looking for the Land Captain. I went to Galina Sekova's cottage. The wolf has killed Sekova, Olga Putina, and her brothers. Blood was everywhere; it was a slaughterhouse."

"The wolf has also killed Gleb Andreev," added a man in village attire as he walked up the church steps. He jerked his thumb to gesture back over his shoulder. "His head is bobbing in the trough at the *Kanti Gans* like a spring gosling."

"This is Igor Balkov, my foreman," Morozov looked from Kirill to Volkov. "He got the job when the wolf killed my previous foreman and a half-dozen other hunters."

"Wolf. Just one?" Kirill looked around the room and raised his finger. "You all believe just one wolf is responsible for all of these killings? Not a pack of wolves?"

"How do you even know it was a wolf that was responsible? Has anyone seen this wolf?" Razin added. "Maybe it's a rogue bear."

"I've been hunting these woods my whole life," Balkov spoke slowly, his face an emotionless mask as he rubbed the side of his crooked nose. "The only creature I have ever seen kill with malice like that was a wolf."

"With malice?" Volkov eyed the man. "What do you mean?"

"Most beasts will eat you, or at least some of you," Balkov shook his head at the memory. "These men's bodies were torn to pieces and shredded as someone would do to an angry note. But it ate nothing. They were all there, just a million pieces of them."

Pavel opened his mouth to say something, but Morozov caught his eye and gave him a slight shake of the head, and the gendarme fell silent. Sergeant Razin noticed their wordless exchange and eyed both men suspiciously.

"What was that?" Razin asked, his gaze bouncing between Pavel and Morozov.

"What's that, Sergeant Razin?" Kirill asked.

"This one was going to speak," Razin pointed from Pavel to Morozov. "Then this one shook his head."

"He's right, Sir; I saw it too. He nodded," added Herzen, nervously adjusting the rifle slung over his shoulder.

"You. Speak," Volkov pointed at Pavel, his tone commanding.

Pavel sighed and looked toward Volkov without meeting his gaze, "One of the hunters, a man named Sleptsov, had an irregularity on his body."

"An irregularity?" Kirill asked.

"What manner of irregularity?" Batu's voice was quiet and steady as he intently eyed Pavel.

"He was eviscerated and then garroted by a wire snare looped around his neck," Pavel made a slicing movement across his neck. "Like the note in Dimitri Volkov's mouth, it indicated the wolf had a human accomplice."

"The wolf... the wolf had a human accomplice?" Kirill snorted, looking more perplexed by Obrechen by the moment, "This is all too much; I need a drink."

"Gentleman, I would like to extend to you the hospitality of my estate," Morozov stepped forward and opened his arms in welcome. I believe you will find my guest quarters more agreeable than any accommodations in Obrechen."

"Do you have wine?" Kirill asked, the cheer returning to his voice.

"I have plenty of wine," Morozov smiled and bowed slightly, delighted at the prospect of having a Romanov beneath his roof.

"Volkov, it's been a long couple of days," Kirill looked over to Volkov. "Let's get some food and rest. We can figure this out tomorrow with fresh minds."

Volkov, eager to begin hunting the beast, was about to voice his disapproval, but Batu spoke up.

"I think that is an excellent idea," Batu looked to Volkov and slightly nodded. "We need a better understanding of this beast. I want to go with the gendarme and the gentleman to examine the site of the latest attack."

Pavel looked at the tracker and nodded in agreement. However, McMurrough protested, "I need to return to Count Guriev and report what has happened; he will be very interested in learning of Sekova's death."

Volkov looked at the floor for a long moment, remembering his brother's gregarious laugh as they hunted together as children. He turned toward the priest, "What did you do with my brother's body?"

"We buried him in the church graveyard," Father Grigori answered solemnly. "I gave him a Christian burial."

Volkov nodded, then looked to Batu. "Go with the gendarme and see if you can pick up a track on this wolf, find its den. I will pay respects to my brother and then join the others at the Land Captain's manor. I trust your estate is easy to locate?"

"Of course," Morozov beamed. "There is no place like it in Obrechen."

Chapter 2

I went to Galina Sekova's cottage. The wolf has killed Sekova, Olga Putina, and her brothers. Blood was everywhere; it was a slaughterhouse.

Oksana staggered back from the crack in the wall; her chest felt so tight she could not breathe. The world seemed to spin, and she reached a hand out to brace herself against the church.

Galina dead. The thought was dizzying. And what of Bogdan? There was no mention of the forester. He would not have abandoned Galina in the face of peril. Could he have been one of the others, mistaken for one of Olga's brothers? What was Olga Putina doing at Galina's? The woman hated Galina.

Oksana began to stumble away from the church and then run. She ran as fast as her legs would take her toward the only place she could think of in Obrechen. The village passed by as a blur before her tear-filled eyes. She was only vaguely aware of the people and homes she passed, her mind an abyss of despair. As the crushing darkness closed about her thoughts, her body guided her onward like a homing pigeon returning to its roost.

Alexei was gone. Galina was dead.

She collapsed onto the ground beside the porch, only vaguely aware of the voices around her. The tears flowed unbidden, and a howl of despair escaped her lips as she clawed at the dirt. The cruelness, the unfairness of the world, was overpowering her. Oksana could hear Leo, his voice concerned, but she could not make out the words. Then, muscular arms were wrapped around her, rocking her. She listened to the soothing words and felt the warmth of a cheek against her forehead. When Oksana blinked away the tears and looked up, she saw Bogdan's face, grief-stricken and tear-streaked, looking down at her.

"Oh, Bogdan," Oksana wrapped her arms around his neck and buried her face in his shoulder. "She's dead. Galina's dead."

"It's going to be okay, child," Bogdan said as he rocked her. "Everything is going to be okay."

Oksana sniffled loudly and looked over Bogdan's shoulder at Leo; he sat in his wheelchair, his familiar blanket covering his legs. She could see Leo's face etched with sadness and worry, but he managed to muster a weak gap-toothed smile for her, and Oksana loved him for it.

She pulled back from Bogdan and stared into his face, "What happened? Where were you?" Oksana hated the accusatory sound of her voice, and the hurt look it invoked in his eyes.

"Galina was sick. She needed medicine and sent me to Kalinin," Bogdan shook his head. "I don't know why Olga Putina and her brothers were at the house; I believe they went there to do her harm."

"Olga hated Galina," Oksana's mind reeled.

"How did you hear?" Leo craned his neck to see her over Bogdan's shoulder. "Bogdan only just made it to town."

"Your father and McMurrough were at the church. They told the Land Captain about Galina and the others. And Gleb Andreev."

"What happened to Andreev?" Bogdan cocked his head sideways.

"The wolf killed him. Left his head in the trough at the Kanti Gans," Oksana replied, wiping away her tears.

"What?" Leo exclaimed, his eyes opening wide in surprise.

Bogdan looked deeply troubled, lost in thought, as he stared at the ground.

"There are strangers in town." Despite the cool weather, Oksana's dark hair lay matted to her head with sweat. She had washed the manure from her face in the church's watering trough but still felt like she could smell it in her nostrils. "There's a Romanov. He has soldiers, the Tsar's huntsman, and a wild nomad from Siberia with him. I think they came to hunt the wolf."

"Romanov? The Tsar is here in Obrechen?" Leo bobbed so excitedly that he seemed like he would topple right out of his chair.

"I said a Romanov, not *the* Romanov," Oksana shook her head. Despite her sadness, she had to repress a smile at Leo's never-ending childlike wonder.

"And he has one of the nomads from Siberia with him? What did he look like?"

"He had short black hair and almond-shaped eyes," Oksana squinted her eyes in imitation. "The man carried two long knives in his belt and had a hunting bow on his back."

Bogdan's head had snapped up, and he studied Oksana sternly, "Oksana, how do you know it's the Tsar's huntsman?"

"The Romanov introduced him to Morozov that way. I think he said his name was Artemy," Oksana searched her memory; the name sounded close but not quite right.

"Was it Arkady? Arkady Volkov?" Bogdan's voice sounded cold and breathy, like a wind across the tundra.

"Yes," Oksana nodded. "Yes, that's it. Arkady Volkov. Do you know of him?"

"Where are these men now?" Bogdan asked as he stood.

"They were at the church," Oksana replied, confused by his sudden change in demeanor.

"If there is a Romanov in town, he will be staying at the Land Captain's manor for certain," Leo added.

"Oksana, I need you to stay here with Leo. I'll come back for you as soon as I can," Bogdan said, turning to run toward Obrechen.

Oksana turned and looked at Leo in surprise, but the boy only shrugged. They watched Bogdan jog off toward the village and quickly disappear from view.

***

"Here he is," Father Grigori gestured toward the mound of earth and the unmarked wooden cross. "I will leave you alone with your brother."

The priest bowed his head solemnly to Volkov, then looked at the grave and made the sign of the cross before returning to the church, leaving Volkov alone standing beside the grave. The village cemetery was silent except for the receding crunch of the priest's feet upon the dry earth and the whisper of the wind among the stoic crosses.

Volkov looked at the rough-hewn wooden cross and smiled wryly. He knew he should have a tombstone crafted in Kalinin and placed here to mark his brother's grave. A testament honoring Dimitri that would stand here long after the other wooden markers in the grave rotted to dust. But why? Volkov would never return to this place again. No, he would let his brother rest as he had lived among the common people of Russia.

"Brother, I am not surprised that you wound up in a place like this," Volkov said, kneeling beside the grave and looking around the cemetery. "I always figured it would be someone sick of listening to your big mouth or some angry husband who laid you low for mounting his wife like a prized pony but never a wolf of all things."

"I'm not a religious man, little brother, you know that. Though Mother would have wanted me to say a prayer for your soul," Volkov felt a slight tightness in his chest at the finality of the moment. "Say hello to Father; I hope wherever you both are now is filled with lots of vodka and whores."

"Things were not always good between us," Volkov slipped the folded note from his pocket and glanced at the bloodstained paper, "but I wanted you to know I got your note and came to kill this beast for you. I will do this thing because we are blood, and blood avenges blood."

Volkov slid the note into the dark earth of the grave, "Goodbye, little brother."

***

As the small band of riders made their way to Morozov's estate, they rounded a bend in the road and found a dark-haired man standing in the middle of the path, waving his arms above his head as if signaling to the horsemen. The man was tall and broad, wearing a forester's dark green shirt and brown trousers. Sergeant Razin reined his horse forward to place himself between the man and Kirill.

"I think he's signaling for us to halt," Herzen eyed the man.

"Could be brigands; keep your eyes on the woods for an ambush," Sergeant Razin ordered as all three soldiers unslung their rifles.

"Igor, who is that man? He looks familiar." Morozov squinted to see the man better.

"A Romanian woodsman," Balkov snorted a wad of phlegm and spit off to the side. "Bogdan Negrescu; he worked as a hand for Galina Sekova."

"The dead girl?" Kirill asked, and Morozov nodded.

"Go see what the man wants," Sergeant Razin gestured toward Tyutchev.

The young soldier galloped his horse forward, rifle leveled at Bogdan. The riders watched as Bogdan kept his hands visible, showing Tyutchev he was unarmed. Sergeant Razin's eyes alternated between watching Tyutchev's exchange and scanning the woods for danger.

"Tell me more about this splendid wine you say you have at the manor," Kirill glanced sidelong at Morozov.

"For such esteemed guests," Morozov smiled broadly, "I will have dinner served with a bottle of Hungarian Tokaji."

"Hungarian Tokaji," Kirill's eyes alighted at the mention of the fine wine. "However does a Land Captain in Obrechen acquire such a delicacy?"

"A merchant from Kalinin donates a bottle to Father Grigori whenever he passes through," Morozov appeared well-pleased by the young Romanov's appreciation of his prized wine.

"Tyutchev, what are you doing?" Sergeant Razin muttered as he watched the soldier returning with the forester walking alongside him.

"Sergeant Razin, we need to get moving again. The Land Captain has a bottle of wine that urgently awaits uncorking," Kirill called to Razin as Morozov grinned widely.

The Cossack looked annoyed at the men before turning to level his rifle at Bogdan, "That's far enough."

Bogdan halted and nodded his understanding as Tyutchev brought his horse up alongside Razin. The forester looked over the riders, craning to see past them.

"Sergeant, he wants to speak to the Romanov," Tyutchev informed Razin in a hushed tone.

"Why's he looking like that?" Razin gestured toward Bogdan with the barrel of his rifle.

Tyutchev looked back at Bogdan, "He was asking about the Tsar's huntsman. I told him Volkov was following behind us."

"You. Speak your peace," Razin shouted to Bogdan.

Bogdan took a step forward, however, he halted when Razin raised the barrel of his rifle, "My name is Bogdan Negrescu; the wolf has killed my employer, Galina Sekova."

"I bet she made a tasty morsel," Balkov said loud enough for all to hear, however, he fell silent when his gesture failed to garner any snickers.

"My condolences for your loss," Kirill said, reaching into his coin purse, intent on demonstrating Romanov generosity. "Please allow me to relieve the sting on your family until you can find new employment."

"Sir, I seek no coin," Bogdan waved off the gesture. "I would like to aid you in hunting the wolf and avenge my employer."

Kirill raised an eyebrow at the rejection of his generosity and glanced at Morozov.

The Land Captain shook his head, "We have our own hunters."

"Sir, I have hunted wolves in the Carpathian Mountains. I know the beasts as well as I know myself," Bogdan protested. "I will hunt the wolf and find its den, then report the location to your huntsman."

"We're more likely to find the wolf gnawing his bones," Balkov smirked.

Kirill appraised the forester and nodded slowly, "No, I like this plan. Tsar Alexander's personal huntsman and tracker are traveling with us; however, if you find the wolf's lair first, I want you to report directly to me. If it proves true I will pay you handsomely. We will be staying at the Land Captain's manor."

Bogdan nodded his agreement and stepped to the side of the road.

"Well then, Land Captain, shall we attend to that Hungarian Tokaji?" Kirill spurred his horse forward, followed closely by Morozov, Balkov, and the two soldiers.

Sergeant Razin continued to eye Bogdan suspiciously, his rifle still pointed at the forester, "The Romanov is my charge. I am the danger to all that threatens him."

"I assure you. I mean the Romanov no harm," Bogdan met the man's withering gaze.

Razin held the forester's gaze a moment longer and then urged his horse forward after the riders. Bogdan stood in the road, watching the horsemen disappear around the bend, then stepped into the woods and began running.

***

The scent of blood was maddening to Alexei. His senses tingled, his legs shook, and his body ached to feast upon warm meat. He paced back and forth in the wooded brush across from Galina's home, the aroma of human flesh calling to him. Ever since he tasted the blood of the Chernyshevsky brothers, the ache for human flesh had become constant.

Alexei's father once told him that a dog that bites a human needs to be put down because once it has tasted blood, something feral awakens inside it; the dog is never the same. Alexei never understood that until now. Since his transformation, he had fed upon deer and rabbits, and they filled his belly, but they never satiated his hunger like feeding upon the Chernyshevskys, Gleb Andreev, and the Cossacks.

The stench of fresh blood, fresh human blood, in the air propelled him through the woods. The aching hunger of the wolf drove him forward, a mindless ravenousness that possessed his body, mind, and spirit. Only with the vaguest recollection did the human part of his mind recognize Galina's house and pull him back from his feral state. Alexei's mind screamed with the horrifying image of charging into Galina's house and feeding upon his friends.

There was a wrongness about the aroma of blood wafting from Galina's house like waves against the shoreline. The blood smelled lifeless, and fear grew within him that his friends lay butchered inside. Another faint and fading scent hung about the house—the smell of the other wolf-beast. It had been here; it had killed.

Alexei had searched for the beast every night, catching only distant traces upon the wind. However, the scent around the cottage was intense; the wolf had been here recently. The more pressing concern was the source of the human blood inside. He could smell four sets of blood, two men and two women, one of which bore a scent of something foul and tainted. His mind raced with the possibilities: could it be Galina, Oksana, Bogdan, and another man? Perhaps Leo?

Alexei wanted to race inside and see, but he feared stepping into the blood-soaked cottage. The thought of the wolf's primal hunger consuming him and devouring his friends' bodies before he even realized what he was doing terrified him.

Suddenly, he picked up a fresh scent, men approaching with horses, and lowered himself to the ground, his gray fur blending with the branches and brambles. Alexei watched as two men, Pavel Verenich and an Asian man who wore a bow and quiver of arrows across his back, rode up to Galina's house. He felt the fur along his spine bristle, the image of his powerful jaws closing on Pavel's throat floating through his mind in a way that pleased both his wolf and human sides. Alexei would have charged across the distance between them and claimed the gendarme as his prey, however, there was something dangerous about the Asian man that gave him pause. Something instinctual within Alexei recognized the man as a predator, and he crouched lower in the brush.

Alexei watched as the two men entered the cottage, Pavel drawing his pistol. A few moments later, Pavel exited quickly and violently wretched off the porch. His shoulders heaved as he disgorged his lunch in a bile-filled, pungent stream that splashed noisily to the earth. The acrid smell of the gendarme's vomit stung Alexei's nose, making it twitch with disgust.

Pavel sat heavily in a chair on the porch, his pistol in his lap, as he wiped his mouth with a handkerchief. Alexei watched and waited until the Asian man slowly exited the house, his eyes scanning the wooden floor of the porch as if he were following a trail. The man stopped and looked at Pavel, a hint of annoyance in the man's posture that Pavel had disturbed something with his boots.

Alexei watched as the man continued to follow something he saw on the ground, hopping off the end of the porch to examine the earth beyond it. The man landed as gracefully as a cat, then knelt to examine the ground more closely. He looked from the ground to the forest, then studied the ground intently. Pavel asked the man what he was looking at, but he ignored him and continued studying the earth. He looked about and leaned to stare at several other spots on the ground.

When the man finally stood, he said something to Pavel, and the gendarme gingerly got to his feet. They walked toward their horses, and then the man stopped. He turned and stared into the woods at exactly the spot where Alexei crouched. Alexei felt as if the man was looking directly at him and held his breath, afraid to move a hair.

Pavel climbed atop his horse and said something to the man, who reluctantly broke his gaze away from the forest and mounted his horse. As they rode away, the man looked back again, staring at where Alexei lay concealed, before following Pavel from sight.

Once the man disappeared from view, Alexei exhaled deeply, and the tension finally released from his body. He felt exhausted from the strain and got unsteadily up onto all four legs. With one last look at the cottage, Alexei turned and disappeared into the forest.

Chapter 3

Volkov rubbed his hand between Nar's eyes, smiling as the brown stallion plucked the slice of apple from his hand. Morozov had given Kirill and his party choice spots within the estate's stable and promised that his groomsman would diligently look after the horses' care and feeding. The huntsman insisted on choosing Nar's stall himself before feeding, watering, and brushing the stallion as the nervous grooms looked on, unsure how to handle Volkov's presence in the stable.

He heard footsteps approaching, human and horse, and smiled; Volkov would recognize the sound of Batu and Sar in the middle of a raging storm. Batu wordlessly walked Sar into the stall beside them and situated the stallion. Like Volkov, Batu had a routine he liked to follow to feed, water, and groom the horse. They often joked that the fervor they dedicated to such equine routines was the closest either man had to religion.

"However, whereas I am just a priest in this religion, you are the Pope," *Batu chided Volkov for his fanatical devotion to the horse as the two sat*

side-by-side before their campfire during a hunt in Vladivostok. "I just hope you never have to choose between me and Nar."

"I would choose you, of course," Volkov had feigned looking hurt, then smiled as he added. "I think."

Volkov glanced at Batu as the man knelt and inspected Sar's hooves. The Mongolian tracker appeared deep in thought and quiet. Batu was naturally stoic however, the tracker's conduct seemed too deliberate.

"Did you examine the site of the wolf attack," Volkov leaned against the stall wall and folded his arms across his chest.

"I did," Batu nodded but did not look up from examining Sar's front hoof.

"What are your thoughts?" Volkov studied the tracker; Batu was acting strangely.

Batu sighed as he released the horse's hoof and stood, turning to face Volkov, "The beast killed four, as McMurrough stated; the bodies of two men and a woman were still in the house, and the wolf dragged off the fourth body.

"Did you follow the blood trail?" Volkov felt a surge of adrenaline course through his veins.

"No," Batu shook his head. "The gendarme was eager to leave, and I thought it prudent not to track it alone."

Volkov narrowed his eyes, "You've told me what you saw; I asked you what you thought. What is it, Batu? You're acting strangely."

"The prints the beast left," Batu hesitated. "They were irregular."

"Irregular? In what way?" Volkov cocked his head, intrigued.

"The prints varied greatly, and many of the wolf's rear paw prints appeared to have increased in length and width at times," Batu's eyes met Volkov's and for the first time, the huntsman saw uncertainty there.

"As if there was a rider?" Volkov asked.

Batu shook his head, "No, that would have made the prints broaden and slip. The prints look as if the wolf walked on its hind legs."

"What?' Volkov could not hide his surprise. "Walked? Like a person? Not just reared up on its hind legs?"

Batu nodded, "Yes, and the front paws were all wrong."

"Wrong?" It made no sense as Volkov tried to envision a wolf walking upright.

"The front paws were long and finger-like, like a giant raccoon," Batu said, holding his hand and wriggling his thumb. "But unlike a raccoon, the paw had a thumb, like a human."

"Are we dealing with a killer wearing a wolf skin?" Volkov's jaw tightened at the thought of his brother murdered by some madman.

"Arkady," Batu's voice grew grave, and his eyes searched Volkov's face, "there are stories among the Turkic people of the steppe, tales of shamans who could perform rites that would transform them into wolves. They call them *Kurtadam*, wolf men."

Volkov opened his mouth and closed it, unsure what to say.

"Amongst my people, too," Batu continued, "there are tales of the *Itbaraks*, dog-headed men, who appeared as half man and half beast."

Volkov would have laughed if not for Batu's dire look. "You think we're hunting one of these wolf-men?"

"I do," Batu spoke with a tone of finality that left no room for questions.

"So the gendarme, Verenich, was on the right track with his belief that the wolf had a human accomplice. Except, you're saying the wolf and his human accomplice are one in the same, one of these *Kurtadam*?" Batu nodded in agreement.

Volkov had known Batu too long and trusted him too much to question something the man felt so strongly about, even something so outlandish as wolf men, "If what you believe is correct, could this man walk amongst us when he is not in wolf form?"

"He could, and I believe he does," Batu's eyes grew very hard.

Volkov studied the man's face, "You think you know who it is." It was a statement, not a question, and Batu nodded. "Who? I have not seen anyone Turkic in Obrechen."

"I have extensively questioned the gendarme, Verenich," Batu lowered his voice to a whisper, and Volkov involuntarily leaned in conspiratorially. "The attacks in the village appear to have coincided with the arrival of the Irishman, James McMurrough. Verenich confirmed that he was often seen with Olga Putina, one of the latest victims, and had business dealings with Galina Sekova, the other murdered woman."

"Does Verenich suspect McMurrough as well?" Volkov ran a hand over his beard as he thought.

"No, Verenich thinks it is a wolf working in league with anarchists," Volkov looked up, shock written across his face. "The man is an idiot."

"What did he know of McMurrough?"

"Very little; the man is an Irish mercenary or British Army deserter. He works for Gennady Guriev, the Count of Kalinin, and handles unseemly work for the man." Batu's jaw was tight. "I believe he is the *Kurtadam*."

"We need to proceed carefully," Volkov said, touching Batu's shoulders. "If this is a *Kurtadam* and we are wrong about McMurrough, the real wolf man may already be among us. We cannot trust anyone but the men that came with us."

Batu stoically nodded his agreement.

"Morozov has invited some men to dinner with us tonight to discuss the hunt with Kirill; I don't know if McMurrough will be among them, but we must observe everyone's reactions," Volkov worked through the suspect list in his head.

"Arkady," Batu's voice suddenly softened and gentled, "thank you for believing me. I know this sounds outlandish."

Volkov cupped Batu's face and leaned his forehead against the tracker's, "Batu, there is no man I trust more than you. If you say this is what we are up against, I will not question it."

"Sergeant Razin's premonition..." Batu began.

"Razin predicted Kirill's doom, not ours. Fuck the Romanov, we will kill the *Kurtadam* together." Volkov stared into Batu's eyes, overly aware of the heat of the tracker's forehead against his own.

"I would die for you, Arkady Volkov," Batu's words were barely audible.

"And I for you, Batu."

***

The scent of roasted meat and the murmur of conversation greeted Volkov and Batu as they entered the main dining hall. Three serving girls, a blonde and two brunettes that Volkov assumed came from Obrechen and the surrounding areas, attended to the guests, bringing fresh bottles of wine and platters of food. The two dark-haired servants, girls in their late teens, laughed and smiled at every gesture or comment from Kirill, while the blonde girl appeared a few years older and hovered near the blue-uniformed gendarme Verenich.

Kirill sat at the head of the table, no doubt at the insistence of Morozov, who sat to the Romanov's right. The two men were engaged in animated conversation, likely fueled by the two empty wine bottles that Volkov observed before them. At Morozov's side sat a young, attractive woman who picked sparingly at her food as she listened intently to the priest, Father Grigori, seated beside Kirill.

Pavel Verenich sat to the priest's right, blocking Volkov's view of the man between them. The gendarme was craning his head, trying to listen to the conversation between Morozov and Kirill, and appeared annoyed at his placement further down the table. Volkov gestured to the two vacant seats beside Morozov's wife, and Batu followed behind him as two servant girls quickly approached with plates of savory meat and vegetables.

Volkov placed his hand upon the seat and halted, stunned to see the man seated between Verenich and the priest, Valerian Rostov. The man was eating a large piece of meat he had skewered with his knife and froze mid-bite at the sight of Volkov, his eyes opening wide in surprise and then narrowing with contempt.

"Volkov, there you are finally," Kirill called from the end of the table. Then, he saw the hostile glances exchanged between Rostov and the huntsman.

"Come now, gentlemen. We have all come together for a common purpose. Let us sit, drink, and plan this hunt."

Volkov and Rostov glared at each other a moment longer, and then Rostov nodded slightly in agreement.

"Kirill was just telling us a thrilling tale of riding alongside Tsar Alexander during a fox hunt," Vera Morozova looked awestruck.

"Is that so?" Volkov replied and caught Kirill's conspiratorial wink. Volkov fought the temptation to call out the young noble for the fraud that he was, knowing the Tsar had a bad experience on a horse as a child and was deathly afraid of the creatures. Tsar Alexander would not ride in a horse-drawn carriage, let alone on the back of a steed. However, he let Kirill have his moment among these glorified peasants.

"As the Imperial Huntsman, you must spend a great deal of time with the Tsar. What is he like?" Vera asked as the serving women stared at him with such wide-eyed enthusiasm that Volkov felt like a street performer ogled by the crowd.

Volkov paused to compose himself, then looked at Vera. "He is a powerful man, built from sturdier stuff than his father; I have often seen him tear a pack of playing cards in half with his bare hands to delight his children. Some think him brutish because he does not embrace the refinement and delicateness of European royals. However, Tsar Alexander prides himself on being rough-hewn like the people of the empire."

Father Grigori stroked his beard, "I once heard the tale of a painter who encountered the Tsar at the Mariinsky Theater; he described Tsar Alexander as an imposing man with eyes as cold as steel but who appeared to carry a monstrous burden born from an ever-present fear for his life and the lives of those closest to him. I pray daily for the Tsar's safety."

"Can you blame the man?" Pavel paused, momentarily distracted by a blonde serving girl who smiled flirtatiously at him as she stepped forward to place a fresh bottle of wine before him. "Jewish anarchists brutally slew his father."

Murmurs of agreement rippled through the assembled guests.

"Will Mr. McMurrough be joining us?" Batu asked as he settled into the chair beside Volkov.

"He returned to Kalinin to advise Count Guriev of Galina Sekova's death," Pavel responded, delighted that meaningful conversation had reached his end of the table.

"It's just terrible what happened at that cottage," Vera Morozova held her hand to her chest, looking genuinely distraught. "I hope they find peace in heaven."

"The wages of sin is death," Father Grigori added as he cut into a potato. "Galina Sekova lived like a harlot and died like a sinner. I find it unlikely she reconciled with the Lord Almighty in her final moments."

"Not Sekova," Vera shook her head. "Olga Putina and her brothers."

"Ah, yes, of course. You have such a kind Christian heart to keep them in your thoughts," Grigori corrected himself, and Vera flushed red at his praise.

Volkov watched as Rostov stared lasciviously at Morozov's wife as she spoke, his eyes running up and down her body with a wolf-like hunger. Rostov noticed Volkov's stare and gave the man a little smirk, the kind men give when they seek to enlist others in their lewd thoughts. Volkov glared back disapprovingly, and Rostov just shrugged and returned his gaze to Vera Morozova, his tongue flicking to wet his lips.

"If the *Kurtadam* is not McMurrough, I pray to God its Rostov," Volkov leaned over and whispered to Batu.

"Perhaps the wolf will just move on and leave us be," Vera offered as she picked up her wine glass and frowned, seeing it was empty.

"Let me get that for you, Missy." Rostov quickly rose to his feet, grabbed the bottle before him, and leaned over the table to give her a fresh glance.

Volkov noticed the priest scowl at the copious amount of wine Rostov poured into her glass and the way the man angled himself to get a better look at her bosom. He glanced at Morozov, but the man was oblivious to the happenings around his wife as he chatted amiably with Kirill.

"So Rostov," Father Grigori interrupted the man's leering, "how does one go from beating Jews in the streets of Kalinin to hunting wolves?"

"It's not what I do; it's how I do it," Rostov sat back in his seat and glanced at the priest before pointedly making eye contact with Vera. "I'm very good at whatever I put my mind to."

Vera sipped her wine, oblivious to the man's suggestive comment. Rostov's face soured at her disinterest, and he ran a hand over his bald head before picking up his fork and skewering another chunk of meat on his plate.

"Count Guriev needed me to take care of the Jews in Kalinin, so I was good at killing Jews," Rostov shoved the wad of meat into his mouth, chewing loudly. "And now Salamonsky needs me to capture this wolf, so I'll be good at trapping wolves."

"Maybe the dreadful thing will just return to where it came from," Vera sighed and shook her head.

"From your lips to God's ears, sweet angel," Father Grigori added, making the sign of the cross, which Vera quickly repeated, a slight smile on her lips.

"I am afraid the wolf will not leave," Batu leaned over to look down the table at Vera, his face impassive.

"Why?" The distress on her face made Vera look small and childlike, sitting next to her husband's sizeable bulk.

"Because it's a man-eater," Volkov looked up and saw Rostov nodding in equal understanding. "Obrechen is its new hunting ground."

"My farm will provide you with all the sheep and goats you need to hunt this wolf," Morozov puffed out his chest in self-importance. "Whatever you need, I will see that you have it."

Volkov shot Morozov a withering look. "Are you not listening? It has acquired a taste for humans. You cannot lure it in with livestock."

"Arkady, I believe our host is only graciously extending an offer of assistance," Kirill shot Volkov a disapproving, glassy-eyed look.

Volkov felt his ire rise at the young Romanov's chastisement; however, a gentle tap of Batu's foot against his own stayed his tongue. He glanced sidelong at the tracker, who met his gaze and held it until Volkov's shoulders sagged slightly, resigned to letting the matter with Kirill pass.

"Are you saying you must use human bait to lure the wolf?" Father Grigori was aghast.

"Unless we can track the beast to its lair, which could take weeks, the only way to lure it out would be with human bait," Volkov looked up at Pavel. "Are you currently holding any prisoners?"

Pavel shook his head as he carefully sliced his meat, "We don't usually have anything more than the occasional unruly drunk from the *Kanti Gans.*"

"Pity," Volkov quipped.

"They used to have a Jew," Rostov gave a cruel smile as he chewed a mouthful of food and elbowed Pavel.

"Arkady, the Land Captain, has offered us the services of his foreman, Balkov, and some of the local hunters in his employ who are familiar with the surrounding forests," Kirill held up a hand when Volkov leaned forward to protest. "I have already accepted his offer, as well as the hospitality of his home."

"Very well," Volkov gave Kirill a tight-lipped nod, then turned to Rostov. "However, I do not believe we need the services of Rostov's Cossacks."

"I did not offer them," Rostov sneered. We will conduct our business on our own."

"If I may be so bold," Morozov interjected as he tipped the wine bottle to refill Kirill's glass. "I would be honored if I could accompany you with my son; I believe the experience would be good for the boy."

"Of course," Kirill responded, lifting his glass and tipping his head toward Morozov. "It will be something he will tell his grandchildren about someday."

Over the crackling fire and sounds of dining and drinking, Volkov caught the faint noise of men shouting in the distance. He lay down his utensils and cocked his head to listen, noticing Batu also had picked up on the voices. Across the table, Pavel was too distracted whispering to the blonde serving girl to notice but, Rostov perked up from his meal.

"What is that?" Rostov narrowed his eyes as he strained to listen.

A hush slowly fell over the dining table until the only sound in the room was the crack and pop of the burning fire. Kirill and Morozov seemed to have difficulty focusing in their wine-laden state. Still, Vera and the priest exchanged apprehensive glances as the sound of heavy boots in the corridor overtook the din of men shouting outside.

Suddenly, the doors to the dining room burst open, and the serving girl closest to Kirill screamed as Sergeant Razin and his two soldiers burst into the room, their rifles in their hands. Herzen and Tyutchev took defensive positions on either side of the door, facing out into the corridor, while Razin ran up to Kirill.

"Sir, it's the wolf. There's been an attack," Razin reported, breathing heavily.

"What?" Kirill was having difficulty processing the sudden change in events.

"An attack at the estate? How? Walls surround us," Morozov looked around in disbelief.

"Where was the attack?" Pavel leaped to his feet, his hand going to his holstered pistol. Something in the man's movements seemed too theatrical to Volkov, who suspected the gendarme was putting on a show for the young servant girl rather than getting ready to charge into danger.

"It was in the barn," Razin responded.

The sergeant's eyes briefly touched upon Volkov, then darted away. It was only a split-second movement, but the huntsman caught it, and a cold wave of fear knotted his guts. Volkov leaped to his feet, Batu trying to grab him as he ran for the door.

Herzen and Tyutchev looked from the huntsman to Razin, unsure what to do as Volkov raced past with Batu close behind him. Volkov was only vaguely aware of his surroundings as he rushed from the manor house into the night air. Men with torches gathered about the stable as he ran toward it, pushing past all who stepped in his way, ignoring their curses and shouts as he shoved through the throng.

Balkov knelt beside a groomsman, a young boy no more than twelve, who sat sprawled on the ground. The boy's eyes were wide with fright, like two shining coins in the night, and his body trembled so violently that it rattled the wooden board behind him.

Balkov looked up grim-faced, "The beast walked right by him. It scared the shit out of him."

From the stench rising from the boy, Volkov did not think Balkov was speaking figuratively. Despite the rising fear and dread, Volkov asked, "Who did the wolf attack?"

Balkov stared up at Volkov, then flicked toward the stable and back to the huntsman as Batu and the two soldiers pushed through the crowd. Volkov glanced at Batu, a lump in his throat as he swallowed, and the tracker read the apprehension on his face.

"Arkady, let me go first," Batu reached out to grab his arm, but Volkov was already pushing into the barn.

Several men milled about inside, talking amongst themselves and peering into one of the stalls. "Get out!" There was a terribleness to Volkov's command that the men did not question.

The men moved quickly past Volkov, and he roughly shoved any man not shuffling by fast enough. Behind him, he heard Batu telling Herzen and Tyutchev to keep everyone back. Volkov heard Batu's quiet footfalls approaching as he walked slowly past the horse stalls. The animals were agitated, snorting wildly and pawing at the ground. The metallic scent of blood filled the air.

Volkov walked forward, stumbled, and braced himself against the wall. Batu was close now; he felt the man's presence as much as he heard it. The jet-black head of Sar came into view as he walked past the stallion's stall; the horse's eyes were wide and white, its nostrils flaring as its breath came in snorts and pants.

Before he reached Nar's stall, Volkov spotted the stallion's brown leg lying taut and motionless on the straw-covered floor. The world seemed to darken and swoon as he spied the large pool of wine-colored blood in the stall. As Volkov entered the stall, he fell to his knees, and Batu rushed to his side, kneeling beside him and putting an arm around the huntsman. Batu was speaking his name, but his voice sounded far off.

Nar, the horse that had carried him across the empire, lay sprawled on the ground of the stall, the dark brown orbs of his eyes staring sightlessly. The stallion was untouched except for a gaping wound across its throat, severing both carotid arteries, too ragged to be a blade but quick and clean. Volkov felt like a light went out inside him, replaced by a blackness filled with rage and hatred. He would not just kill whoever or whatever did this; he would destroy it. His breaths came in shuddering gusts as the tightness of grief clutched at his chest. Batu sat down beside him, quietly staring at the slain horse.

"Batu, I believe you were right," Volkov said when he finally spoke. "This is no mere wolf, it's a *Kurtadam*. Look at the tracks on the stable floor; they are just as you described."

The tracker turned to him and stared.

"The wound that killed Nar was from a claw, not a weapon," Volkov's hand touched his arm, where the tiger's claws had marked his flesh. "The beast walked past the groomsman and all the other horses and slew Nar with a single blow. Not out of hunger. No, it did it to hurt me; it did it to send me a message. It left the boy alive, so there could be no doubt as to the culprit."

Batu nodded his head in agreement, "But why? Because of your brother?"

"I don't know, Batu. But what this creature did tonight was call holy hellfire down from the heavens," Volkov turned to face Batu, his voice cold and filled with hatred. "And by God, I will rein fire upon this beast until the earth is scorched bare."

Chapter 4

The bright moon shone through the room window, cascading rays across the girl's bare back. Pavel watched the gentle rise and fall of her breathing, her blonde hair strewn across the pillow beside him as she slept. Morozov had sent the serving girl up to his room after the commotion surrounding the slaughter of Volkov's horse had died down; just another perk of the new life he had carved for himself.

Colonel Zelyabov and Major Sazhin had scoffed at his investigation, mocking and dismissing him. Yet, now, here he was, a trusted associate of the Land Captain, dining with Romanovs and the Tsar's huntsman, bedding young serving girls. Pavel's future seemed clear; he was on the cusp of wealth and greatness. All he needed to do was shed the last vestiges of his old life and ingratiate himself with these men.

Pavel slipped out of bed and picked up his discarded uniform from the floor beneath the girl's dress. He glanced back at her; perhaps he would wake her for another romp when he returned. A smile crossed Pavel's face as he pulled on his boots. Yes, he would wake her when he returned.

***

Batu sat on the edge of the bed, watching Volkov. The huntsman had positioned a chair by the window, his rifle across his lap, and stared silently into the moonlit night: the stable where Nar lay, a dark silhouette in the distance. Two figures, Herzen and Tyutchev, stood guard at the entrance to the stable, guarding the body of the slain horse and its sibling against the beast's return.

The Mongolian tracker felt a general sense of unease as he watched Volkov. The two had been together a long time, personally and professionally, and this was not the reaction Batu expected at the loss of Nar. Batu knew Volkov better than to think he would hold the man through the night as he wept for the lost stallion. The Arkady Volkov he knew would have raged into the night, cursed God, smashed furniture, paced the floor, and maybe even drank himself blind drunk. However, Volkov did none of those things; his anger and pain had turned him cold and quiet. This man was not the Arkady he knew, and that had Batu concerned.

In every hunt the two had undertaken, Volkov approached it with a single-minded purpose: to kill their quarry. In Batu's estimation, it made him the best hunter in the empire. Volkov possessed an iron will; hardship, deprivation, or weather would not deter him; he would drive on until he achieved the kill. It is what almost got them killed when they hunted the tiger, but it is also why they survived the encounter. A keen hunter's mind always tempered Volkov's will.

Batu knew and accepted that Arkady was a selfish man. He was generous with wealth and material things, but his pride made him a selfish man, selfish lover, and selfish hunter. There could be no hunter greater than Arkady Volkov and no beast that Volkov could not hunt and slay. The *Kurtadam* had slain Dimitri, but Arkady did not come to Obrechen out of grief for his brother; he came to kill the beast to show that he was the most formidable creature in the forest and, more importantly, for all to know it. Word that Arkady Volkov, the Tsar's huntsman, had slain the Beast of Obrechen and avenged his brother was the stuff of court legends and fairy tales. That was the logic of how Arkady Volkov's mind worked.

However, Volkov now appeared possessed of a fanaticism Batu had never seen in the man before. Volkov's thinking was not cold and calculating but passionate and reckless. Arkady had loved Nar, which was without question, but what he loved most about the stallion was what it meant to his mythos. He was the great hunter who returned from the western tundras on his legendary Siberian stallion with exotic furs and a Mongolian tracker. Arkady coveted Nar, and the *Kurtadam* appeared to know that and took the horse from him as a challenge, which was something Volkov's pride could not bear.

Batu wanted to kill the *Kurtadam* for the pain it caused Arkady; the creature had hurt the man he loved, and for that, Batu would see it vanquished. However, Batu had to admit that there was a more profound resentment in his heart; by killing Nar, the *Kurtadam* had unleashed a wellspring of emotion within Arkady that the tracker had jealously sought for himself. Would Arkady have reacted as strongly if the *Kurtadam* had slain him instead of Nar?

A knock at the door shook both men out of their thoughts. Volkov impassively glanced at Batu and nodded for the man to answer the door. Batu was surprised to see Pavel Verenich standing in the hallway in his uniform at this late hour. The man seemed surprised to see Batu as well, but quickly recovered.

"I would like to speak to Volkov," the gendarme's voice held a hint of eagerness.

"Let him in Batu," Volkov called without turning around.

Batu opened the door, and Pavel strode in with barely a dip of his head to greet the tracker. Volkov remained seated, staring out the window, while the gendarme waited for the huntsman to turn around. Pavel looked questioningly at Batu, but the tracker silently stared back at him.

"What is it, Verenich?" Volkov's voice was short and impatient.

It took Pavel a moment to realize Volkov was watching him in the reflection in the window, "I have a son; the boy is a cripple."

"My condolences," Volkov replied without sincerity.

"You said only human flesh could lure the wolf. I want to offer the boy as bait." Pavel said it as casually as if he was offering someone an apple.

The offer broke Batu's normally stoic demeanor, and he looked agape from Pavel to Volkov, who stared intently at the gendarme's reflection in the window.

Volkov nodded, "I will provide recompense to your family."

"Thank you, that is very generous of you," a self-satisfied grin crossed Pavel's face.

"Arkady!" Batu rushed over and knelt beside Volkov's chair but, the hunter's gaze remained fixed on Pavel.

"Wipe that smile off your face," Volkov barked, his tone harsh and cruel. "You just consigned a boy to near-certain death. Your own flesh and blood, and you smile?"

The smile quickly evaporated from Pavel's lips, "The boy has no future. I do it for the good of the Empire, to slay the wolf."

"For the good of the Empire or Romanov gold?" Volkov's eyes bored into gendarme, and Pavel looked away from the huntsman's harsh reflection.

"Sir, I asked for no gold." Pavel sputtered a protest.

"And yet you gladly accept it," Volkov's voice was cold as ice. Pavel appeared ready to protest, but Volkov raised a hand for silence. "Bring your boy tomorrow and you'll get your gold; now leave me."

Pavel nodded uncertainly and left the room with a forlorn look as he glanced back at the reflection as he exited.

"Arkady, this is monstrous; you cannot do this," Batu grabbed Volkov's arm, but the huntsman pulled it away and rose to his feet.

"I decide how we hunt the *Kurtadam*," Volkov walked to the bed and lay atop the sheets without undressing. "Come to bed; tomorrow we hunt."

***

Oksana laughed as she brushed a speck of dried porridge from Leo's cheek, "For someone that eats so little, how do you manage to get so much of it on you?"

"I consider it my special talent," Leo gave her a broad, self-satisfied smile as he leaned his face up to feel the warmth of the morning sun.

Oksana straightened the blanket covering his legs and sat beside him on the porch, her legs dangling off.

"You know, I bet my father will really impressed those men," Leo's gaunt face beamed with pride, and he showed all his crooked teeth in a wide grin. "The Romanov will see what an important man he is in Obrechen, and the Tsar's huntsman and the Siberian will probably want his advice on hunting the wolf!"

Oksana gave Leo a sad smile as she watched her friend talk glowingly about his father. Leo loved his father dearly, even though the man had never shown the boy an ounce of love or compassion. She remembered how Leo's father had been the day her father had surprised Leo with a wheelchair he made for him from old wood and wheels. The man was furious when he heard Leo's mother intended to take him into the village market and "parade the family's shame for all to see."

Somehow, Leo never let his father's cruelty phase him, at least not that Oksana had ever seen. Despite his small, withered, misshapen body, Leo had been an indefatigable well of good nature for as long as she could remember. He could see something good in even those villagers, boys like Petr Morozov, who ceaselessly mocked and mistreated him. Oksana loved that quality in Leo and hoped she could someday be that way. Most nights, she lay in bed and envisioned enacting her revenge on her uncle and Father Grigori for their mistreatment and cruelty.

"What are you two talking about?" Leo's mother stepped out onto the porch and smiled warmly at the two as she wiped her hands on her greasy apron. Oksana thought Anya Verenicha was a kind woman who may have once been beautiful but aged prematurely from a hard life in Obrechen, made even more difficult by caring for a sickly son and living with a cold, heartless man.

"We were talking about Father," Leo's eyes twinkled with delight as he stared at his mother.

"Is that so?" Leo's mother looked concerned. "I just hope he's safe with whatever business kept him out all night. This wolf has killed so many people."

"Here he comes now," Leo smiled and waved vigorously as his father came into view, riding his horse from the village toward his home. The man did not return the wave or smile as he approached.

Leo's mother frowned deeply at the grim look on her husband's face.

***

"Where are you taking him?" Leo's mother pulled at her husband's arm as he rolled the boy's wheelchair down the dirt road into town. Pavel shrugged off her grip and continued to push the wheelchair.

"Mother, please. It's okay." Leo turned to look back at her and gave her a nervous smile. "Father is just taking me into town."

Oksana walked alongside Leo and stared at his father; his face was dispassionate, and his eyes unreadable. Leo's mother was utterly distraught as they passed the wooden homes that comprised most of Obrechen. As they turned toward the village square, Oksana could see a crowd formed around the Romanov and his companions, who all sat on horseback.

The blonde-haired Romanov and the huntsman each sat atop large white horses while the Siberian rode atop a shorter, thickly built, black horse with short, stout legs. The horse had thick hair on its body and legs that gave it the appearance of fuzziness.

Oksana could see the three Russian soldiers seated disinterestedly on plain brown horses alongside an empty donkey-drawn cart driven by Morozov and his son. To her surprise, she saw that it was Seryy and Galina's cart; Oksana had ridden in it often enough to unmistakably recognize both, though how they had wound up in the hands of the Morozovs, was a mystery to her. Oksana also saw that Leo recognized the donkey and cart and craned his neck to look at the crowd—searching for Bogdan, she supposed.

The red-haired Petr Morozov spotted Leo and pointed as he leaned over to say something to his father. Oksana did not like the boy's malicious smile as he watched them, filling her with unease.

Several of the village's woodsmen stood in the square, carrying packs and long rifles. Oksana noticed that her uncle, Igor Balkov, was among them.

"Oksana, it's the Romanov and the Siberian," Leo's face beamed excitedly. "And that must be the huntsman alongside him! See, Mother, I told you Father knew them." Leo's father shared nothing of his son's excitement and remained stone-faced as they approached the crowd.

"Pavel, you need to tell me what's going on right now," Leo's mother grabbed the man's arm with all her might and jerked him around to face her.

Leo's father's face became a mask of fury and embarrassment as he saw several of the men from the village watching them and whispering amongst themselves, sly grins crossing their faces at his manhandling by the more petite woman. He shoved her hard with both hands with such force that she stumbled backward and fell, landing hard on the ground with a cry of shock and pain.

"You keep your hands off me, woman," Pavel pointed his finger at her menacingly. "I'm doing what's best for this family. There is barely enough food for us in the winter, yet you waste what we have on this boy. This is for the best."

"What are you saying?" her eyes filled with tears as she sat on the dirt road. "Pavel, what have you done?"

"I have done what I should have done fourteen years ago," Pavel's eyes were cold and heartless as he looked at her, then turned back to continue pushing the wheelchair.

Leo looked back at his mother, his momentary excitement replaced by fear as tears began to roll down his cheeks.

"Oksana, go get Father Grigori," Leo's mother said in a voice filled with fear and desperation. "Hurry, please hurry."

Oksana's eyes met Leo's briefly, and her heart broke at seeing the desolation in his eyes. Gone was her friend's boundless good cheer and optimism, replaced by a look she had seen only once before. The day soldiers traveled through Obrechen with a man they said was a member of *Narodnaya Volya*, caught trying to plant a bomb on train tracks. The man wore shackles on his hands and feet as they led him through the village to his hanging in Kalinin. Oksana saw the world-weary look of hopelessness in his eyes as he staggered past her—the same expression she now saw in Leo's eyes.

Oksana began to run for the old church as fast as her legs could carry her.

***

Kirill gestured for Herzen and Tyutchev to block the distressed woman as Pavel wheeled the boy up to the cart. Volkov watched as the soldiers angled their horses to stop her and kicked out with their booted feet when she got too close. The huntsman heard her anguished cries cut short as Herzen delivered a swift kick that sent her sprawling motionless onto the ground.

Pavel Verenich wheeled the vacant-eyed boy up to the back of the cart; the child seemed smaller than his already frail frame as he sank back in his chair. The village men stared pitilessly at the boy as he rolled past them, and Volkov felt disgust rise in his gut for the lot of them. His village in the Valdai Hills would have fought tooth and nail to the last man if outsiders had tried to take even the weakest among them.

Two village men lifted the boy from his chair and deposited him in the back of the cart as if they were loading a sack of grain. The boy did not cry out or whimper as he lay curled in the cart.

As good as dead already. Volkov looked from the prone boy to the red-haired boy seated in the front of the cart with Morozov. He heard the boy say "fresh meat" as he looked back and laughed mercilessly at the frail boy. The smile slipped from the boy's face when he caught Volkov's hard-eyed gaze and quickly turned away.

Pavel stopped beside Volkov's horse, "I need to retrieve my horse; it's still at my house."

Volkov stared into the man's dispassionate eyes, failing to see even a sliver of remorse, "You are not joining us on the hunt."

The gendarme looked shocked and then angry. He opened his mouth to protest, however, Volkov abruptly shifted his horse, forcing Pavel to quickly back away.

"Our deal was for the boy, not you," Volkov glared at Pavel, wishing the man would protest further or try to confront him. He would welcome the chance to beat the man down. Volkov caught Batu's disapproving gaze; the two had spoken little since the night before and he quickly looked away.

Pavel's eyes moved from Volkov to Kirill.

"Arkady, pay the man, and let us get on hunting this beast." Kirill looked bored and eager to get on his way.

Volkov reached inside his thick coat and produced a small leather pouch that he quickly shook so the coins clinked together. Pavel slowly stepped forward to receive it, then watched Volkov let it fall into the muck and manure.

"Wait until we're gone to pick it up, or I'll have Batu put an arrow through your skull," Volkov kicked his horse forward so abruptly Pavel had to jump back.

Pavel stared at the pouch as Volkov and Kirill led the procession out of the village center. The horses' hooves pushed the purse of coins down into the muck. None of the five woodsmen from the village that joined the hunting party looked at Pavel or acknowledged him as they passed. The men did not act so out of objection to Pavel's treatment of Leo; instead, they feared incurring Volkov's ire and risking their place in the hunting party, a venture that could prove very lucrative if successful. Igor Balkov made a show of stomping his foot down hard and grinding the pouch into the muck. He gave a mean-spirited laugh and shouldered past Pavel.

The Morozovs were the last to pass him in their cart, with Leo deposited in the back. The boy lay on his side, unmoving, either too terrified or grief-stricken at his father's betrayal to move. Silent tears streamed from the boy's wide brown eyes as he looked vacantly forward. Had Pavel glanced at him, he would have seen Leo's last desperate, pleading gaze resting on the man he had shown unrequited love and adoration to his whole life.

As the cart exited the village center, only Pavel, the empty wheelchair, and his wife's prone form, who lay crying on the ground, remained. He bent down, digging his hand into the mud, and muck until he withdrew the small leather pouch. Pavel clutched the small fortune in his closed fist as he walked home. He was finished with Obrechen.

Pavel stopped for a moment and stared dispassionately down at his wife. She lay curled in a fetal position, her face screwed into a mask of anguish as tears ran unbidden down her face. Dirt caked her long, dark hair, and a large purple bruise began to swell above her eye from where the soldier had struck her with his boot.

"How could you do this?" she choked between heaving sobs. "Leo loved you."

His eyes were dark and expressionless; Pavel continued without a word, the leather pouch clutched tightly in his hand.

***

Oksana pushed through the door of the dimly lit church, her breath coming in quick gasps after she ran from the village center. The lanterns on the wall illuminated the kneeling beam where she had knelt in pain, seeking penance only days before, however, the church was otherwise empty. Over the sound of her pulse pounding in her ears, she could hear a muffled commotion coming from Father Grigori's private room.

"Father Grigori," she quickly crossed the wooden floor. "Anya Verenicha needs your help. There's trouble in the village square."

Oksana hesitated for a moment before the door, but the desperate look in Leo's eyes drove her onward. The door was unlocked, and she stepped into the priest's private quarters and stopped, confused by the scene unfolding before her as the scent of lavender and lilacs mixed in the air with the musk of human bodies. A woman who leaned face first against the wall, almost certainly Vera Morozova by the richness of the dress, cried out at the sight of Oksana and tried to hide her face. Her intricately stitched blue dress sat hiked up around her hips, and Father Grigori pressed against her, his black frock in disarray.

A look of fear quickly replaced the bewildered look on Oksana's face as Father Grigori whirled on her, an expression of rage so intense on his bearded face that she stepped back out of the room. The priest appeared so furious that he could not speak, his mouth only producing a growl of primal rage as he charged at her.

Terrified by his reaction, Oksana turned and fled through the church with Father Grigori close behind her. The enraged priest grabbed an empty candleholder from the altar as he pursued her and, to Oksana's dismay, screamed a string of profanities at her as she ran.

Just as her hand closed around the door handle and freedom, the priest swung the heavy stone candleholder in a wide arc. The cold stone impacted the side of Oksana's head with such force that her head jerked sideways. Oksana felt as if struck by lightning as she swooned, her limbs going weak and her vision blurring. She would have toppled to the ground if she had not already gripped the door handle. Warm blood poured down the side of her face and neck as she tottered for a moment and then stumbled forward, the weight of her body pushing the door open.

The bright sunlight hurt her eyes as she staggered out into the street. Her legs bent awkwardly like two blades of grass as she willed them to move forward.

"She will never live to speak of this," Grigori's voice sounded far off, and the she heard a woman's frantic voice, the words trailing off as the church door slammed closed behind her.

Oksana fell to her knees but continued to crawl forward; dark droplets of blood dripped steadily from her head and onto the dry ground in ruby pools. Each step was agony as she crawled to the side of the stable and leaned her back against the hardwood. Her skull throbbed with pain as she labored to breathe. Oksana brought a trembling hand to the side of her head and felt a jagged indentation; her hand came away coated in dark blood.

Her thoughts felt like they were swimming in a dark sea; she struggled to grasp fleeting words and images as they slipped from her mind. She looked out onto the street at the procession of men and horses heading toward the woods. A cart trailed with something small in the back. Her vision was beginning to go black, shrinking to a small circle of light as if she were looking at everything from a vast distance.

Then something clamped down on her shoulder and yanked her from behind. Her mind vaguely registered pain in her shoulder as if a dozen knives pierced her. Oksana's eyes lazily watched her legs bounce along the ground as the backs of the houses of Obrechen receded from sight, replaced by the green of the woods.

Then all went black.

***

Leo felt numb with sadness as he watched the image of his mother curled motionless on the ground and his father standing unmoving in the village square grow further away. Tears rolled from his eyes and dripped off the tip of his nose as the cart rolled and jolted over the rough dirt road leading to the woods. He could hear the harsh words and malicious snickers passing between Petr Morozov and his father as they drove the cart onward.

He could almost laugh; the last time he had ridden in this cart was the happiest day of his life. What a grand adventure that had been.

Leo saw something small and broken propped against the church stable and wondered what it was. Then his heart leaped momentarily as a dark-clad figure ran out into the road behind the cart; Leo could swear it was Alexei. Was his friend alive, or had his specter returned from the dead to rescue him? Leo stared at Alexei and felt their eyes meet—it was really him. He could sense Alexei wanting to help him.

Alexei looked toward the broken thing by the stable and then back to Leo as if torn by a weighty decision. Leo wanted to cry out, take me away, save me, as Alexei gave him a last desperate look and then turned to run toward the church stable.

Desolation and hopelessness filled Leo as the cart left Obrechen behind. His father had delivered him into the hands of men who would see harm done to him, and his mother was now far away. Nobody would come to rescue the frail boy from Obrechen with a weak body and twisted legs. He would die surrounded by those who laughed and jeered at him his whole life.

Then, the fire that was Leo reignited deep within him, and he wiped away his tears with his thin hands. Leo's eyes took in the forest's tall trees, the green leaves, and the smell of the mountain pines. He listened to the birds that sang as they flitted in the trees. Leo would not waste a minute; if this were all the time remaining for him, he would drink in all the beauty of the world he always dreamed of getting off his porch and seeing.

The cart rolled on as the procession made its way up the old forest road.

***

The sun was beginning to journey low in the sky as Volkov walked into the makeshift camp, Batu trailing silently behind him. The cold fall breeze had brought the scent of the camp's burning fires to Volkov far into the forest, invoking his ire. As he stepped into the clearing, he pointed to the knot of village hunters sitting around their campfire quietly talking, and Batu gave a curt nod of acknowledgment.

As the Mongolian hunter moved purposefully toward the villagers, Volkov stalked angrily toward the fire, where Kirill lounged, talking to Morozov and his son. Morozov's stocky, red-haired boy was kneeling by the fire and cutting pieces of dried meat that he added to a steaming cooking pot.

"Arkady, how did your scouting go?" Kirill's grin quickly dissipated as Volkov planted a boot in Petr Morozov's back and shoved the boy away from the fire.

As the boy cried, startled, Volkov upended the cooking pot, dousing the fire with its contents. The fire hissed and died as the stew soaked the flaming branches and cooled the burning embers.

Across the clearing, the villagers protested as Batu stomped their fire out. Sergeant Razin and the two soldiers eyed the events with slight interest as they guarded the horses and the cart containing the prone Verenich boy.

"I can smell the fires halfway to the kill spot," Volkov said, grinding the last of the fire's embers into the dirt with his boot and ensuring his voice was loud enough for all the men to hear. "This wolf will not come near the bait if it smells our fires. If you must eat tonight, eat your food cold."

"Is there a problem?" Volkov's eyes shot angrily toward the knot of villager hunters who grumbled quietly amongst themselves and stared darkly at Batu.

"Your man did not need to come stomping on our fire," Igor Balkov gave Batu a hostile glance. "He could have just asked us to put it out."

"In the future," Volkov sneered at the suddenly silent villagers, "I encourage you to take your etiquette concerns directly to Batu."

"If you're so worried about scaring off the wolf," Andrei Morozov looked from his spoiled stew to Volkov, "why are we sitting here and not out hunting for it? Throw the cripple into the woods, and let's kill this beast."

"Even the sheep on your farm know that wolves primarily hunt at dawn and dusk," Volkov stepped menacingly toward the taller man. "They don't begin hunting until twilight. We'll bait our trap then."

***

"There's a small meadow about a half mile east of us." Volkov used a stick to draw a circle representing the meadow in the dirt and then indicated two places along the west side of the perimeter. Batu and I will be positioned here and here. This will provide us with good visibility when the wolf comes for the bait."

"And?" Kirill let a look of annoyance show on his face.

"And our Romanov friend will be here, of course," Volkov pointed to a third spot on the perimeter without acknowledging Kirill's sour look, then gestured to Igor Balkov. "I need you to position your hunters one hundred paces behind us, taking advantage of the crosswind to avoid the wolf detecting your scent. Circle around when you hear me shoot or yell for you, so the wolf cannot escape."

"How do you know the wolf will not come from behind us?" Balkov looked sidelong at Volkov.

"The village is west of us," Volkov gestured toward Obrechen. "The wolf will be moving toward the food source, so it will be coming from the east when it picks up the scent of the bait. It will enter the clearing from the north, south, or east approaches, which is why we position ourselves along the western perimeter of the clearing."

"Ever the master tactician, Arkady," Kirill gave the huntsman a wry smile. "The Tsar should make you a general one day."

"I want my men and me with the Romanov," Sergeant Razin interjected, frowning.

"You can stick with Kirill and provide supporting fire from here," Volkov said, pointing to a spot in the clearing to the right of Kirill's position. "But your men stay here with the horses."

"Yeah," Igor Balkov said with a wicked smile, "We may need more bait for the trap."

Kirill gave Razin a reassuring nod, and the soldier reluctantly agreed.

"Where will I be?" Morozov peered down at the drawing in the dirt.

"You and your son will remain here with the horses and Sergeant Razin's men," Volkov held up a hand as Morozov began to object. "I do not need anyone traipsing through the woods like a lost cow."

Morozov's face reddened angrily at the slight, but Volkov abruptly ended the discussion. "We must get moving before the wolf starts hunting for the night."

"You carry the bait," Volkov poked Balkov hard in the chest.

"Why me?"

"Because any man that runs his mouth as much as you must have a tremendous excess of energy," Volkov glared hard at Balkov until he looked away and nodded his acquiescence.

"Romanov!" An angry-looking man in a long brown coat and dark green trousers walked briskly up the road from the village. His shoulder-length black hair was wild and unkempt. "Romanov!"

"Tell your friend to shut his mouth," Volkov watched as Herzen and Tyutchev unslung their rifles and positioned themselves to block the man from entering the clearing.

"He's a foreigner. Bogdan Negrescu," Kirill looked uncertainly at the stranger. "I hired him to track the wolf."

"You didn't think to mention this to me?" Volkov turned on Kirill, eyes flaring angrily, as Batu put a restraining hand on the huntsman's chest.

"Slipped my mind," Kirill gave Volkov a dismissive look and shrugged.

"He has been seen around Obrechen the past few days," Balkov slipped his rifle from his shoulder. "He was a hired hand at Galina Sekova's cottage."

"He looks upset," Morozov eyed the man.

"Romanov, where's the boy?" Negrescu stopped as Herzen and Tyutchev barred his entrance and scanned the clearing with dark menacing eyes. "Leo, where are you?"

Negrescu's eyes searched the camp for Leo and locked onto Volkov's gaze. His nostrils seemed to flare wide at the sight of the huntsman, and a look of feral rage contorted his features.

"Arkady, do you know this man?" Kirill looked from the stranger to Volkov.

"I have never seen that man before in my life." Volkov's eyes narrowed as he studied Negrescu.

Without warning, Negrescu surged forward, crashing into the two soldiers and sending them sprawling to the ground. The village hunters leaped out of the way as Negrescu moved like an enraged beast with incredible speed and agility, closing the distance to Volkov. Kirill fumbled to unsling his rifle and bring it to bear on Negrescu but, the man swatted him out of the way like a straw doll. The Romanov tumbled across the clearing and landed hard on the ground.

Volkov drew a long knife from his belt and crouched to meet Negrescu's charge, a stance that had served him well in the past when predators had charged at him. Even the tiger that raked its claw across his arms died on the sharp steel of this hunting blade. He would meet Negrescu's charge, and the man would die like any other wild beast.

As Negrescu was almost upon him, Volkov thought the man's face took on an even more feral, almost lupine appearance. Negrescu's lips rose to reveal teeth that suddenly looked more animal than human as he snarled at Volkov. Then Negrescu was tumbling as Batu crashed into the man's side, wrapping his arms around the charging man and sending both to the ground. Batu held Negrescu tightly as the man struggled to break free. Volkov circled the pair looking for an avenue of attack when Balkov stepped forward and cracked Negrescu hard on the back of the head with his rifle butt.

Negrescu stopped struggling, and his body went limp and lay motionless in the dirt. Batu drew his long knives and rolled the unconscious man onto his back.

"Wait," Volkov grabbed Batu's shoulder and stopped him from driving the blades home into the man's chest.

The Mongolian hunter looked questioningly at Volkov, who bent to pick something off the ground beside Negrescu.

"I know this knife," Volkov stared solemnly at the deer bone-handled blade and then down at Negrescu, unconscious. "This was my brother Dimitri's knife. I gave it to him for his thirteenth birthday."

"Get a rope," Kirill, blood streaming from his swollen nose, gestured to one of the soldiers. "I want this man hanged immediately."

Herzen retrieved a length of rope from his saddlebag as Balkov roughly pulled free Negrescu's belt and bound the unconscious man's hands behind his back.

"The bastard broke my nose," Kirill dabbed blood from his nose with a handkerchief as Herzen looped the length of rope seven times to make a hangman's knot and slipped it over Negrescu's head.

"Not yet," Volkov slapped at Negrescu's face, unsuccessfully trying to bring him back to consciousness. "I need to ask this man how he came into possession of my brother's blade."

"He probably found it in the woods after the wolf killed your brother," Kirill tilted his head back to stop his nose from bleeding.

"Sir, we are ready," Herzen slid the noose into place.

"It's almost twilight; we need to see to the wolf first. We can hang him when we return. After I ask my questions." Volkov gave Kirill a hard stare.

"Oh, very well," Kirill threw the bloody handkerchief away in disgust and retrieved his rifle from the ground. "We shall hang him when we return."

"You men," Volkov gestured to Herzen and Tyutchev, "guard the prisoner until we return."

Morozov watched as the two soldiers grabbed the unconscious Negrescu by his feet and dragged him toward a tall tree, his dark-haired head bouncing and jostling on the rough ground. A thin trail of dark blood followed, undoubtedly from the blow to the head the man received.

Petr Morozov came to stand beside his father, his attention drawn to the party of men preparing to depart to the clearing where they would await the wolf. The Mongolian hunter was the first to slip into the woods, followed by Volkov, who traded his coat for his hunter leathers, and the Romanov, in an imperial blue jacket with gold buttons. The four village hunters followed behind solemnly, looking beggarly in their ordinary peasant clothes. Igor Balkov reached into the back of the cart and picked up Leo Verenich, carrying the frail boy over his shoulder like a grain sack.

As Balkov headed into the woods to follow behind the others, Leo looked up with wide, melancholy eyes and stared at Petr. The red-haired boy gave Leo a wicked smile and made an exaggerated biting and chewing motion with his mouth that he punctuated with mean-spirited laughter.

***

Leo's ribs ached as they bounced roughly against Balkov's shoulder as they made their way through the forest. His spirits had soared when he heard Bogdan calling out to him, but that hope was short-lived as he listened to the man's beating. Leo's heart ached for the fate of his friend, a man he barely knew, but one brave enough to risk his life for him. It greatly saddened Leo that Bogdan would likely meet his fate alone and surrounded by such heartless men. He silently prayed that Bogdan would somehow escape or not suffer greatly. Leo did not know if Bogdan Negrescu had any people, but when he reached whatever awaited him after this life, he would wait for and greet Bogdan so the man would not be alone on the Otherside.

Balkov carried him past the four village woodsmen who had stopped walking, their eyes darting nervously around the woods. None of the men looked at Leo. Leo looked skyward; the sun was getting very low, and the air was cooling. He wondered if he would be able to see the moon tonight. It would be nice to see the moon one last time.

The greenery of the forest receded as Balkov carried Leo into a large clearing where the Romanov and his three companions awaited. The world spun as Leo felt himself briefly falling and then he abruptly struck the hard ground. He let out a little cry of pain and surprise as he hit the firm earth, and the air rushed from his lungs. His back and hip throbbed with pain from the impact as he rolled onto his back and gasped air into his lungs.

"Was that necessary?" Kirill looked at Balkov with distaste, but the man only shrugged his shoulders.

"Go wait with the others," Volkov let his dislike for Balkov show clearly in his voice.

Leo stared at the four men as Balkov slipped back into the woods. The bearded soldier, Volkov, and the Mongolian stared back at him with hard, cold eyes.

"I'm going to find a spot with a good field of fire," Kirill said, looking at Leo with pity, then he quietly walked into the woods with the Cossack sergeant beside him.

Volkov and Batu exchanged a knowing look, and the Mongolian gave a curt nod. Leo stared at the darkening sky and smiled as he saw the faint outline of the moon. It was a perfectly round circle and pale milky white in the twilight haze—a full moon and cloudless. Leo's eyes scanned the dusk sky; the moon would shine brightly tonight.

Leo stared at the sky, amazed at how the moon brightened while the sun retreated as Batu slid the cold steel blade into his side.

✳✳✳

Volkov pressed his cheek against the stock of his rifle and waited for the wolf to arrive. The Verenich boy writhed and moaned in the clearing, his twisted legs moving fruitlessly as blood pooled around the frail body. He sighted the rifle above the boy, expecting the wolf to pounce upon the wounded boy at any moment.

A rustling noise to his right drew his attention, and a look of irritation crossed his face as Kirill pushed his way through the forest brush toward him.

"Get back to your shooting position," Volkov's words came out like a rough hiss.

"Is this necessary?" Kirill gestured toward the Verenich boy's anguished moans. "I understand we need the boy's body to bring the wolf, but does he need to suffer like this?"

"I'm sure the Russian Empire will survive with one less crippled boy," Volkov resumed his vigilance for the wolf.

"I don't care if you use a hundred such boys to catch your wolf, but making him suffer like this is inhumane," Kirill balled his fists in anger and frustration at the hunter's dismissive tone.

"This is a necessity," Volkov said, giving Kirill a withering look. "Fresh blood will attract the wolf. It will sense his pain and suffering and be drawn into the clearing."

"I am in charge here, and I say his dead body will attract the wolf all the same," Kirill broke from the tree line and stepped into the clearing.

"Kirill, get back here," raged Volkov at the arrogant Romanov's impertinence. *The fool will ruin everything!*

Across the clearing, Sergeant Razin stood from his hiding place and gave Volkov a questioning look. Volkov seethed with anger as he watched Kirill draw his ornate hunting knife and approach the writhing boy. The Romanov knelt beside the boy and rolled him onto his back; the boy's twisted legs weakly thrashed against the blood-soaked earth.

Just as Kirill began to bring the knife up toward the boy's throat, a light-brown wolf of enormous size leaped from the clearing to land just in front of the Romanov. Volkov had never seen a wolf of this size before; it was twice as large as any he had ever encountered. It bared a mouth full of razor-sharp teeth at Kirill as the Romanov fell backward in surprise and tried to bring his rifle up for a shot.

A loud boom rang through the forest as Razin fired at the wolf as it leaped at Kirill. The wolf moved so impossibly fast that Razin's shot went wide, and the soldier scrambled to find a better angle for his next shot. Volkov was trying to fire upon the wolf, but Kirill was in his line of fire.

Kirill screamed as the wolf closed its jaws onto the space between his neck and shoulders. The wolf shook him violently, and blood poured down the Romanov's blue coat as he beat the beast with his bare hands; his knife and rifle laying beside the wounded boy.

Batu let loose an arrow, grazing the wolf's shoulder, drawing a line of thick glistening blood in its light-brown fur. The wolf gave a whelp of pain and released Kirill, who crumpled to the ground in a bloody heap, spurts of lifeblood spewing from his tattered neck. The beast raised its head and howled a deep primal sound that echoed through the forest. Volkov's blood went cold when he heard a responding howl come from behind him. *Two Kurtadam?*

Volkov quickly raised his rifle and aimed directly at the wolf's mid-section, firing off the shot and promptly chambering another round. Whether it was the good fortune of the wolf or the ill luck of the Romanovs, Kirill sat up just as Volkov's shot sailed through the clearing. The Romanov's head jerked back as the bullet struck him in the forehead, and Kirill Vladimirovich Romanov, the second cousin to the Grand Duke and sixty-eighth in line to be the Tsar of Russia, was dead before his head hit the ground. An anguished cry rose from Sergeant Razin as he watched Kirill tumble lifelessly to the ground.

"Dammit! Balkov, get those men up here," Volkov could hear village hunters running through the woods as a cacophony of shots and gunshots rang out behind him.

In the clearing, the wolf ran for the woods, moving with speed unnatural even for such predators. Batu let fly another arrow, missing the beast, as did Volkov's second shot that trailed behind the fleeing wolf.

Then the wolf turned back and ran for the boy, zigging and zagging. Volkov cursed as his next shot kicked up dirt in front of the wolf, and in his haste to load another round, the cold metal bullet slipped from his fingers. The wolf snatched up the Verenich boy in its jaws and bounded into the woods, leaving only the fallen Romanov sprawled in the clearing.

There was a commotion as Batu suddenly tumbled from the wood line, grappling with a giant black wolf. The wolf was immense, even larger than the light brown wolf in the clearing. It stood erect on its hind legs as it raked the Mongolian's chest with long, fingerlike claws, tearing so deep into his flesh that Volkov thought he could see glimpses of the white bone of the tracker's ribs amid the curtains of torn skin.

***

"We are missing everything," Morozov stared into the woods at the sound of the first gunshot. "We should be out there."

"The Romanov told us to wait here with the prisoner," Tyutchev's voice was deadpan and dispassionate.

"What if he is in trouble? Will you answer for the Tsar's huntsman getting killed?" Morozov saw the seeds of doubt festering in the soldiers' eyes. "Maybe even the Romanov?"

The soldiers looked at each other questioningly.

"Look, I will hang the man myself. No blame will be placed on you," Morozov leaned in close to the soldiers. "You could be heroes for saving the Romanov."

A second shot rang out in the distance, and the heads of both soldiers shot up in alarm. They peered at the woods apprehensively, and then the Tyutchev looked to Morozov and gave a quick nod.

"Good," Morozov smiled broadly and gestured to his son. "Petr, throw that rope over the branch there."

The red-haired boy looked down at the unconscious Negrescu, smiling as he grabbed the rope's end and tossed it over a thick branch about eight feet off the ground. Morozov took the rope from his son and pulled it taunt as he gestured for the soldiers to help him. The three men pulled the rope until it jerked Negrescu into the air.

The man's eyes flew wide open as he regained consciousness, the noose tightening around his neck. The Morozovs and the soldiers pulled harder as Negrescu's legs frantically kicked and his body jerked and swung in the air. The dark-haired man's face reddened, and his eyes bulged as the rope constricted tighter. They tied the rope to the wagon wheel as more shots rang out in the distance.

"It sounds bad," Herzen picked up his rifle and stared into the woods.

"We should get moving," Morozov squinted into the darkened forest.

Behind them, the swinging Negrescu started to twitch and jerk spasmodically as his hands elongated into wolf-like claws. The bones of his face began to shift and stretch into a canine snout as thick black hair sprouted all over his body, and his teeth grew long and razor-like. The sound of Bogdan's clothes tearing drew the younger Morozov's attention; however, by the time the youth turned, only an enormous black wolf hung from the noose. Fear gripped Petr so intensely that he could not speak. He feebly tugged at his father's tunic as the giant wolf shredded the rope, pounced to the ground, and stood upright on its hind legs.

The wolf ran toward the men, moving incredibly fast for a beast of its enormous size. It batted Petr with its massive paw, sending the red-haired boy hurtling across the clearing. The Land Captain turned just in time to see the wolf's massive jaws, with threads of saliva dripping from its knife-sharp teeth, close on the head of one of the soldiers, Herzen, crushing it like a fragile eggshell. The beast then struck Tyutchev in the head with its paw, crashing the soldier into the side of the wagon, where he lay with his neck jutting at an unnatural angle.

Morozov did not even have time to raise his hands before the wolf raked its claw across his neck as it hurtled by and disappeared into the woods. He dropped to the ground as he clutched at his neck, waves of blood pouring down over his robust belly. He tried to scream, but his shredded vocal cords failed to produce a sound as he tumbled face-first into the dirt.

The wolf bounded through the woods at an incredible pace, racing toward the sound of the gunshots as a howl rang out. The great beast reared its head and howled an answering cry as it crashed through the frightened assembly of village hunters. Human bones shattered as the wolf crushed two men to the ground, his vicious claws felling two others as he bound past. The hunters' voices cried out in fear and confusion as they fired wildly after it. His nose picked up the smell of blood, that of the Verenich boy, Leo, and the new-made she-wolf, and he quickened his pace. More gunshots rang out as a shape moved on the edge of the clearing before him.

Leaping through the air, he bared his teeth in a feral snarl and reached out with his front claws as he crashed into the Mongolian hunter. Surprise and terror crossed the man's face as the wolf's claws tore through the fabric of his outer garments and into his flesh, shredding the tracker's skin. The hunter dropped his bow and raised his arm to protect his face and neck as his other closed around one of the long knives on his belt.

The wolf swung a hand toward the hunter's head, gouging into the man's scalp and coming away with gore and clumps of hair falling from its claws. The hunter grunted in pain but stepped into the wolf's next strike as he drew the knife. The downward arc of the creature's arm prevented the tracker from stabbing upward into the muscular torso of the beast, so he sidestepped and plunged the blade toward the soft flesh between its hind leg and hip. The wolf felt the blade slice deep, but the blade glanced off the beast's hipbone and was jerked out of the hunter's hand.

The beast roared with pain, a sound of anguish and rage, as it lashed out at Batu. The wolf's hand raked across the tracker's face, one claw sinking deep into the man's eye, which burst in a spray of blood and fluid that soaked the man's mangled cheeks. The hunter reeled, moaning and disoriented, as he staggered back, clutching his face, his other hand groping for his remaining blade as the wolf leapt upon him again, pressing its advantage.

Batu struggled to hold the creature's jaws at bay with one hand as he desperately reached for one of his knives with his other. As his body trembled beneath the onslaught of the wolf, Batu's remaining eye met Volkov's horrified gaze. The huntsman saw in the tracker's eye the resignation that he would not win this fight. He would sacrifice his life so that Volkov, the man he loved above all else in this world, could flee and live to hunt the beast another day. Amidst the blood and anguish marring Batu's features, Volkov saw the depth of love that resided within the man. The need for Volkov to be the last sight he saw before his life was extinguished.

"Arkady, run!" Batu screamed as his strength gave way.

The wolf thrust its massive skull down in a ferocious headbutt that struck the left side of Batu's face just as the Mongolian pulled back the knife for a second thrust. Bone met bone with a sickening crack as the knife fell from Batu's fingers. The tracker's arms went limp and his face slack as his eye rolled up into his head. The black wolf gripped Batu firmly as it brought its head down repeatedly against the tracker's skull, until the sounds of shattering bone gave way to a damp, squishing sound like stomping through mud. Volkov stared in horror as Batu's head lolled lifelessly upon his shoulders, and he dropped to the ground like a marionette with its strings cut. As Batu's head thudded upon the ground, his sightless eye stared directly at Volkov from a skull horribly crushed and misshapen.

The wolf snarled and glared balefully at where Volkov hid in the woods, and the huntsman tried to sink further into the shadows. Blood dripped from the knife wound on the wolf's side, but it showed no sign of weakening. It gave a guttural howl that turned Volkov's intestines watery, then bounded off into the woods, trailing the other wolf.

For the first time in his life, Volkov sank to his knees, shaking in terror as he tried to swallow down the bile that rose in his throat.

***

Volkov retrieved Batu's bow and knife and knelt beside the tracker's body. He slid the blade back into its sheath and placed the bow on Batu's torn and bloodied chest, folding the man's arms over it. Batu's hands were still warm as Volkov ran his fingers over them. The skin on

Batu's hands was rough and calloused, but the hands themselves were delicate.

Hands made for art, not death.

He forced himself to look at Batu's face; this was not how he wanted to remember his friend, his lover. The tracker's face was an utter ruin. The skin was torn and ragged where the *Kurtadam* had raked its nails across his face, covering Batu's weather-tanned skin in a sheen of quickly drying blood. Batu's left eye was a gaping hole, the remnants of his eyelids sunken in like a deflated balloon and crusting over with blood and fluid. The man's remaining eye was wide open and rolled backward, white as an egg, in a head now noticeably concave with jagged edges of fractured skull poking through torn flesh. Volkov wanted to lean down and kiss the man one last time, however, the tracker's top lip was severed into two halves by the *Kurtadam*'s claw.

"Goodbye, Batu," Volkov reached a hand out and closed Batu's remaining eye.

"You fucking killed him," a ragged voice yelled from behind Volkov, who turned and saw Sergeant Razin staggering toward him, his rifle pointed at the huntsman. "You fucking shot him. You killed him, you bastard."

Volkov glanced toward the crumpled body of Kirill Romanov and then back to Razin, who had stopped a few paces before the huntsman. "The Romanov was dead before the shot rang out; the beast had split him from stem to stern."

Razin raised the rifle to his face as he sighted Volkov down the barrel. The barrel wavered, and Volkov could see the man's eyes briefly flick to Batu's body and then back to the huntsman. Then, the man's shoulders sagged, and he sank to his knees with a pitiful moan. Razin drove the butt of the rifle down hard against the earth and leaned his head against it.

"This is not over, Sergeant Razin," Volkov eyed the man.

"The Romanov is dead; the tracker is dead; everyone is dead," Razin did not lift his head from its resting place on the rifle.

"We're alive, and so are the beasts that did this," Volkov said, getting to his feet. "One is wounded; I will track it to its lair and kill them both."

Razin looked up and watched Volkov retrieve his rifle and head into the woods after the wolf without glancing back at the Cossack sergeant. He glanced over at the lifeless body of the Romanov, despondent over his failure to once again protect his charge. Then, leaning heavily on his rifle, Sergeant Razin pulled himself to his feet and followed Volkov into the woods.

Chapter 5

The dream felt so real. Oksana opened her eyes and lay in the old barn at Galina's cottage. The hay rustled beneath her body as she sat up, and the unmistakable scent of manure assailed her nostrils. She heard movement behind her, something else moving among the hay. Oksana turned to see what was making the noise when a terrible pain doubled her over. She wrapped her arms over her stomach and bent over so far her forehead nearly touched her knees as a hunger so intense it felt like it was clawing at her insides. Her body began to shake, and she opened her mouth and screamed, a scream that turned into a howl.

Oksana raised her hand and watched as her fingers elongated and sharp, curved claws grew from the tips. Her clothing tore along the seams as muscular limbs covered in long golden fur burst forth. She clamped her eyes shut as an intense feeling of heat radiated over her body and she rolled over onto all fours. When she opened her eyes, a figure stood on the other side of the barn. It was a man standing in the shadows. However, although he stood in darkness, her eyes could see him clearly, as if it were daylight. She felt the air escape her lungs—it was Alexei.

It is a dream. This is a dream. I am not some beast. Alexei is not alive. Wake up. Wake up. Wake up.

Oksana's mind screamed the words. Alexei moved quickly toward her; something dangled in his hands. Her nose discerned it before her eyes fully registered what it was—a rabbit.

The expression on Alexei's face was unreadable as he stepped forward and threw the rabbit toward her. Oksana snatched it from the air without thinking, grabbing it with a long lupine mouth. Salty blood filled her mouth as her teeth sank into the soft fur and punctured the tender flesh beneath. She tore into the rabbit, muscle, and sinew shredding beneath her sharp teeth. Oksana swallowed chunks of meat, barely chewing them as she sought to satiate the painful hunger. Alexei threw another rabbit, its limp brown body landing alongside the torn carcass of the first. She devoured them both until the darkness took her.

***

Oksana stirred to wakefulness; her head throbbed, and she reached up to tentatively run a finger along the spot Father Grigori had struck her. She ran her hand along her scalp and, although her head felt tender where the priest had struck her, Oksana's head seemed relatively unscathed. Something thin and rough poked at her feet, and it took Oksana a moment to place the sensation.

Straw.

Oksana's eyes flew open, and she took in her surroundings: the wooden plank walls, the earth and straw floor, the unmistakable scent of manure. She was in a barn, but not just any barn; she was in Galina's barn.

Oh my God, I'm back in the dream.

She sat up and felt cool air on her back and shoulders as the blanket that had covered her slipped off. In sudden horror, Oksana realized she was naked beneath the woolen blankets and quickly held it tight around her. Her head throbbed. This made no sense. How had she gotten here? Why was she naked? Oksana forced herself to focus; she remembered something sharp tearing into her shoulder and dragging her. Her hand reflexively went to her shoulder. However, there was no wound, just small, pink circles of skin in the shape of a bit – an animal bite, wolf or dog.

I was hurt. Father Grigori struck me as I ran. Why was I running?

The image of Father Grigori and Vera Morozova came flooding back to her: their writhing bodies, the moaning and thumping of Vera's body the wall, her milky white breast in the priest's hands.

He tried to kill me because I saw them together.

The thought filled Oksana with anger. How many times had the priest punished her and Alexei for the most minor infraction? Yet here was the pious Father Grigori breaking multiple commandments with the ease of shattering glass against the wall. She hated the priest now more than ever.

Why was she in the church?

The thought nagged at her momentarily; then, her blood ran cold. *Leo!* Oksana stood up quickly, perhaps too fast, as she swooned off balance and barely managed to keep the blanket around her. Then she froze.

Beside where she had lain, tiny red dots sprinkled the straw. Oksana bent to inspect the hay, her fingers brushing the earthen floor, which felt damp. When she turned her hand over, she saw her fingertips were pink. Oksana sniffed her fingers and smelled the metallic scent of blood. Something caught her eye: an irregularity among the slim stalks of straw. Oksana dug her hand into the straw until her finger felt something firm and slender. With growing apprehension, Oksana lifted her hand and saw a small, thin, white bone—the unmistakable leg bone of a rabbit. A wave of nausea rose in her gorge, and she had to fight back the urge to vomit as she let the bone tumble to the earth.

What the hell was going on?

"You're awake," the voice was soft and uncertain.

Oksana whirled and saw Alexei standing in the doorway, a small bundle of her clothes in his hand. She was too stunned and confused to speak.

"I know; this is a lot to take in," Alexei raised a hand and tried to calm her.

"What am I doing here?" Oksana felt tears sting her eyes, and she did not understand why. "Why am I naked, and how are you alive?"

He entered the room and offered her the bundles of clothes, "Here, get dressed first. I'll explain everything, or at least I'll try."

Oksana held the blanket tightly around her thin frame and snatched the clothes from him with her other hand, suddenly feeling her anger rising. "You let me think you were dead!"

"Please, Oksana, just get dressed, and I'll tell you everything I know," Alexei backed out of the room. "You're in Galina's barn; I am just next door in the space Bogdan turned into a room. Please just get dressed, and we'll talk."

He shut the door, leaving Oksana glaring at oaken boards as she pulled on her clothes.

***

Alexei sat on Bogdan's bed and ran his fingers through his hair, trying to think of a way to explain recent events to Oksana. He wondered what had become of Bogdan; the woodsman was not among the dead in the cottage, and his ever-present bulging backpack was absent from its peg on the wall.

The cottage. The thought of that cursed place sent a shiver of revulsion and shame down Alexei's spine. He forced his mind back to the issue at hand. There was no rational answer for what had happened to him and now Oksana. Alexei wished Leo was here; he always thought about how things would work, and something like this was right in Leo's bread basket. A smile crossed Alexei's face. Leo would say this was the work of Baba Yaga.

Hell, maybe it was.

The door to Bogdan's room opened, and Oksana stepped in; Alexei could see her lips were tight, something she always did when she was mad. He stood and offered her the best smile he could muster.

"Hey," Alexei greeted her. "It's good to see you."

"Go to hell," Oksana's jaw was so tight she barely got the words out. "You broke my heart. You let me think you were dead and that it was my fault. That you died running off to confront my uncle."

"I did," the words had struck Alexei like a physical blow. "Your uncle, Rostov, and the others grabbed me; they shot me and killed Ivan."

"You look pretty healthy for someone who got shot," Oksana spat the words.

"I did! I healed," Alexei said, pulling down the collar of his shirt. He pointed to the faint red circular scar on his shoulder.

"You're pathetic," Oksana turned to leave.

"My shoulder healed, just like your head," Alexei stepped toward Oksana when he saw her hesitate and reach a hand up to touch the back of her head.

"How?" She turned to him, still rubbing the spot on her head where Father Grigori had struck her.

"I don't know exactly," Alexei shook his head, then met her gaze. "The night your uncle and the others attacked me, I escaped and made it back to my house. My shoulder was bleeding badly, and they had broken my hand. The wolf followed me home; it must have been the scent of the blood."

"Why didn't it kill you?" Oksana narrowed her eyes as she looked at him.

"Ivan showed up. Rostov's men had shot him, too, but he made it home. He spent the last of his energy chasing the wolf off," Alexei had to fight back tears at the thought of the dog's bravery. "But the wolf bit me, and its bite seems to have changed me. It somehow healed me."

"I think it bit me, too," Oksana remembered the pain in her shoulder as something dragged her from the village. "Father Grigori had hurt me. I thought I was dying, but now there's no sign of even a cut."

"No," Alexei shook his head and looked away from her. "The wolf didn't bite you."

"No, Alexei, it did! I remember its teeth sinking into my shoulder," Oksana stepped toward him. "The wolf bit me, and then I had a crazy dream, but when I awoke, I was here and fine."

"Oksana, the wolf didn't bite you," Alexei looked into her face. "I did."

"What?" Oksana stepped back as her face became a mask of confusion. "Alexei, what are you saying?"

"When the wolf bit me, the bite healed me, but it also changed me," Alexei's stomach knotted as he finally worked up the courage to tell Oksana everything. I think the wolf is some half-man, half-beast werewolf, a *volkolak* like in Leo's stories. After it bit me, I changed. At least, I think I died first and then came back changed."

"Alexei, you're not making any sense," Oksana's hazel eyes searched his face.

"I awoke in the grave next to Ivan, and as I fought to get out, I changed into a wolf, just like you did last night." Alexei saw the shock and horror on Oksana's face. "I found you when you were hurt and brought you back here. I thought you died, you were so cold and still; but then you returned and became a wolf with golden fur. My bite affected you like the wolf's bite did me."

Oksana backed away from him, shaking her head in disbelief. She pointed at Alexei, "Stay away from me, Alexei. I don't know what kind of cruel game you are playing; stay away from me."

"Oksana, think. I know it sounds crazy, but you know I'm telling you the truth. You are just like me; if I didn't have those rabbits last night, you would have attacked me. I saw it in your eyes," Alexei pleaded with her. "You are a *volkolak*, just like me."

"You're sick, Alexei," Oksana backed toward the door. "I don't know what kind of insane fantasy you have created in your head to keep me with you, but you're sick."

Alexei feared it would come to this as he reached back into his mind to the door. He could feel the wolf on the other side, its hot breath blowing through the cracks, eager to be released. The transformation came more effortlessly now, as if his muscles and bones remembered. Alexei flung the door open wide.

Oksana moved away from him until her back was against the wall as she watched Alexei change. His limbs grew long and muscular, tearing through his clothes as thick gray hair covered them. The shirt on his back and the trousers he wore shredded and fell to the floor as Alexei's body took on the shape of the wolf, his ears and snout elongating and becoming lupine. Oksana screamed and ran for the door as Alexei reached a clawed hand out to prevent her from fleeing. She batted the fur-covered hand away and fled the room.

Alexei was devastated; she saw him as a monster. He backed away as if mortally wounded as she fled. Alexei had believed she would see the transformation and understand what he was telling her was true; maybe it would bring them closer together—two *volkolaks* against the world. Together, they would find the wolf and discover what was happening.

He had to go after her, but not like this; his *volkolak* form terrified her. The wolf needed to return behind the door. He could be Alexei again to show her he was still the boy she knew. Alexei needed to go after her before she ran too far before she got to...

The cottage.

*****

Oksana backed away from the immense wolf that stood on its hind legs amid the torn remnants of Alexei's clothes. She wanted to scream but feared it would turn into a howl, just like in her dream.

Dream? Had it really happened?

Inside her skull, Oksana felt a primal presence yearning to be free to run through the woods with this wolf—to hunt and feed. She felt like it howled inside her head and clawed at her brain for release. Oksana fled the barn into the cool, dark night and reeled under the myriad of sounds and scents assailing her senses. She felt as if she could hear the footfalls of beetles upon the trees, and the aroma of the forest built the growing storm of the beast inside into a tempest.

Oksana ran toward the cottage, the only place that had felt like home since her parents died. She needed the comfort of her bed to see the fine things that Galina had filled the house with. Her keen ears picked up the sound of Alexei's pursuit before she saw him.

"Oksana, come back," Alexei raced out of the barn, a boy again, his pale chest bare and a blanket held tight around his waist.

She ran faster for the cottage, a feral growl escaping her lips that frightened and flushed her with adrenaline. Alexei was calling to her, yelling for her not to go into the cottage, almost begging her. Oksana cleared the steps up the porch in a single bound, threw open the door, and staggered back. The odor of death that wafted from the house made her gag; the smell of stale blood permeated the air, and she heard her inner beast's howl echo inside her skull.

Her eyes, more attuned to the dark than ever before, peered inside the house as Alexei came up behind her, however, her brain struggled to comprehend what it saw.

"Oksana, please, don't," his voice was soft and mournful as he walked up the steps and reached for her.

Oksana shook off his hand and stepped into the doorway. Amid the overwhelming scent of blood, the overturned furniture, and the destroyed painting, lay a pile of bones—human bones by the look of the three skulls she saw. Something had picked the skeletal pile nearly clean of flesh, cracking the longer bones and sucking the marrow out. The scene reminded her of a dragon's lair from one of Leo's fairy tales.

"Is Galina in there?" Oksana asked, her voice cracking.

"No," replied Alexei softly. "It's Olga and her brothers. The wolf took Galina's body."

"The wolf did this?" Oksana could not tear her eyes from the macabre scene.

"No," Alexei's voice was barely above a whisper.

"No?" She turned to him, eyes welling with tears.

"No," he repeated, not meeting her gaze.

"Alexei?" the first tear ran down her cheek.

"When I brought you back here, the taste of your blood in my mouth drove me insane. I was afraid I would hurt you," Alexei's bottom lip quivered with emotion. "They were already dead, Oksana."

Oksana could not speak as she sank to her knees, her hands coming to her face at the incomprehensible horror.

"You don't know what it's like; once you taste human flesh, the wolf inside you craves it like an insatiable hunger," Alexei's bare chest heaved as he fought back the tears. "I'm not a monster."

She looked up at him with wide, tear-filled eyes that were fearful. "They are not the first?"

Alexei could only shake his head.

"Who?" she breathed the question, needing to know, yet at the same time fearing the answer.

"The Chernyshevsky brothers, Gleb Andreev, and the Cossacks that killed Ivan," Alexei sat down on the steps and stared at the ground. "Oksana, it was the *volkolak*; I could not control myself."

"Is this what you have done to me?" Oksana's voice was a mix of rage and despair. "You've turned me into a *volkolak*? Will I spend my nights snatching children from their beds and eating them under the moon?"

"No," Alexei shook his head. "I don't crave other meat like I do human flesh, and I didn't crave human flesh until after I bit the Chernyshevskys. I think as long as you don't bite another human, you won't hunger for it."

"And what about you?" Oksana whispered.

"I don't know." He glanced sidelong at her and noticed she was shaking. "Are you okay?"

"No, I'm very not okay," Oksana half-laughed. "I think the smell of blood from the house is awakening the *volkolak* inside me. I feel like it's in a forest running toward me in my head."

"For me, it lurks behind a door in my head; if I open that door, I become the *volkolak*. But I think I can control when I change now. I can teach you how to control it," Alexei looked at her and saw the hesitant acceptance in her hazel eyes. "We should leave here now and hunt in the forest. It will be better for you to be away from the scent of people. There are deer and rabbits."

She slowly nodded. In her mind, Oksana could feel the *volkolak* approaching through the forest. She felt as if she could feel the beast's breath within her warm upon her neck. Her will was crumbling, and she could not resist the primal call of the *volkolak* much longer.

Suddenly, Alexei stopped and tilted his head upward as he sniffed the air. Oksana would have thought the sight comical if not for their present situation and his look of deep concentration.

"What is it?" Oksana felt his unease and wondered if this was how animals in a pack grew attuned to each other.

"There's a smell on the wind; it's blood. Human blood. I've smelled it before," Alexei could see the confusion on her face. "I've smelled this person's blood before."

"Is it Galina's?" Oksana stood up and looked toward the forest. She tried smelling the air, but the myriad scents, coupled with the stench of blood from the cottage, were still too overwhelming. "Is she alive?"

"No, it's not Galina," Alexei shook his head as he probed his memory. Then his head snapped up, and his eyes flew open in alarm. "The night I became the *volkolak*, I went to Leo's house for help. He cut his finger on the window. Oksana, it's the same scent; it's Leo's blood."

"Oh my God, Alexei," the sudden realization was jarring to Oksana. "Pavel was taking Leo; I think he meant to hurt him. His mother sent me to find Father Grigori for help. How could I have forgotten? If something happens, it will be all my fault."

"It's not your fault, Oksana. That goddamned priest scrambled your brain when he hit you," Alexei let out a feral growl. "You must trust me. We will move faster as *volkolak,* and I can track him better as a wolf."

Oksana nodded, "I trust you, Alexei."

Alexei stepped forward, grabbing her hand and giving her a half smile, "Don't be afraid."

"I won't be," Oksana smiled back, and in her heart, she knew she could trust Alexei to keep her safe.

Alexei stepped back from her, releasing her hand as he shifted into the *volkolak.* Oksana closed her eyes and envisioned the forest in her mind. She could hear the beast approaching, its yellow eyes staring at her from the forest's edge, and Oksana realized the wolf was waiting for her. Whether it would wait until she summoned it forward or become impatient and surge forward to exert its control over her body, Oksana did not know.

Oksana extended her hand, and the golden-brown wolf stepped out of the woods. It strode forward, head raised and eyes bright, padding across the dark earth to stand before Oksana, just short of her hand. The wolf radiated a feral power as it stared intently into her eyes, but Oksana felt no menace from the creature. As she searched the wolf's eyes, Oksana understood that she needed to take the final steps forward.

With her hand still extended, Oksana walked toward the wolf, and it raised its head to meet her. Her fingers, tingling with the sensation of unseen primal energy, ran along the soft golden fur of the wolf's head. The wolf reared its head back and howled, then as if in response, Oksana did the same; their voices united into one howl that sprang up from the core of each of them and intertwined. Oksana felt her eyes close as if blinking in slow motion.

When Oksana opened her eyes again, the wolf stood before her ,only further away now, its coat transformed from golden-brown to steely gray. She blinked, momentarily disoriented, and then realized it was Alexei standing before her in his *volkolak* form. Oksana could see her golden-brown muzzle extending from between her eyes. Looking down, Oksana saw her arms covered in the same golden fur; long fingers, tipped with sharp black claws, extended from palm-like paws that dug into the soft earth.

Alexei stared at her, waiting until she looked up again. She met his gaze and dipped her head in understanding. The large gray wolf dipped his head in acknowledgment and turned, running off into the forest, his nose held high to follow the scent of Leo's blood upon the wind. Behind him, the golden-brown wolf followed.

***

"Fuck," Rostov kicked a booted foot against the forest floor as he leaned against the tree.

More gunshots rang out in the distance, a tell-tale sign that that bastard Volkov had located the wolf before him. Rostov and his men had set and baited spring net traps along an arc between the site of the last wolf attack at the cottage and what he believed was the likely direction of the animal's lair in the hills surrounding Obrechen. Now, those efforts seemed futile; Volkov had beat him to the quarry.

He leaned his head back against the tree and swore again. The bounty on the wolf would have set him up nicely. However, losing to the arrogant Volkov was what really boiled his blood. After this debacle, he might head to Tula, where factories always needed someone to get striking laborers back to work, or he could convince Count Guriev that Kalinin's Jews needed another lesson in Russian might. Either way, he needed to find somewhere to crack some skulls after this. He spit, trying to clear the sour taste from his mouth.

Maybe sampling that tasty little morsel of a wife Morozov kept at home would make him feel better. Rostov licked his lips and smiled as he ran a hand over his bald head. Yes, that would lift his spirits.

He thought there might still be time to visit the Morozov manor while the men were out and try his luck with the wench. The sound of gunfire had died, but Morozov might still be gone for hours. Rostov had picked up his rifle and was ready to call to his men when he heard the shouting.

It was the voice of the cook, Yermak, yelling as a torch sprang to life to Rostov's right. Something had sprung a trap. Hope swelled inside him, and he began to move toward the light.

If this is over a deer that wandered into the trap, that shitty cook will feel the blunt end of my Jew hammer, Rostov thought as he made his way through the darkened forest.

The unmistakable howl of a wolf tore through the night, a desperate mournful sound. Rostov's heart began to thunder excitedly, and he ran through the forest. One of his men, Kyrylo, fell in close behind him; the man's torch illuminated the forest around Rostov as the two ran for the clearing where Yermak bellowed excitedly in triumph.

As he entered the clearing, Rostov's eyes opened wide in surprise; an immense golden-brown wolf hung suspended in the net, which swung wildly as the creature struggled to free itself.

"It's beautiful," Rostov grinned. Whatever Volkov and his men shot at this evening, this was undoubtedly the Beast of Obrechen. He laughed out loud and slapped Kyrylo on the back as the bearded Cossack grinned back.

"We get good pay for this, yes?" Kyrylo pointed at the wolf.

"Oh yes, Kyrylo. We're going to get a lot of money for this," Rostov could not take his eyes off the giant wolf.

Matiev, the youngest of Rostov's Cossacks, stood almost under the swaying net, staring at the wolf. "I have never seen paws like that on a wolf," Matiev pointed upward, then turned to Rostov. "It looks like it has fingers."

Rostov watched as the net swayed back and forth, and the thick sapling attached to the net's rope bobbed and creaked. His euphoria gave way to the immediate need to secure his prize.

"Yermak, Yemelyan," Rostov called to the two men celebrating with swigs from Yermak's ever-present bottle of vodka. "Bring up the cage; we must get the wolf secured."

Yermak yelled something unintelligible back at Rostov and Yemelyan laughed uproariously. Rostov's brows knitted in irritation; he would not let these fools cost him his prize. Reaching for his hammer as he started across the clearing, Rostov would smash that bottle from the man's hand and get him back to work. Hell, maybe he would cave the man's head in as a lesson for the others. He doubted the other men would mind splitting Yermak's share of the money.

Rostov had barely taken a step when an immense gray shape burst from the woods behind Yemelyan and Yermak. He stood agape and blinking, unsure of what he saw—a gray wolf, at least seven feet tall, charged on its hind legs directly toward Yemelyan and Yermak. The beast's mouth twisted in a feral snarl, revealing jagged teeth glinting in the torchlight as it reached for the two Cossacks with dark human-like hands tipped with razor-sharp claws. As the wolf ran between the two men, it swept one hand across Yemelyan's midsection and the other across Yermak's throat, nearly decapitating the man.

Yemelyan sat down hard on the ground, his torso opening as if unbuttoned, as his innards cascaded out before him. Beside him, Yermak dropped like a felled tree, the bottle of vodka still gripped in his hand. Rostov, too stunned to bring his rifle up, could only watch as the wolf leaped skyward. Its claws slashed quickly through the rope that suspended the net, sending the trapped wolf crashing to the earth atop Matiev.

Rostov backed away, barely registering Matiev's screams, as the gray wolf landed a few feet before him. The beast stared directly into Rostov's eyes, and the man saw a depth of malice and hatred he had never encountered before. It turned his legs weak, and he felt the hot wash of urine soak his crotch and legs. Rostov turned to run and collided with the terrified Kyrylo, sending both men tumbling in a frantic tangle of scrambling limbs.

Rostov rolled onto his stomach and tried to crawl to the safety of the woods while Kyrylo frantically tried to crawl over him.

"Get off of me," Rostov yelled and bucked, trying to throw the young Cossack off him.

Kyrylo let out a blood-curdling scream so close to Rostov's head that his ears rang. The Cossack's nails dug into Rostov's shoulders as the man clenched at him. Rostov looked over his shoulder and saw the gray wolf standing over Kyrylo, its claws tearing into the Cossack's back as the man screamed. The beast grunted as it broke free two of Kyrylo's ribs and tore dark handfuls of meat from the man's body.

Kyrylo's grip slackened on his shoulders as the Cossack vomited blood down Rostov's neck, his screams fading into a whimpering gurgle. Rostov felt the back of his tunic soak with the man's warm blood as Kyrylo's body turned into a dead weight on his back.

The wolf tore Kyrylo's body from Rostov's back and flung the lifeless Cossack through the air. Rostov heard the man's body strike a nearby tree with a bone-shattering crack and thud to the forest floor. He leaped to his feet and tried to run, as the wolf raked a claw across the top of his bald head so deeply that Rostov heard the beast's nails scrape against the bone of his skull. He clenched his teeth so hard against the pain that one of his eye teeth cracked off in his mouth and a river of blood ran down his face and into his eyes from his tattered scalp.

In a desperate attempt to escape the wolf, Rostov drew the hammer from his belt and swung it at the beast as he turned to face it. The wolf easily batted his arm away, dislocating his elbow, and stepped forward to grab Rostov by the head and shoulder. He could feel the wolf's hot breath against his face as it lunged toward him and sank its teeth into the curve of his neck. The wolf's jaws tore through flesh and ligament, snapping his collar bone, as he screamed. He felt his feet leave the ground as the wolf swung its head from side to side, shaking him like a dog with a rag doll, until he blacked out from the pain.

Rostov's eyes fluttered open; his body torn, shredded, and covered in blood and gore as he lay sprawled on the forest floor. Through half-lidded eyes he watched the two wolves, one gray and the other golden-brown, run off into the woods on all fours, leaving a scene of utter carnage behind them. Then all went dark.

Chapter 6

Bogdan ran through the woods despite the burning pain in his hip from the Mongolian's blade. He raised his dark muzzle, picked up the scent of Leo's blood, and adjusted his path. His eyes, sharper at night than a human's, made it easy for him to weave through the dense trees and brush that would delay his pursuers.

It would have been so easy to hunt the surviving hunters down and finish them, even with his wound. However, Bogdan needed to be certain Leo was alright. The amount of blood that trailed behind the injured child and the other wolf was alarming, and he said a silent prayer to the gods that the boy's wound was not yet fatal.

When he reached the river, he stopped and drank deeply from the cool water. The chill fall waters cooled his overheated body. His hip throbbed, and he looked over the wound; it was deep but would heal quickly. One of the blessings of his shapeshifting ability was that his hybrid body seemed to recover at a remarkable rate. In his native Romania, they would call a creature like him a *pricolici*, though he preferred the German term, *werewolf*, wolf man.

Bogdan stepped into the river; the water was only a little more than a foot higher than his paws, and he was thankful that the seasonal flood had not yet begun. He examined the far side of the bank and smiled when he detected no sign of Leo or the other werewolf.

Good. Following the plan.

He had warned that if they became separated, they would keep to the water to hide the trail and then reach the den by traveling through the windward side of the hills so the high winds could further disperse their scent. Bogdan had not seen or smelled any dogs among the hunters but there was no telling what their next move would be.

The moon shone bright overhead, and that concerned him. He would be easy to spot as he traveled through the river, an easy mark for one of the hunters in the tree line. Bogdan had no idea how many still lived; he was sure only of Volkov.

The massive black wolf hunched low and moved quickly, taking care to step softly to avoid splashing noises that could draw attention to his passage down the shallow river. Bogdan traveled the cold river waters, sometimes up to his shoulders when he traveled on all fours. In those places, the current grew strong, and he worried about how the other had made the journey with the wounded Leo. The chill waters would have been dangerous to the frail boy even if he was uninjured, and Bogdan began to fear Leo may die before he could reach him.

The moon was beginning to wane on its nightly journey as Bogdan reached the rocky steps of the hills. He dragged himself out of the river, his dark fur cold and wet. Exhausted from the journey and weakened by his wound, Bogdan wanted to rest on the riverbank and recover his strength. However, he pushed forward, refusing to let pass even a moment he could be by Leo's side, providing the boy his only chance to live.

As he scrambled among the rocks, Bogdan picked up the familiar scent of the other. With growing dread, he realized the smell of Leo's blood had grown faint, and the droplets upon the rocks were few and far between. With renewed urgency, Bogdan scrambled up the hidden pathway, marked only by scent. He had chosen the location carefully: over a mile from the river, surrounded by natural shelters, cliffs, and dead-ends, the cave was nearly impossible to see until you almost stood atop it.

Bogdan scrambled down the steep rock climb to the entrance on the side of the hill. His keen lupine sight quickly discerned the three small excursions leading from the cave mouth. He took the opening on the right, a narrow tunnel with an increasingly sloped ceiling requiring an ordinary-sized man to crawl over fifty feet in total darkness to reach the end. It was a tight fit for a wolf as large as Bogdan, though his night vision made the journey less daunting in the enclosed space. The tunnel ended in a wall with a narrow crevice along the base, too small a space for the massive wolf.

Bogdan shifted back into his human form. After all these years, the transition was as easy as donning a coat. The cave floor was cold against his bare hands and feet, though he was thankful the wolf's enhanced night vision remained. He rolled onto his back, the only way to traverse the aperture, the stone scraping his naked body as he pulled himself through the narrow opening. Bogdan grimaced as the pain in his wounded hip ached as he used his legs to push his body further into the crevice.

He felt his head clear the opening on the other end and push into the thick woolen blanket hung to prevent any light from escaping. Bogdan blinked against the sudden onset of light from several lanterns as he pulled aside the blanket and birthed his body through the opening into the room behind.

The room was high enough for him to stand, and the woodsman quickly reached for one of the blankets piled by the opening and wrapped it around the lower half of his naked body. Turning from the opening, Bogdan's heart sank as he saw the pale, lifeless form of Leo, wrapped in blankets, his head propped on a makeshift pillow of clothes. Beside him, the brown wolf, now transformed back into the human form of Galina Sekova, knelt beside Leo, examining one of the boy's frail arms. She wore one of the dresses he had recovered from the cottage, a simple blue fabric with yellow flowers, and turned to him with sad, worried eyes.

"How is he?" Bogdan had trouble keeping the emotion from his voice as he approached them.

"The wound was so terrible. How could anyone be so cruel?" Galina's eyes filled with tears. She turned back to look at Leo. "He gave a shuddering breath and went still as we crossed the river."

"So I am too late," Bogdan felt his chest tighten with a sharp pang of grief. "I had hoped to reach him in time to deliver a bite and give the wolf a chance to save him like it did you."

"Bogdan, I bit him," Galina turned to the woodsman, tears streaming down her cheeks, and lifted Leo's pale arm. "I remembered what you told me, and I bit him on the arm as we fled, but he still died. I fear I did it wrong, and the added loss of blood only made him worse."

"Let me see," Bogdan rushed forward and knelt beside Leo, examining the boy's arm. "There's no right or wrong way to bite someone; you gave the boy his only chance at survival."

"It seems I was too late," she turned sad eyes toward Leo's pale face. He looked so peaceful and still.

"I'm not so sure about that," Bogdan peered closely at the bite mark on Leo's arm and pointed to the wound. "These punctures don't look fresh to me."

"I bit him no more than an hour or two ago," Galina leaned over to look at the wound.

"Exactly," Bogdan said with a faint smile. "The healing process started. We won't know for a few hours whether he passed before the wolf could heal him or this is part of the transformation."

A gentle scraping sound drew Galina's attention toward the crevice, "Bogdan, someone's coming." Her voice was hushed and worried.

Bogdan's brows furrowed, and he gently set Leo's arm down and returned the blanket over the limb. He turned toward the opening, shifting into wolf form as he moved. Beside him, he heard Galina's dress tearing as she shifted and moved protectively in front of Leo's body.

The black wolf rose onto his hind legs and stealthily moved to stand beside the entrance to the room. Raising a clawed hand, he prepared to strike. Anyone coming through the opening would have to travel on their back, exposing their head and throat to him as they emerged into the room. Across the room, Galina hunched low, her body blocking Leo from harm while she prepared to spring forward at any intruder.

The blanket covering bulged slightly as the top of a head pressed against it, and Bogdan poised to deliver a kill strike. He looked toward Galina, who dipped her head in acknowledgment that she was ready. Bogdan raised his other hand to thrust aside the curtain as the intruder pushed further out of the opening. He wanted to land a killing blow before the intruder could bring any weapons to bear against them.

The problematic entrance to the chamber had cemented Bogdan's decision to use the cave as a haven. He had hoped the narrow tunnel and even tighter crevice would deter interlopers. If any brave soul got too adventurous, Bogdan could readily handle them as they entered the chamber.

A disquieting thought entered the woodsman's mind: the chamber's greatest strength might also be its greatest weakness. The crevice was the only portal in or out of the cave chamber. Attackers could starve them out or even collapse the tunnel with explosives; either way, they would be trapped. If Bogdan tried to bring the fight to them, they would likely kill him as he exited the crevice on the other side before he shifted into the wolf.

Bogdan knew he would have a short window of surprise when the sudden bright lantern light of the room blinded and disoriented the intruder. His hip ached as he positioned himself for the attack. The werewolf's preternatural healing had stopped the bleeding, however, standing upright was still extremely painful as it put more pressure on the injured hip.

The dark woolen blanket suddenly bulged outward as the intruder thrust its heads and shoulders into the chamber. In one fluid motion, Bogdan ripped aside the curtain and brought the razor-sharp claws of his hand down upon the intruder's neck. He felt the tips of the claws press into the soft, exposed skin of the intruder's throat as the man gave a startled cry.

Through sheer force of will, Bogdan managed to hold back from opening the man's windpipe as he stared into Alexei Kaminer's dark, startled eyes.

***

The four surrounded Leo's still form, all human again since shifting back from their wolf forms. A palpable air of hostility hung between them. Galina had resumed her vigil by Leo's side, accompanied by Oksana, who now wore one of the older woman's dresses. Alexei looked somewhat comical in Bogdan's oversized clothes but there was no humor in the boy's dark expression.

"So it was you all along?" Alexei folded his arms and gave Bogdan an accusatory stare.

"Alexei, please, let Bogdan explain," Galina said, trying to ease the boy's ire.

"Explain?" Alexei snapped back at her. "Explain how he tried to kill me until Ivan chased him off?"

"Boy, I went there to help you," Bogdan glowered back.

"By attacking me?"

"Alexei, I bit you to save your life, the same way I did for Galina. You both would have died from your wounds," Bogdan's features softened. "The only way I could help you was by making you like me, a werewolf."

"It's true," Galina got to her feet. "Olga Putina had stabbed me; I was dying when Bogdan found me."

At the mention of Olga Putina, Alexei looked away, masking his expression. The images of tearing into the bodies of Olga and her brothers were still vivid in his memory. To his horror, the thoughts were not wholly unpleasant, and he felt the desire to satiate his hunger again gnawing at his mind. Bogdan caught Alexei's sudden change in demeanor and eyed the boy, studying him. Alexei saw the man's inquisitive gaze and quickly averted his eyes.

"But why hide this from us?" Oksana stood as well, her eyes moving from Bogdan to Galina.

"I am sorry for the pain this has caused you," Galina said, grasping Oksana's hand. "Bogdan had good cause for his actions; please just let him explain."

"One moment. I wish to have a word in private with Alexei," Bogdan added without taking his eyes off Alexei.

"More secrets?" Oksana shook her head, a wistful expression crossing her face.

"It's okay, Oksana," Alexei glanced toward her; his face looked so scared and childlike that she was momentarily taken aback and could only nod.

Bogdan put a hand on Alexei's shoulder and led him across the cavern chamber to where they could speak in private. He studied the boy's face and sighed, nodding sadly.

"I am sorry, Alexei," Bogdan's eyes held genuine sorrow as he looked at the boy. "Not for making you like me, but for not being there when you first shifted. This transformation is difficult to understand, especially for someone so young and alone."

Alexei swallowed hard but said nothing. He looked from Bogdan's eyes to the floor, having trouble holding the man's gaze.

"I returned to your cabin the following day but honestly thought you had died before the wolf's power could take effect and save you," Bogdan's eyes flickered to Leo's still body and then back to Alexei. "I thought the shift would occur more quickly, but now I am learning that in some, the transformation happens more slowly than in others. For a time, it is impossible to tell the dead from the transforming. You were the first person I have ever passed this along to."

"Oksana shifted only a few hours after I bit her," Alexei nodded and then looked toward Leo. "How will we know if Leo is truly dead?"

"His body shows no signs of decay or stiffening, so I am hopeful that Leo may still return to us if he received the gift in time," Bogdan glanced over at the boy as Oksana and Galina adjusted the pile of clothes used as a makeshift pillow into a shape they thought would be more comfortable.

"Gift?" Alexei gave a bitter laugh. "Or curse?"

Bogdan turned back to Alexei, his eyes growing stern, "It is truly a gift, Alexei. You will not age or sicken. Your wounds will heal quickly. But if you cannot control yourself, yes, it will become a curse."

Alexei appeared ready to give a hot retort, then his shoulders sagged, and he nodded knowingly.

"There have been several men killed that I was not responsible for. Was that you, Alexei?" Bogdan's voice softened, sounding almost fatherly, and Alexei nodded without looking at the woodsman. "I see."

Bogdan took a moment to collect his thoughts before continuing as Alexei shifted his feet uncomfortably.

"Did you consume any of the bodies of the men you killed?" Bogdan's voice was barely above a whisper.

"I did," Alexei nodded as he finally met Bogdan's gaze, tears welling in his eyes.

"It's okay, son," Bogdan placed his hands on Alexei's shoulders. "It's not your fault; the wolf in you made you do it."

"Bogdan, I crave human flesh now. I have eaten deer and rabbit, but nothing quells the hunger inside me now except people," Alexei tried futilely to hold back the tears. "I cannot be near a person without thinking about what their heart and liver taste like. Even you and the girls; I can sense the blood pumping in your veins. If you left me alone here, I would eat Leo's body like I did Olga and her brothers. I'm a monster, Bogdan; a fucking monster."

"You're no monster, Alexei; you are a hunter," Bogdan gripped the boy's shoulders more firmly. "But you MUST control this craving, or it will consume you and destroy you."

A loud gasp of air echoed through the cave, accompanied by startled cries. The two men turned to find Leo sitting up, as the two women exchanged shocked looks and then broad smiles. Leo stared around in bewilderment, blinking rapidly.

"Leo," Bogdan gave a smile that reached up to his eyes.

Alexei, too, smiled at the sight of his friend alive. But then a look of confusion came over his face and he turned to Bogdan, "why didn't he shift? Oksana and I both shifted as we awoke from our injuries."

Bogdan shrugged, "Who knows how this gift works or where it truly came from? Aside from the four of us, I know of only three other such creatures, and at least two are dead."

"Others?" the thought shocked Alexei. It had never occurred to him that there could be others like them in the world.

Bogdan gave Alexei a resigned smile and clapped him on the back, "Come, Alexei, I think it is time for me to tell all that I know from the beginning."

The two men made their way toward Leo and the women, who were alternating between laughing, crying, and hugging the boy. Leo smiled broadly as Bogdan and Alexei approached, though he still looked confused.

"Alexei, Bogdan! Am I in heaven?" Leo stared at them in wonder. Then his eyes grew wide, and he looked around the cave. "Are we in Baba Yaga's hut?"

***

Bogdan sat back against the cave wall and sighed heavily as four pairs of eyes watched him expectantly. Alexei and Oksana flanked Leo, sitting wrapped in a blanket and munching noisily on an apple. The boy had refused the dried venison Bogdan stored in the cave but readily accepted an apple to ease his incredible hunger. The wound on the boy's side had healed, though the skin around it was still bright red and sore to the touch.

Bogdan's wound had already closed, thanks to the preternatural healing abilities of his werewolf body, though no healing was ever as quick as that which occurred during the first transformation. He looked at Galina, her eyes meeting his, and she gave him a faint smile and nod of encouragement. The woodsman returned the smile and nodded slightly before turning to look at the others.

"I was a soldier once," Bogdan began. *"I fought with Prince Vlad and King Carol against the Turks at the Battle of Pleven in seventy-seven..."*

***

I was a soldier once. I fought with Prince Vlad and King Carol against the Turks at the Battle of Pleven in seventy-seven. We were in the thick of it; I held the line alongside Prince Vlad. That man was a sheer terror on the battlefield, a sight to behold. It was bloody work, and we won the day, but I had had my fill of war and missed my young bride, Ana. So I took my pay, and I bought us a small farm in the foothills of the Carpathian Mountains.

It wasn't much, but it was ours, and it produced enough food for us to live on and still have some to sell at the market for some extra money. Life was good, and we were happy. Very happy. But as life would have it, that's when things turned to shit."

Ana got sick first. It started as just a slight cough here and there. She would tire more quickly than usual. By the time we figured out she was really ill, I had it as well, and it was too late for either of us—tuberculosis. We hugged, cried, and made love like each time would be our last.

We came up with a plan. When the time came that we were too sick to go on, we would drink a small vial of poison that Ana would craft from some local plants and curl up for one last long night's sleep together. I never thought much about death and dying, but Ana did not like the thought of being buried in the ground. The idea of becoming worm food terrified her, and she did not want us to be separated, even in the grave.

Ana did not believe in heaven or hell; she had an idea that when we died, she wanted our bodies burned. Ana thought that when we turned to smoke, our bodies would mix, and we would travel together on the wind until the end of time. I loved that thought; there was a beauty in it. So, as Ana mixed the poison, I made a lantern that would burn slowly as the poison took effect and then explode and set the house and our dead bodies ablaze. We set them aside and we waited.

Summer turned to fall, and then fall turned to winter. The illness slowly ravaged our bodies, and we knew our time was growing very short. Then, one day, a man sought shelter in our barn—an Irishman and former soldier, like myself, just finding his way in the world. I would learn later that his name was Cillian O'Rourke.

I gave Cillian food and shelter and showed him kindness, something he was unaccustomed to. He saw that we were deathly ill and sought to repay our kindness with a remarkable gift. Cillian bit and transformed us. It healed our bodies; the tuberculosis was gone.

Cillian had come with the British and fought in the Crimea. One night, a giant wolf, a werewolf, attacked the trench where he and his mates slept. Cillian killed the beast, but not before it bit him and killed the other men. He shifted that night in the medical tent and fled into the night. Cillian spent the next two decades searching for others like him. He never found another living werewolf. However, Cillian found the archives of Europe filled with tales and encounters with the creatures. He scoured records and private libraries, learning all that he could.

Cillian believed that once bitten, the blood became infected, and the victim would soon die. However, it was a faux death, like the caterpillar in the cocoon. He came to believe that the victim went into limbo, neither truly dead nor alive, as the wolf toxin and the human body reformed and was reborn as a werewolf. The metamorphosis into the werewolf had remarkable healing effects that cured diseases and healed even the most grievous wounds. It cured our tuberculosis.

Cillian was our mentor and teacher in this bizarre new world, and we traveled all over Europe, joining him in his quest for knowledge. We saw all of the great cities as we hunted for any word or tale of werewolves. He taught us how to live and hunt while hiding in plain sight among normal humans and gave us rules to strictly follow in order to avoid detection, survive, and control the beast within us.

However, in time, we knew it was time to part ways. Cillian had learned that some of his kin, his brother and two sons, lived in America and had settled in Florida. He wanted to see them if they still lived, and he wanted to investigate the Native American legends of skinwalkers, creatures he believed were a form of werewolf. Ana and I yearned to return to our farm. Traveling and seeing much of the world makes you truly appreciate the simple things in life. We had not aged since our transformation, so we thought we would have forever together, and that would be perfection.

We would shift into wolf form and hunt together for food, taking only what we needed. A single deer could fill our bellies for two weeks or more. However, game became scarce one winter, and we hunted deep into the Carpathian forests.

We followed the rivers and streams, knowing that deer would come to drink. That is when we came across them; two majestic red deer bucks with immense racks of eight or ten points each, drinking deeply from a shallow stream. Ana and I stared at them in awe; they were beautiful creatures to behold as the sun shone down on them—like forest gods.

We must have tarried too long watching them because they caught our scent on the wind and ran. The forest thundered with the sound of their hooves as one ran east and the other west.

Ana turned to me, and I could see the look in her eyes as she issued the silent challenge. My heart surged with love for the woman, and I wish to all the gods that I had shifted back into a man and made love to her all afternoon by that stream instead of giving chase to those bucks. However, that is precisely what we did. I gave chase to the one who ran east and Ana, the one who fled west.

That buck ran like the wind, never slowing or faltering. I closed on him several times and half expected him to turn and charge at me with those tree-branch antlers, but he found the will to run faster and gained on me again. In time, we broke free of the forest, and I caught up to him as he clambered up the rocky slope of a mountain.

He had run his race and had nothing left to give as he turned to confront me. I thought he lowered his head to charge and then realized the beast was too exhausted to keep his head up. The buck's breath game in noisy snorts, his nostrils flaring. I could see him watching me, his eyes so wide that his pupils looked like a brown island in a white sea. He stood there, and I could smell his fear of the pain and death that was to follow. The buck slowly raised his head until the sunlight glinted off those majestic antlers; he was spent but would meet his death with dignity and defiance.

I stared at him for a long moment; he looked as regal as a king and, in my mind, I imagined all that he must have experienced in his lifetime to reach this moment standing before me—all the joys, sorrows, fears, and triumphs he had experienced.

Humans sometimes forget that animals live lives as rich and meaningful as our own. The Bible says that humans have 'dominion over the fish of the sea, and over the fowl of the air, and over the cattle, and over all the earth, and over every creeping thing that creepeth upon the earth,' but that's not true. This world is as much theirs as ours, maybe even more so, and this forest was as much the buck's as it was mine. Because I had the means to hunt and kill for my food did not give me the right to slay this majestic creature. After all, was I not as much a beast of the forest at that moment as he was?

So I turned and left him standing there. He must have stared at me dumbstruck because it was several minutes before I heard his hooves upon the stones as he departed. My stomach ached with hunger from the exertion of the hunt, and I hoped that Ana would be waiting at home with her kill.

Without the thrill of the hunt, the way back felt tediously long and, though I caught the scent of other prey, I was too exhausted to hunt. It was nearly dark when I returned to our cottage, and I was surprised to have returned before Ana, though if her pursuit were anything like mine, she would have had to carry that large deer a long way home.

I shifted back to human form, dressed, and awaited her on the porch, sniffing the air for any scent of her approaching. The sun ceded the day to the moon; still, there was no Ana. Terrible thoughts ran through my mind: perhaps she had become injured during the pursuit, or the buck had turned on her with its antlers.

Shifting back into the wolf, I headed out in the direction of her pursuit. As I ran through those darkened woods, I felt a terror unlike anything I had ever experienced. The thought of some injury befalling my beloved nearly crippled me with fear, but I ran on searching through the night.

It was several hours before I caught Ana's scent on the wind and the iron stench of blood. There was so much blood that it felt as if the air was permeated with it. When I found her, what remained of her, my mind could not process what I was seeing. Cillian told us that we revert to human form when we die unless death occurs immediately when we are wolves. Since Ana was still in her wolf form, I took solace in knowing that her death was likely instantaneous.

I could see a large bullet wound in her chest; from the location, I believe it struck her kind heart. She was likely dead before her body hit the ground. The hunter had skinned her for her coat of wolf fur and left her to rot, a discarded mass of bone, flesh, and sinew. I curled up with her on that cold earthen ground, my fur sticky with her blood as I wrapped my arms around her and wept. The howls that escaped my mouth were such that no creature dared approach us despite the smell of fresh blood.

I shifted back into human form at some point, though I could not tell you when that happened. I laid there for days, at least, my mind overcome with grief. Finally, I could no longer bear the thought of Ana lying on that cold forest floor, and I carried her back to our home. As I walked with her remains in my arms, my grief turned to despair, and I welcomed every sharp cut of a branch or rock on my naked skin. Had I not left her on my pursuit, I believed she would still be alive, or I would be dead beside her. I could not bring myself to look at the mangled thing in my arms.

Once we were home, I built a funeral pyre, placed her body upon it, and set it ablaze just as she had desired. I cannot describe to you the overwhelming desire I had to throw myself atop the blaze alongside her; to have our bodies consumed by flame and turned to smoke together on the wind. I wanted to feel the pain of the fire boiling my blood and rending my skin as punishment for allowing Ana to come to this end.

However, as I watched the flames lick at the wood, inching closer to what remained of my beloved, I was filled with unfathomable rage.

Just as the fire consumed her body, my rage consumed my despair. Whoever had done this to Ana needed to die; they needed to die screaming in pain and begging for mercy. I could not leave this world while Ana's death went unavenged.

For weeks, I searched the surrounding villages for any word of hunters who had killed a wolf or tried to sell a wolf pelt at the market but found nothing. I began to despair of ever locating the savages who killed my Ana when I came across a man in a tavern in Sibiu. He told me that two Russian brothers had come to him with an incredible-sized wolf pelt for him to make into a coat for one of the men. The man directed me to the Hermannstadt Inn, where he believed the brothers had stayed, and for a bit of coin, I learned their names from the clerk—Arkady and Dimitri Volkov.

The brothers had left Romania weeks earlier, and their trail had gone cold, so I set out for Russia. Information on the brothers was elusive at first, and I spent several months chasing false leads and cold trails. After the assassination of Tsar Alexander the Second, I stayed away from cities and towns for almost a year. During those turbulent days, it was too easy for a foreigner to find himself mistaken for a revolutionary or anarchist.

However, things began to calm again, and I discovered an interesting article in the newspaper. The new Tsar had taken an interest in restoring the Romanovs' ancestral hunting lodge in Byelovvyezh and had sent his huntsman, Arkady Volkov, to assist. It was my first concrete lead on the brothers in over a year.

After that, it was easy to find gossip about Arkady Volkov in the taverns of Saint Petersburg. The man's legendary exploits, his mysterious tracker brought back from the court of the Chinese emperor, and, of course, his pride and joy, the famed Mongolian stead, Nar. However, if you plied the right man with enough vodka, you could hear stories of the man's peasant brother, Dimitri, an ill-tempered brute who eschewed the Tsar's court for village whore houses. Dimitri was said to hunt in the forests around Kalinin, so a plan formed in my thick skull.

I believed that if word of a wolf terrorizing a nearby village spread, Dimitri would leave Kalinin to hunt for it; and so he did. When I found him, he wore the coat he had crafted from Ana's fur. I am not proud of what I did to him, but I will go to my grave believing he deserved every moment of pain. I retrieved the coat; it is in my backpack, and I will burn it over Ana's grave so that she will be whole again in this life and the next.

I found a letter from Arkady among Dimitri's things and placed it in his mouth, hoping that when they discovered the body, word would reach Arkady, and he, too, would come to Obrechen.

"And so he has," Galina chanced a glance over at Leo, who was examining the raw red scar that had formed over the place the Mongolian tracker had stabbed him.

"And so he has," Bogdan nodded.

"After what he did to Leo, Volkov will have to deal with all of us," Alexei said in a low growl as he put a hand on Leo's shoulder.

"I'm sorry, Alexei, but I don't think that is a good idea," Bogdan leaned back and sighed.

"What? So only you get to avenge Volkov's wrongs?" Alexei's eyes narrowed as his temper flared.

"No, that's not it," Bogdan shook his head. "I will not risk any of you. It would be a pyrrhic victory to exact revenge on Volkov but see harm come to one of you."

"We won't let you confront him alone," Galina reached out and touched Bogdan's arm.

Bogdan turned to her, a sad smile crossing his weathered face, "I don't want to confront him at all. What Volkov and his brother did to Ana was barbaric but no less brutal than the things I did in my search for revenge." Bogdan shook his head, "No, this ends now; we escape this place and find somewhere we can live in peace."

Alexei laughed, a harsh, cynical sound, "Ha. We'll just be the nice werewolf family that lives down the lane."

"Alexei," Oksana glanced, her voice a pleading whisper.

"No, Oksana, there is truth to what he is saying," Bogdan's shoulders slumped in resignation, "That night we celebrated Leo's birthday was the most perfect night I can remember in a long time. It felt like the family Ana and I had always wished for."

"So you, what? Turned us all into werewolves so we could be your perfect little family?" Alexei's voice was heavy with suspicion. "And if you were to be our Papa Wolf, who would be your Mama Wolf? Galina? I think we all know that's unlikely. Then who? Oksana?"

"Alexei, enough! Please," Oksana's rebuke was harsh enough to stun the boy into silence.

"Alexei, I came to you when you were hurt. You likely would have died without attention to your wounds; and if you lived, your hand certainly would have been crippled," Bogdan's countenance was grim as he stared at Alexei.

"Very convenient that you arrived in time to save each of us. I guess it's our misfortune that you did not show up in time to prevent our injuries," Alexei sneered back at the woodsman.

"No different than you did for me, Alexei," Oksana shot him a withering gaze. "It would have been very fortunate if you arrived before Father Grigori struck my head like a blacksmith's forge."

Bogdan glanced over at Galina, an unspoken question passing between them. When she nodded slightly, Bogdan's gaze returned to the others, "Galina was already dying when I arrived in Obrechen. She had an illness within her; I could smell it."

As all eyes turned toward her, Galina flushed with embarrassment at the admission that Bogdan could smell the rot within her body.

Oksana grabbed the woman's hand, her voice laced with concern. "The pain in your stomach?"

Galina nodded and squeezed Oksana's hand, smiling at the comfort the girl's touch brought her.

"I admit that I sought to stay with Galina for this reason," Bogdan looked at her, a gentleness filling his eyes as he smiled at her. "She has a good heart and deserves a long life. I thought I could repay some of the kindness Cillian showed Ana and me when he healed our tuberculosis."

"Leo, you've been very quiet; what are your thoughts?" Oksana leaned over and looked at the boy, who had been quietly watching as he ate his apple.

Leo smiled as he swallowed a mouthful of apple. "I am very grateful that Galina saved my life," Galina returned his smile, and then Leo's face grew serious as he looked at the surrounding faces. "My father sold me to men who stabbed me and left me for bait, and now I am a magical creature with all of my friends. I will leave this place with you, Bogdan, and I hope all of you will come too. Though, I would like to tell my mother goodbye before I leave."

"Of course, Leo," Bogdan smiled at the boy and nodded in agreement.

"There is one more thing," Leo's ever-present grin returned. "I can feel my toes."

"What?" Galina and Oksana exclaimed in unison as everyone leaned in, and Leo slid the blanket up to reveal his feet.

Leo's toes were dirty, the nails gnarled and long overdue for a trim, but all ten flexed and wiggled.

"My god, Leo, wolf paws are going to be a vast improvement over those things!" Alexei joked, eliciting a loud laugh from his friend.

"Leo, there's no doubt that you have the wolf blood in your veins just like the rest of us," Bogdan grinned so wide his eyes wrinkled at the corners.

"I'm going to try and stand," Leo's eyes opened wide with excitement as the others greeted the comment with enthusiasm and nervous caution,

Alexei leaped up to help steady his friend. Leo turned to look at him questioningly, and Alexei nodded his encouragement. With Alexei's arm under his left shoulder and Galina scrambling forward to support his right elbow, Leo slipped his feet under him and slowly straightened his legs. Oksana's hand flew to her mouth, and tears streamed down her cheeks as she watched Leo Verenich stand for the first time in his young life.

Leo beamed with happiness and wonder as he stood amongst his friends, then he reached deep within his diaphragm and gave his best imitation of a wolf's howl.

***

Sergeant Razin gripped his rifle tightly, eyes scanning the woods, with his back to the flickering light of the campfire. The fire illuminated the small clearing he and Volkov had chosen for a camp but, the light also played tricks on his eyes as he watched the forest. Every shadow became another wolf gazing at him from the black, impenetrable night of the forest.

Opposite him, Volkov also sat with his back to the fire, eyes staring out into the darkness. They each covered a one-hundred-and-eighty-degree field of fire, guarding against attack.

"What did you say Batu called these creatures?" Razin kept his voice low as he called over his shoulder.

"*Kurtadams,*" Volkov answered back, his voice flat and emotionless.

"And he said they were half-man, half-wolf?" Razin glanced back over his shoulder.

Volkov sighed, and Razin could tell the man was tired of explaining things to him. "It is a man who could take on the form of a wolf. His people knew of holy men who could do such things."

"And you believe this too?" Razin peered into the darkness, squinting to discern anything beyond the firelight.

"No wolf could do what those things did today, so yes, I fucking believe it," Volkov snapped back.

"Can they be killed?"

"Yes," Volkov stared into the forest. "They can be killed."

Razin sat quietly and nodded, "Then I will kill the *Kurtadam* for what it did to the Romanov."

Volkov glanced back at the sergeant, his expression irritated, and then he turned back to the woods without saying anything more.

Razin waited for the huntsman to respond, then asked, "If we stand watch all night, how will we be able to hunt the beasts tomorrow?"

"We won't," Volkov's tired voice still held an air of authority. "We've lost the *Kurtadams'* trail. They are probably back in human form by now. So tomorrow, we'll return to Kalinin and get more men—the whole fucking gendarme garrison. We'll surround Obrechen and search every house, burn them to the fucking ground; there'll be nowhere for them to go and nowhere for them to hide. I'll interrogate every man and woman in this shithole until we find the *Kurtadams.*"

"No," Razin yelled as he jumped and turned to face the huntsman. "I will not leave without the *Kurtadam's* head."

"You can stay if you like and wander this forest until the *Kurtadams* gets hungry again and find you," Volkov said, turning to stare at Razin, the firelight dancing in his eyes. "But know this: for what they did here today, I will parade their bodies through the streets of Saint Petersburg and have them stuffed as a gift for the Tsar."

Volkov turned and returned to his vigil of the darkened forest, saying nothing more. Razin looked from the huntsman to stare into the fire, watching the burning embers glow a vibrant red below the yellow-orange flames. The Cossack sergeant wanted to cry in shame and frustration; he had failed again.

We will leave, and the Kurtadam will flee. There will be no honor. I should have died beside the Romanov.

The thought filled Razin with a depth of despair that surpassed even the death of the Tsar. He felt cursed, a blight upon his family's name. Razin's name would become forever associated with failure among Cossacks—a cautionary tale for young Cossack soldiers, a slur used to disparage the incompetent.

Razin looked toward Volkov; Batu's blood stained the huntsman's clothes in dark blotches. The man was a hunter, as much a predator as the *Kurtadams*, and Razin was only a soldier. He knew war and battlefields, but this man knew how to hunt and kill. Who was he to disagree if Volkov believed they could return and trap the *Kurtadam*? Razin chided himself for his childish outburst and misplaced bravado.

"This is the *Kurtadam's* hunting ground. They will be here when we return," Razin murmured as he sat heavily on the ground.

"What's that, Sergeant Razin?" Volkov looked sidelong over his shoulder at the Cossack.

Razin did not realize he had spoken the words aloud and was surprised by the question, "I agree that the *Kurtadam* will be here when we return. It's their hunting ground. Batu told me that wolves return to the kill sites when they kill more than they can eat. That's certainly the case tonight."

Volkov stared at Razin, his face unreadable, but the sergeant could tell thoughts were churning behind the man's dark eyes. Then, wordlessly, the huntsman turned away from Razin. The sergeant stared at the man's back, waiting for him to say more, and when no further conversation was forthcoming, he, too, returned to guard the woods.

Chapter 7

Deep within their cave sanctuary, lit by the flickering lights of half-dozen oil lanterns, the small group laughed and clapped as Leo danced a jig. Leo's elbows jutted out as he swung his arms back and forth; his knees popped, and his ankles clicked as he hopped around. It was as awkward and spasmodic a dance as ever was danced, however, the grin on Leo's face and the sparkle in his eyes as the sound of his laughter reverberated off the cave walls spoke volumes about the joy the boy felt. After a lifetime of inability to use his legs, he could walk, run, and even dance.

He had taken the first unsteady steps of his life after standing, hobbling with his friends at his side as the wolf blood coursing through his veins breathed life into muscles long withered and atrophied. Soon, he was running from one end of the cave to the other in a series of sprints that culminated in the wild jig and ended when he collapsed to the ground, grinning and panting heavily.

"I can't believe it," Leo wiped a hand across his face to brush the sweat from his eyes. "This is amazing!"

"Believe it, Leo," Bogdan said as he laughed, making a deep-rumbling sound, and clapped the boy on the shoulder.

"Bogdan, if Leo has the wolf blood within him, why hasn't he changed like the rest of us?" Alexei asked as he took a seat beside Leo.

Bogdan leaned his head against the cave wall and shrugged, "Leo's wounds and childhood infirmities have healed, so I have no doubt that the metamorphosis has occurred. As to when his wolf will emerge, there is no way to know. Cillian believed that the wolf within us is a distinct entity with thoughts and feelings. The creature formed as much from us as we are of it, so it bears much of the personality traits of the human host. Leo can be timid, so too might be the wolf within him."

"Have you ever heard from Cillian again?" Galina asked as she sat cross-legged on the floor.

"Not since we parted ways in Paris," Bogdan shook his head, then a faint smile crossed his lips. "Sometimes, I like to picture him in America, spending his days playing in the sunshine with his nephews, Jack and Liam."

Alexei picked up a hint of sadness in the woodsman's voice, "And other times?"

Bogdan blew out a deep breath, "Other times, I hope he gave up his quest for knowledge of our kind and found a quiet place alone in the woods."

"That sounds terribly lonely," Galina frowned. "Why would you wish that upon him?"

"There is something you need to understand, Galina, something you all need to understand," Bogdan's dark eyes met each of their gazes. "The transformation makes us remarkably resistant to illness and disease; we heal quickly and age very slowly. You will likely measure your lifespan in centuries rather than decades. All the humans around us will grow old and die, and we will only age a few years. I would spare Cillian the pain of seeing those he loves fade and pass from this world before his eyes."

"So my mother will age and die, and I will remain the same?" the smile had faded from Leo's face, replaced by a forlorn look.

"I'm afraid so, Leo," Bogdan nodded.

"Bogdan, you said Cillian taught you rules?" Seeing Leo's crushed look, Oksana wanted to change the topic quickly.

"Yes, Cillian had five rules he said we needed to adhere to to survive in this world as werewolves," Bogdan said, holding up his hand and splaying out his fingers. "First, never reveal your secret to a normal human. Never tell them, and especially never let them see you change. Not a friend, not a family member—no one. Our greatest defense is secrecy. Werewolves need to stay a thing of nightmares and fairytales. If our existence ever became known, the woods would fill with hunters, and the Church would institute trials and executions of suspected werewolves on a scale that would make the Würzburg witch trials look like a Sunday school class."

Alexei looked at Leo and silently mouthed the words "Würzburg witch trials?" but Leo shrugged, equally clueless to the reference.

"Is that why you never told us?" Galina studied him carefully.

"Yes, and I apologize for that. However, to survive, we must abide by these rules like a religion. The archives are full of accounts of how dangerous this world can be for our kind." Bogdan's words came out sterner than he intended but he needed to impart the importance of this lesson.

Seeing the understanding on the faces of the others, Bogdan continued, "Second, life is precious. We do not hunt for sport like Volkov; we kill only what we need to survive and do it as mercifully as possible. Every creature has an equal right to live in peace. We must hunt because we cannot survive on grass like deer and rabbits but make no mistake, that does not make us better than the animals we hunt; their sacrifice is the gift of life to us. It is a sacred act, and we do not profane it with cruelty."

The woodman touched a place on his neck to demonstrate, "For large prey like deer or elk, you slice through the neck here, severing the artery. It will cause massive blood loss and death. For smaller game like rabbits, you snap the neck. Do you understand?"

The four nodded, focusing on Bogdan with rapt attention.

Bogdan scanned each face as if to will the importance of the rules into his young charges, though conscious or otherwise, his eyes stayed the longest on Alexei's, "Third, we never feed upon another human. Human flesh is like a drug to our kind, and it becomes like an addiction. Cillian believed very strongly we could control our wolf side as long as we stay away from human flesh. However, once consumed, the wolf's cravings become so great that it becomes uncontrollable. In every case we found of a werewolf discovered and killed by humans, it all started with an attack on a man, woman, or child."

Oksana caught Alexei looking away and not meeting Bogdan's gaze. She knew Alexei had partaken of human prey on several occasions and now struggled with the shame of that admission. He had told her at the cottage of his inner struggles with the wolf's ever-stronger cravings for more human flesh. The way Bogdan's eyes lingered on Alexei, she suspected the woodsman knew too; or at least had strong suspicions.

"Fourth," Bogdan tapped a finger against his index finger. "We only hunt in the wild. Don't get lazy and snatch some farmer's goat; it's too easy to get spotted, and once a village loses a cow or goat, they will begin setting traps.

"Cillian, my wife and I had dinner in Paris with a priest from England, from Devonshire I believe, who specialized in the study of werewolves. Father Baring-Gould had investigated stories of werewolves in Iceland and Norway where the people believed that some people were *eigi einhamir*, not of one skin. He learned the Norwegians believed that if a person takes on the bestial form of a wolf, they go on a *gandreid*, a wolf's ride. When in this state they believed that the person was subject to the feral urges and instincts of the wolf without recourse. I am telling you now that this is incorrect. The wolf's instincts are strong, there is no doubting that. You and the wolf are two halves of the same whole now. However, you are the greater half and will always be in control unless you relinquish it."

"What happens if you relinquish control to the wolf?" Leo asked, enrapt by the conversation.

Bogdan's countenance darkened, "If you do, you will become more beast than man. From everything we discovered in the archives, and what Cillian believed to be true, once you give control over to the wolf there is no return. The wolf will become too dominant, and you will fade into a shadow of yourself. In every instance of this we uncovered, the creature was hunted down and destroyed."

Bogdan looked at the four sets of eyes intently watching him, this was more than his family, they were his pack, and he needed to ensure that they understood these rules if they were to survive.

"Fifth, and I saved this one for last because it's the most important," Bogdan lowered his voice, forcing the others to lean in and listen more intently. "We kill another person only if we have no other choice—to protect our lives or our secret. And if you must kill a human, use only your claws, not your teeth. If you bite a human and they survive the attack, they will become like us, so it is essential that if you must use your teeth, you make sure the person is dead. Tear out the heart or remove the head, so there is no doubt."

Bogdan tapped a hand against his heart and then gestured toward his neck.

"If we don't, they will become like us?" Leo interjected.

"Worse, Leo," Bogdan's countenance grew grim. "We live by our rules to control the wolf within us; this person would be a rogue. Without any guidance, they would likely give in to their primal instincts, and the carnage they created would continue until they were hunted down and killed. They would likely reap a sizeable death toll of innocent lives and alert the empire to our kind. A werewolf like that could endanger us all."

Oksana looked toward Alexei and suddenly became alarmed by his expression. Alexei had gone deathly pale and clenched his fists so tightly that his knuckles had turned white. The boy's eyes were wide and fearful; looking at him filled Oksana with a terrible dread.

"Alexei, what is it?" Oksana could not suppress the alarm in her voice, causing the others to turn their eyes upon him in concern.

"Back in the clearing when they tried to trap us," Alexei turned to Oksana, his eyes filled with uncertainty, "I killed the others with my claws, but Rostov, I bit. I think I killed him."

Bogdan leaned forward, his eyes searching Alexei's face, "Alexei, are you sure he's dead? You must be certain."

"I'm not sure," Alexei shook his head, his visage a mask of dread.

"We must go and check," Bogdan said, rising to his feet. "And then we must leave Obrechen immediately; this place is too dangerous for us."

"My mother," Leo looked up and swallowed hard. "I have to say goodbye to my mother."

Bogdan nodded to Leo and then turned to Oksana. "Oksana, go with Leo; your presence won't arouse any suspicion. Be quick about it."

"Anyone seeing Leo walking is going to run to Father Grigori and tell the priest that Leo's possessed by the devil. I should go too; it may get dangerous," Alexei insisted.

"Let Father Grigori come," Oksana's face soured at the priest's mention.

"No, Alexei. I need you to show me where you left Rostov. Galina will come with us. The three of us stand a better chance of hunting down Rostov if he still lives," Bogdan looked to Galina, who rose and stood beside him. "We will meet at Galina's cottage and then head west to my farm in Romania. It will be safe there; no one will find us."

***

Leo's gait was still a little awkward as he grew accustomed to walking, however, the sight of him doing so still amazed Oksana. They had left the cave behind, squeezing their way back through the crevice. Oksana had never liked close spaces, and the thought of that dark, confined journey still gave her prickles of cold sweat down her neck. The first time Oksana entered the cave, she had frozen in the tight opening, her breath coming in rapid pants as it felt like the mountain would bear down and trap her in the dark, crushed between the cold rocks. The thought had been suffocating, the sheer terror of being trapped in the darkness, her chest unable to expand, to gasp in the air as her lungs fought futilely to expand. The fear was overwhelming, and just as her mind was about to succumb, a hand reached through the darkness and grasped hers. The warm touch of fingers against her sweat-slick hands had jarred her from her panicked stupor. Light streamed in from the end of the narrow opening, and Oksana could hear Alexei's voice calling, reassuring her as he squeezed her hand and rubbed it gently with his thumb, urging her forward.

When it came time for them all to leave the cave, Alexei traversed the narrow opening backward, one hand always grasping hers as she slithered forward. It was the most valiant thing Oksana had ever seen, and there, in the darkness, she began to wonder if everything that transpired had changed Alexei or if it had changed the way she saw him. Oksana quickly filed the thought away in the back of her mind but felt a rush of excitement about exploring the idea further as she slid across the cold rock and into the opening on the other side.

There was little time for anything before Oksana and Leo parted ways with the others, who went off to confirm Rostov was still among the dead. The two walked through the forest, headed for Leo's house and what Oksana knew would be a difficult parting with his mother. She had tried to bring up the subject, but Leo quickly brushed aside the topic and asked her about her experience with the transformation.

"In my mind, the wolf waits in the forest. She's always there watching. But not in a bad way, more like a guardian angel," Oksana explained as she walked beside Leo. "Alexei's wolf waits behind a door, and Galina says she feels hers always walking beside her."

"What about Bogdan?" Glanced sidelong at her as they walked.

"Galina told me that Bogdan's wolf waits atop a mountain," Oksana smiled and looked toward the distant treetops, imagining the mountains beyond. "I suppose one of his Carpathian Mountains."

Leo's forehead furrowed in disappointment, "I don't feel anything like that. Sometimes, I feel like someone or something is watching me, but nothing like you or the others describe."

"It's okay, Leo," Oksana placed a hand on Leo's shoulder and gave him a reassuring smile. "Your wolf will come in time."

Leo returned the smile, though Oksana detected a hint of sadness. Then, a look of excitement came over his face so suddenly that the rapid change startled her.

"You know, I have been thinking," Leo pursed his lips as if he were working through a problematic equation, "I read a story called *Сноха,* by a man named Khudyakov, in one of Galina's books. Baba Yaga had turned wolves into cows so that when the mother's daughter-in-law went to milk them, the wolves would eat her."

"Leo!" Oksana laughed loudly and shook her head. "Your obsession with Baba Yaga is endless."

"If it weren't endless, it wouldn't be an obsession," Leo smiled back and then grew serious. "No, but listen; if Baba Yaga could change wolves into cows, and I read another story where she turned wolves into sheep... if she could do that, why couldn't she change wolves into people?"

Oksana opened her mouth to respond but closed it. Leo had a good point. After all, if werewolves could exist, and they were proof of that, why couldn't Baba Yaga exist? Maybe Baba Yaga did create werewolves.

"Ah," Leo pointed a finger at her and grinned. "I have you thinking about it! I can tell!"

"You're incorrigible," Oksana playfully slapped his accusatory finger away.

"Incorrigible?" Leo looked surprised, which delighted Oksana.

"Galina taught me the word, and let me assure you, it applies to you perfectly," she gave him a very self-satisfied smile.

"I'm looking forward to..." Leo stopped mid-sentence, thrusting his nose into the air, inhaling quick, deep breaths through his flaring nostrils. "Hey, wait a minute."

"What's the matter, Leo?" Oksana asked, suddenly alarmed. She quickly scanned the surrounding woods but saw no sign of danger;

then, she, too, caught a familiar animal smell on the wind. "I know that smell. What is that?"

Leo inhaled deeply again and then smiled, "It's Seryy!"

"Seryy? What is he doing out here?" Oksana was shocked. "Bogdan said he left Seryy and the wagon by the roadside when he shifted to try and save Galina the day Olga Putina and her brothers paid her a visit. Seryy and the wagon were gone when he returned for them."

"The Morozovs had him," Leo's smile dimmed. "They used Seryy and the wagon to transport me out here."

"Oh, Leo," Oksana said, touching his arm. Her heart broke for Leo, she could barely imagine the sadness and fear those memories must hold for him.

"We can take Seryy and the wagon to my mother's house; we'll get there faster," Leo's face lit with excitement, and he turned toward the forest. "Come on, the clearing must be nearby."

"Leo, wait," Oksana tried to grab his shoulder to stop him before he dashed into the forest, following the donkey's scent. She shook her head as she started after him, never imagining she would have to chase after Leo Verenich.

Leo disappeared into the woods, and she heard him noisily traipsing through the brush. She had barely reached the woods herself when the loud crack of a gunshot rang out. Above her, birds took flight, startled by the booming report of a rifle.

"Oh, no," Oksana's mouth breathed the words as the cold grip of dread ran down her spine.

***

Galina stared down at the bodies of the two Cossack men. One man had his midsection torn open, and his neck sliced so deeply to have nearly decapitated him. Beside him was a second man, large and bearded. The man's innards spewed forth from the ragged wound in his torso and produced a stench so pungent that Galina had to cover her nose with her hand as the flies buzzed at his gore. She noticed that, inexplicably, the man clutched a bottle of vodka in one hand's death grip.

"These two are certainly dead," she called across the clearing to Bogdan and Alexei.

The two were looking down at the body of a young Cossack man lying broken beside a thick-limbed tree. Bogdan knelt, examining the body; as Alexei scanned the clearing. The boy looked mildly ridiculous in Bogdan's overly large clothes. He had rolled them up at the sleeves and the cuffs of his trousers to make them more his length, and Alexei had cinched the belt holding up his pants tightly, giving them a clownish pantaloons appearance.

"Rostov's body should be there," Alexei pointed toward the edge of the clearing.

Bogdan's eyes followed Alexei's finger as he stood, a deep frown wrinkling his face. With long strides, he crossed the distance to where Alexei indicated and surveyed the ground.

"You sure this is the spot?" Bogdan's voice was grim as he met Alexei's gaze.

Alexei's shoulders visibly sagged as he nodded, "Yes, I'm certain."

Bogdan knelt and ran his hand through the grass. When Galina watched him raise his hand, she could see the fingertips were dark with blood. The forester rubbed the blood between his fingers and then sniffed them, his features darkening. He slowly scanned the surrounding woods, and when Bogdan's eyes met hers, Galina knew the situation was grim.

"What is it? Where's Rostov?" Galina asked though the look on the two men's faces told her all she needed to know.

"Rostov has shifted," Bogdan replied as he stood.

"I don't know how he could have survived," Alexei's voice was heavy with regret. "His wounds were... severe."

"It's okay, Alexei," Bogdan reassured the boy. "We will find Rostov and end this. He will not be far."

A shot rang out in the distance, loud enough to make Galina startle, as all three heads snapped to look in the direction of the sound. A sudden dread filled her as she looked from the direction of the shot to the others in the clearing.

"That's where Leo and Oksana are," Alexei stared intently at the forest, willing his eyes to see through the ocean of trees and brush to where his friends were.

"I'm sure they're okay," Galina offered but the words sounded hollow even to her ears.

"Alexei, they'll be fine. They can handle themselves. We need to find Rostov," Bogdan said, taking a step toward the boy and urging him not to act rashly.

Alexei looked from Bogdan to Galina with eyes filled with worry and despair, and she could sense the torment of the decisions raging through his mind. He stepped forward and let loose an anguished cry of frustration that turned into a howl as Alexei's face elongated into a lupine muzzle. A muscular, gray-furred torso and limbs tore through the ill-fitting clothes, the fabric falling like leaves to the ground as Alexei shifted into wolf form. Alexei had transformed into the large gray wolf in less time than it took him to take three steps as he began running for the forest.

"Alexei, wait," Galina stepped toward him.

"Let him go," Bogdan said as he watched the gray wolf leap into the forest at a full run. "We need to stop Rostov."

"Forget Rostov; let's get the others and leave Obrechen," Galina said, overcome with worry for her friends, compounded by her hopelessness of finding Rostov.

"We can't leave Rostov on the loose," Bogdan gestured eastward as he walked toward her. "His trail leads that way. What's in that direction?"

"That's not toward Obrechen. The only thing in that direction..." Galina thought for a moment, then looked up, her eyes alighting with realization. "That's the direction of Morozov's estate."

Bogdan nodded, "We must hurry. He's going to feed."

***

Yakov Nikulin's sightless gray eyes stared up at the early morning sky. Flies dotted the dark blood coagulating around the gash that opened his throat and soaked the green woolen tunic his wife had given him as a gift this past Christmas. Rigor mortis had already begun to set in, stiffening his splayed out arms and legs as the stench of his vacated bowels and bladder mingled with the iron stench of blood. Nikulin's body lay atop the remains of two oak trees, fallen side by side the previous winter, his back and ass wedged in the narrow space dividing them. His corpse looked like a starfish trapped between two giant chopsticks.

The body jerked upwards as if an unseen puppet master yanked all his strings at once, causing pooled blood to spill from the cavernous wound in his neck and run down his chest. A second, more violent, upward thrust dislodged it from its perch between the two trees, and a third caused it to tumble from the logs and flop face down on the ground with a heavy thud and sickeningly wet, squelching noise.

Two hands reached out of the space between the trees, followed by the head and shoulders of a man, his face filthy and crusted with dried blood. Igor Balkov stood, breathing deeply of the fresh morning air, and stretched his neck, working the kinks out with loud clicks and pops. Reaching up, he pressed a finger against each nostril, expelling a wad of snot to clear the stench of Nikulin's corpse from his crooked nose. Balkov looked down at the facedown body with disgust and spat a wad of mucusy phlegm onto the man's back.

He bent over to retrieve his rifle and climbed from between the fallen trees, his eyes surveying the carnage. Two other hunters lay dead beside Nikulin, their broken bodies crumpled like discarded paper. Gripping his rifle, Balkov scanned the forest, his trained hunter's ears listening for any sign that the wolf-beasts were nearby.

Satisfied he was alone, Balkov checked each body, relieving them of the few coins concealed in their worn purses.

"Don't worry, I will raise a drink for you at the *Kanti Gans*," Balkov gave a wicked smile as he looked over at Nikulin's body and deposited the dead man's three coins in his purse.

Balkov backtracked his trail through the forest, alert for any sign of the wolf. He chanced across the body of Valery Rodos; the aged hunter's body lay at an odd angle, his back broken. The man's eyes were wide open in death, his mouth agape amidst the tangle of his gray beard, which gave the older man a look of shock as Balkov knelt and rifled through his pockets. A frown darkened Balkov's face as he found the man's purse and pocket empty of coins or valuables.

"You were always a pauper," Balkov stared into the corpse's wrinkled and weather-beaten face as he stood and shook his head.

As he headed back toward the clearing, Balkov felt remarkably good. He had survived the night's calamity unscathed and came away from it quite a bit richer for his troubles. His hand ran over his coin purse, and he smiled, feeling its extra weight.

Balkov's luck seemed to continue as he entered the clearing and spied the two dead soldiers. Kneeling beside the first body, he winced and averted his eyes from the ruined skull of Herzen as he searched through the man's pockets. The young soldier's clothing contained a veritable treasure trove of tobacco, a roll of banknotes, and the topless picture of a young, dark-haired woman, her torso covered by a feather affixed to the picture. Balkov blew on the feather and grinned lasciviously as the thin tendrils of the feather separated to reveal the woman's exposed breasts.

"Maybe I'll pay her a visit for you," Balkov grinned at Herzen's bloody and misshapen face as he slapped the man's leg.

He moved on to Tyutchev, who looked as if he was sleeping peacefully against the wagon, if not for the unnatural angle of his neck and the hint of bone that bulged from the base of his skull. The horses had run off during the night, but the mule remained, harnessed to the wagon. As Balkov approached, the gray mule stared at him with disinterested dark eyes, seemingly unperturbed by the carnage in the clearing.

"I guess we're the lucky ones," Balkov grinned at Seryy as he turned to kneel beside Tyutchev.

Balkov found an ivory-handled pocket knife in the soldier's coat and quickly slipped it into his pocket, along with the man's watch. His eyes lit with excitement as he opened Tyutchev's wallet and surveyed the bulging stack of banknotes inside. The hunter stuffed the bills greedily into his pocket before sliding the empty wallet back into the dead man's pocket. He was studying the man's relatively new black leather boots, comparing his foot size to Tyutchev's, when a dash of color at the edge of the camp caught his eye.

Balkov squinted, trying to get a better look, and his eyes opened wide with excitement. He quickly leaped to his feet and hurried across the clearing, his steps quickening as he approached what he discerned as a body sprawled along the brush.

"You've got to be fucking kidding me," Balkov's grin spread across his face.

He felt almost giddy as he approached the body, his steps quickening until he was staring down at the body of Andrei Morozov. The large man lay face down in the dirt; a small cloud of flies buzzed around the dark pool of blood that formed around his head. Balkov cocked his head and stared at the Land Captain, the crescent moon-shaped bloodstain on the ground circling the man's head reminded him of those halos around the saints in church paintings. Well, Morozov was certainly no saint.

"Hey, Land Captain," Balkov prodded the body with the toe of his boot. "Morozov, you still alive?"

When no response was forthcoming, Balkov knelt and rolled Morozov over. As Morozov flopped lifelessly onto his back, Balkov had to turn away, shielding his face with his hand as a small cloud of flies took flight from the Land Captain's torn throat. The small swarm quickly dissipated, landing amidst the bloody grass or back along the ragged edge of the wound that ended Morozov's life. At the moment of his death, Morozov's face had frozen in shock and horror, eyes thrown wide and mouth open in a perpetual silent scream.

"Serves you right, you rich bastard; you're a fucking mess," Balkov smirked as he stared into Morozov's death mask. Then he squinted at the man as something caught his attention.

Unfolding the ivory-handled pocketknife he had acquired from Tyutchev, Balkov grabbed Morozov's chin and leaned closer for a better look. Ignoring the flies that buzzed up from the man's throat, Balkov reached into Morozov's mouth and worked at one of the man's teeth with the pocketknife. With a grunt, Balkov pulled free the tooth, spit on it, and then rubbed it clean on the Land Captain's shirt. Turning to get a better angle, Balkov held up the tooth and smiled as the sun's rays glinted off the gold filling.

"You won't be needing this anymore," Balkov said, looking down at the corpse's face and grinning as he slipped the tooth into his pocket.

The huntsman slipped a gold ring off Morozov's finger and placed it in his pocket alongside the tooth. He was disappointed to find nothing of value in the Land Captain's pockets until his hand ran over the bulging coin purse beneath the man's tunic. Balkov's mouth fell open in shock when he slid the purse out; it was as large as his fist, with the edges of coins pressing hard against the leather sides. He held a fortune in his hand, even without the money he had pilfered from the other bodies.

What must the Tsar's huntsman carry if the Land Captain carried such wealth? Or the Romanov?

The thoughts raced through Balkov's mind; he already had more money than he had ever seen.

Fuck, Obrechen. I am never going back there. I've got everything I need right here; I'll go to Kalinin or Saint Petersburg.

A moan rose from the bushes, snapping Balkov out of his thoughts and sending a cold chill running down his back. Had someone seen him robbing the bodies? Grabbing his rifle, Balkov edged toward the brush that ringed the clearing. He could see now that something had smashed through a portion of the foliage. Balkov cursed himself for not noticing it sooner; he had been too preoccupied with his newfound wealth. As he edged close, he spied two booted feet lying motionless among the leaves and branches.

The huntsman peered through the bushes and saw a boy lying on the ground with a tangled mess of red hair. The boy's face was swollen and horribly bruised, with thick blotches of purple on one side and down the neck. A whimpering, choking sound escaped the boy's lips, and his head lolled from side to side.

Shit. It's the Morozov whelp.

Balkov pushed through the bushes alongside the prone form and watched Petr Morozov's eyes slowly move to look at him. Only Petr's head moved, and Balkov noticed the boy's fingers did not stir.

His neck's broken. Balkov knew it instinctively.

Fear and desperation filled the boy's eyes as he stared up at Balkov; his lips moved, but no words came forth. Balkov studied him with cold, calculating eyes. Could the boy have seen him? Balkov doubted it, though it was possible. He studied the boy's plump face for a moment then, as casually as crushing a bothersome spider, Balkov placed his boot upon the boy's bruised throat.

Petr's eyes flew wide open in shock and confusion as he tried to shake his head but barely managed any movement. Balkov applied more pressure to the foot, and Petr began to gag and choke. The hunter stared dispassionately at the boy as he felt Petr's throat give in. Tears began to stream from Petr's eyes as his mouth opened, emitting a wheezing, gurgling sound. Balkov pressed down harder, and Petr's throat collapsed in a wet, cracking sound. He held his foot there until the boy's eyes glazed over, and he went still.

I need to find the Romanov's body, and that huntsman's and then get the hell out of here, Balkov thought to himself as he stared down at the boy's broken body.

The loud crack of a branch from something moving through the bushes startled Balkov so severely that he jumped. Cold panic flooded his body as he turned and raised his rifle toward the movement. His finger reflexively went to the trigger, and he heard the rifle boom as he inadvertently fired a shot. Balkov silently cursed himself for his stupidity in making such a mistake; now, he had given away his position.

To his surprise, he heard a grunting sound as the bullet miraculously struck its target, and Balkov quickly loaded another round. As an experienced hunter, he knew an animal was far more dangerous when injured or cornered. He raised the rifle to his cheek, aiming toward the movement as something stumbled through the brush. His eyes frantically scanned the thick foliage for a clear shot as the thing crashed noisily through the branches toward the clearing.

Balkov's hands were sweaty, and he did not realize he was holding his breath until the rifle began to shake. However, as he slowly blew out his breath, he heard a loud thud as if something crashed to the ground.

He waited as his ears tried to pierce the morning sounds of the awakening woods to detect any sound of further movement. He slowly edged back toward the clearing, careful not to step on any dried twigs or forest debris that would crack noisily.

As the brush thinned out along the edges of the clearing, he saw a dark-haired woman trying to crawl on her hands and knees, clawing at the earth. Balkov's eyes quickly scanned the clearing but detected no one else as he stepped out of the woods, rifle still trained on the woman. She wore a simple gray dress, typical of the type worn in Obrechen. The woman stopped crawling and clutched at her midsection as she rolled onto her back. Balkov could see a slick red stain quickly expanding in the middle of her torso, just above her stomach, as blood flowed freely between her fingers. The woman made no sound except for a harsh, ragged breath that escaped her lips as she stared at the sky.

For Christ's sake, Balkov swore as he lowered the rifle and walked toward the woman.

It was Anya Verenicha, the woman must have come out into the forest looking for her boy. As he slowly approached her, she glanced sidelong at him, and then he saw her eyes look toward his rifle.

"I am sorry about this," Balkov came and knelt beside her, placing his rifle on the ground beside her body. She watched him silently, her eyes accusatory and her breathing heavy, as he glanced at her wound. "It's bad. Real bad."

"Leo?" Anya gasped out as she winced in pain.

"The boy's dead," Balkov replied without bothering to look at her. His eyes scanned her body; she was a fine enough-looking woman, wasted on the likes of Pavel Verenich. "They're all dead."

"Dead?" A confused look crossed Anya's face as if the thought was incomprehensible.

"Your boy. The others, all dead," Balkov shook his head. "The wolf got them all."

"Help... me," she gasped through blood-flecked lips. "I need to find Leo."

"There's no helping you," Balkov shook his head. "But I will give you the same kindness I gave the boy."

Balkov slowly got to his feet, shifting his rifle from one hand to the other so that his right hand was closest to the trigger. He looked down at Anya as a thin line of blood slipped from the corner of her mouth and rolled down her face like a thin line of paint. Balkov had watched her in the village market numerous times, thinking what a pretty little thing she was and what he would do with a woman like her.

Now, as he watched her body tremble as the blood ran from the gaping hole in her chest and, she coughed up dark amber fluids that stained her teeth and ran down her chin like drool, Balkov felt nothing for the woman. Her eyes settled on him, and Balkov could see pain, sadness, and grief echoing in the dark depths of her pupils. He thought he detected something else, too—blame. Anger surged within the hunter, and he gritted his teeth.

"This your fault, you stupid woman," Balkov seethed. "You should never have come into these woods. You should have let that boy die years ago."

"Boy," Anya said the words as if dazed when awakening from a dream. "Have you seen my boy?"

"Oh, for fucks sake," irritation filled Balkov as he raised the rifle to his cheek, aiming the barrel at her forehead.

"Mother?" a boy's voice called from across the clearing.

Startled, Balkov lowered the rifle and looked up. Leo Verenich walked into the clearing, his eyes fixed upon his mother's prone form. The sight was so jarring that Balkov lowered the rifle and took a step back, a sense of fear gripped his innards. As if not registering Balkov, Leo ran toward his mother. *He ran.*

"What devilry is this?" Balkov stammered the words out as he took another involuntary step back. The rifle nearly slipped from his fingers, suddenly slack, until he saw the second figure emerge into the clearing—his niece Oksana Nostrova. The girl's eyes met his own, and Balkov saw such hatred in her stare that a chill ran down his back. The girl's eyes flicked to the hunter's rifle and then to Leo as the boy ran across the clearing, and Balkov saw fear in her—fear for Leo's safety.

"Leo, wait," Oksana called out a warning.

Her shout snapped Balkov out of his stupor, and he quickly raised his rifle. The Verenich boy seemed to notice him for the first time, eyes going wide with shock and fear as Balkov aimed the gun at his chest.

"What have you done to my mother?" Leo's voice was laden with accusation as he halted and pointed at Anya.

"I don't know what kind of game you and your little girlfriend are playing," Balkov said, alternately aiming at Leo and Oksana as he spoke, "but you're fucking dead."

Balkov pressed the rifle to his cheek and aimed at Leo. He heard Oksana scream for Leo as his finger slid onto the cold metal of the trigger, and Balkov felt a feral glee as he saw the boy's eyes grow wide and his mouth agape. He would shoot the boy, then his troublesome niece, and if the bitch on the ground still lived, he would finish her too.

Uncertainty filled Balkov, and the smile slipped from his lips as he realized the boy was not looking at him. The sky above seemed to darken like an eclipse, and with sudden dread, Balkov turned and swung his rifle. He gasped in horror at seeing the giant gray wolf hurtling toward him, the beast's massive body blocking the sun as it leaped from the forest.

The wolf's body struck him like a boulder, driving the air from his lungs. The rifle flew from Balkov's hands as his legs splintered like dried twigs, and his head struck the earth with a jarring phenomenal force, dizzying him. The wolf straddled his chest, pinning his arms down with the knees of its hind legs. Balkov could hear screaming in the distance and was astounded to realize it was coming from his own lips.

He could feel the wolf's hot breath on his face as it stared down at him. In the back of his rattled brain, Balkov felt a recognition in the beast's eyes. Something about the wolf's gaze reminded him of the boy

Alexei. Then the creature brought a closed fist down upon Balkov's face, and he screamed as his cheekbone fractured under the blow. A second blow shattered his teeth, sending fragments rocketing into his throat as the creature's fist pulped his jaw. Balkov's head rocked with a third blow that must have dislodged an eye as his depth perception went haywire.

The beast's enraged throttling continued until all Balkov could hear was the cracking of his skull and the gurgling sound that had replaced his screams. Then all went black; forever.

***

Oksana nearly wept with relief as Alexei's wolf form sprang from the woods and assailed her uncle. With the threat of Igor Balkov removed, Leo was again running toward his mother, and Oksana hurried to his side.

As she approached, Oksana tried to ignore Balkov's violent death cries and the sickening sound of shattering bone that filled the clearing.

Leo knelt by his mother, holding her hand as they spoke, tears streaming down his gaunt face. Oksana knelt beside Leo and placed a reassuring hand on his shoulder.

"I'm here, Mother; I'm okay," Leo smiled and gripped her hand despite the tears.

"Leo, you're walking!" Anya's face filled with wonder.

"Mother, I can walk and run," Leo grinned as he stretched his leg out to show her his healthy limbs.

"Leo, it's a miracle! My boy can walk and run!" She smiled and laughed a little. "This is the happiest day of my life. I knew I'd find you."

"You did, Mother; you found me. I'm okay, better than okay," tears streamed from Leo's eyes.

Anya's face screwed in pain as a wracking cough caused fresh blood to bubble from her lips. Her expression grew serious, "Leo, how can this be?"

Leo looked from his mother to Oksana, desperation in his gaze, and she squeezed his shoulder as she struggled to hold back tears.

"What do I tell her?" he whispered.

"I don't know," Oksana shook her head and bit her lip as the sadness welled up inside her.

"Oh," Anya gasped, a look of wonder returning to her face. "Leo, are we in heaven?"

Leo looked at Oksana, and she nodded, trying to give him a reassuring smile.

"Yes, Mother, we're in heaven," Leo nodded and held her hand against his chest. "We're all in heaven together."

"Oh, Leo, are you an angel?" Anya smiled through blood-streaked lips.

"Yes," Leo barely managed the word as his voice broke.

"Will..." Anya's eyes moved from Leo to Oksana before returning to her son's face, "will I be an angel too?"

"Yes, Mother, you will be an angel too," Leo tried to smile as he stifled a sob. "All your pain will disappear, and we will live and play together forever."

Anya smiled, a serene expression smoothing away the pain from her features. "That will be wonderful, Leo."

"I love you, Mother," Leo pressed his face against his mother's hand.

"I love you too, Leo," Anya replied.

When Leo looked back at his mother, her eyes stared sightlessly toward the sky, a beatific smile on her face.

"Mother?" Leo searched his mother's face.

"Leo, she's gone." Oksana wept as she put an arm around Leo.

A terrible cry escaped Leo's lips, a sound so anguished that Oksana felt her heart breaking. Leo pulled his mother close to his chest as he rocked and sobbed, strangled cries all that escaped his mouth. He clutched his mother close to his chest and stared at the sky, a heartrending wail emanating from the boy.

Then the wail transformed, deepening into a howl. Oksana fell backward from Leo as the boy's mouth widened and elongated into a lupine snout. His body trembled as his limbs grew and thickened, a coat of white fur covering his skin as his clothes shredded and tore.

Oksana looked toward Alexei, the gore-covered gray wolf finally abandoning Balkov's ravaged body. Alexei threw back his head and joined his howl to Leo's as he stepped clear of Balkov. When Oksana returned her gaze to Leo, a white wolf with a line of brown fur that ran from its ears down its back stood where Leo had once knelt. Leo turned his gaze to Oksana, and she could still see her friend in the wolf's eyes. Then the wolf turned and, with a burst of speed, ran from the clearing on all fours.

"Alexei, we must go after him," Oksana called to the gray wolf, who padded over to her.

Alexei stopped before her and hung his head, his muzzle thick with flesh and blood. Oksana looked over to Balkov's corpse and could see that the man had been thoroughly gutted. She knew that if she inspected the body closer, she would find several organs missing. There was no time for shame; Leo needed her and Alexei.

In her mind, she stood at the forest's edge and extended her hand, summoning the wolf to come. Alexei waited as she shifted, and then as one, as a pack, the two wolves ran into the forest after their friend.

***

"Kira? Kira?" Vera Morozova called the young serving girl's name as she walked through the dimly lit corridors of her home. She knew all the other servants would be asleep by now, but the young girl was supposed to have stayed awake in case her husband and son arrived home late.

Vera had stayed up late writing a poem for Father Grigori, and now she wanted Kira to make her some tea. The poem had been rather sordid and much crasser in her description of the lovemaking the couple Vera wrote about, but she wanted the priest to picture them in his mind when he read the words. She felt flush with excitement at the words and imagery she put on the page and needed some tea to calm herself.

Annoyance flared in her mind at the girl's absence. It was not uncommon for serving girls in the household to be unaccounted for during the night, but that was always when her husband was home. Vera was well aware of her husband's liberties with the serving girls, and she smirked at Andrei behind his back, thinking she was such a fool as not to know what had transpired in her own home.

The servant girls, too, snickered behind her back, believing they were sly ones getting one over on the lady of the house; as if Vera missed Andrei's fat belly slapping against her as he rutted on her like a wild boar. They could have the Land Captain every night and twice on

Christmas if they liked. She preferred the firm body of Father Grigori, a man who knew how to please a woman.

The flickering shadows of the hearth fire caught her attention; perhaps Kira had decided to keep it ablaze in case the hunters returned.

"Kira?" Vera called as she walked toward the main room.

"I'm afraid the girl is not here; she did make a rather tasty meal for me in the kitchen, though," a raspy voice replied.

The unexpected voice startled Vera, but she quickly composed herself and entered the main hall. She saw a man seated before the hearth, a blanket pulled around his body and over his head.

"I'm sorry. I was not expecting guests this late. Are you looking for my husband?" Vera slowly circled the man, keeping a wide berth from the stranger.

"No, Lady Morozova. Your husband, and the others are still out hunting their wolf," the man replied. "I came here to see you."

"Me?" Something in the man's voice and posture seemed familiar to her. "Mr. Rostov, is that you?"

"Yes," Rostov nodded. "My men and I tangled with the beast this evening; I am the only one to live to tell about it."

"That's terrible, Mr. Rostov. Are you badly hurt?" Vera stepped toward him and gasped.

"No, I am not hurt," Rostov turned to look at her, his voice a low rumble as the firelight glinted in his dark eyes. Something about how the fire cast shadows in the room, or perhaps it was just a trick of the light, gave his face a wolf-like appearance. "I'm just very, very hungry."

Chapter 8

Pavel looked over the contents of the suitcase one last time and, satisfied that he had not forgotten anything, closed the top and fastened the buckles closed. The picture of the two figures hung beside the bed caught his attention. It had been their wedding day, and he remembered it had cost an exorbitant amount of money; however, he had looked resplendent in his uniform, and Anya had been beautiful in her simple white dress.

Picking up the suitcase, Pavel crossed the room to look more closely at the picture. He stared into his eyes, so young and confident on that day, and scoffed.

Pavel, you naive fool, he shook his head in regret. *It would help if you had run when you had the chance.*

It did not matter now as Pavel turned from the picture and strode from the bedroom for the final time. The boy was gone, likely dead by now, and Anya had not returned to the house. Pavel thought it was better this way; he felt sure she would have begged his forgiveness and pleaded with him to stay. Leaving now avoided the whole pathetic scene. As he crossed the main room of their small house, he paused momentarily by the table where they had shared their meals all these years. His hand strayed to the pouch of coins Volkov had paid him, and he briefly contemplated leaving a few coins for Anya. Pavel thought a few coins would make her life easier through the winter, especially without a man in the house. Then he thought better of it and headed out the front door.

As he stepped onto the front porch, he paused; during the evening, some of the village kids had returned Leo's wheelchair to the porch to taunt him. He had noticed it earlier with mild annoyance, but now one of them had gone so far as to sit in the wheelchair on his porch; he could see the top of their dark head seated in the chair. This insult pushed him too far. A dark anger roiled in his gut. As Pavel took another step forward, one of the floorboards creaking loudly, and the child's head turned slightly.

Pavel paused; something in the manner the boy cocked his head struck him as eerily familiar. The dark, close-cropped hair was so like Leo's as the head turned toward the sound of Pavel's footfall. He watched in shocked horror as one pale, bony hand came to rest on the arm of the chair. Pavel narrowed his eyes and scanned the thin arm that ran up from the hand; it was bare and shirtless despite the chill in the air. He slowly tried to step sideways, craning his neck to get a better look at the chair's occupant, and winced as the floorboards gave another loud creak.

The sound of his heart beating pounded in his ears and almost drowned out the groan of the floorboards beneath his weight. Whether it was the thundering beat of Pavel's heart or the protestation of the floorboards, a sound made the boy in the chair sit bolt upright. The wheelchair whirled around so suddenly that Pavel nearly tripped over his feet as he backed into the doorway. His eyes grew wide in horror as he stared into the pale, gaunt face of his son. The boy sat naked in the chair; a blanket across his lap was all that separated his pale, sunken chest from the spindly white legs that now hung straighter than Pavel had ever recalled.

"Father," the familiar grin crossed Leo's face, quickly fading. "Father, I have some bad news for you."

"Leo, how did you get here?" Pavel's voice was sharp and direct, to hide his shock at seeing the boy. His eyes scanned the road, looking for any sign of who could have deposited the boy on his porch.

"Why I walked, Father; ran actually," Leo's voice grew cold, and his eyes narrowed in uncharacteristic sternness.

"What?" Pavel thought he had misheard the boy, then felt a flush of anger when he realized Leo must have been jesting him. "Don't test me, Leo; how did you get here?"

Leo's eyes trailed to the suitcase, "Are you going somewhere?"

"Listen here, I asked you a question: how did you get here?" Pavel shouted and took a menacing step toward Leo.

Leo shrank back, a time-worn habit when his father raged. Then his eyes grew hard, and he placed both his hands on the arms of the wheelchair. "I told you, I ran."

Pavel sneered, stepping forward to strike the boy for his impertinence, then froze as Leo placed one foot and then the other on the floorboards and stood. He gaped at his son in disbelief, his eyes running from Leo's face to his legs as the boy stood holding the blanket around his waist.

"How? How is this possible?" Pavel uttered the question as much to himself as to Leo. Then his eyes narrowed as he looked at the impossibility of his son standing before him. "What kind of devilry is this?"

"You sold me like a fatted calf for slaughter," Leo's voice held more sadness than anger. "Me, your own son."

"Leo, the Romanov needed your help," Pavel tried reasoning with the apparition before him. He knew there was no way Leo could be standing in front of him; this had to be a specter of the dead boy, some ghostly echo. "You could save Obrechen, be a hero; just like in those stories you love."

"The Romanov is dead," Leo worked his jaw as if to say more, but he was struggling with his emotions.

"Dead?" Pavel could not hide his shock.

"Mother is dead too," Leo said through gritted teeth, his voice cracking as he tried to hold back the tears. "Killed by Igor Balkov as she searched for me in the forest."

Leo stepped toward Pavel, his pale, thin leg growing long and muscular as white fur sprouted from the limb like spring wheat. Pavel's eyes opened wide in disbelief as he let the suitcase slip from his fingers. He was so unnerved that the thudding of the suitcase on the wooden boards made him jump. Pavel backed away from Leo, his hand reaching for the holstered pistol on his belt.

As Pavel slowly backed through the doorway into the house, Leo took another step toward him. The boy's other leg transformed into a lupine limb mid-stride and slammed down so hard upon the floorboard that Pavel heard it crack under the force of the blow. Leo let the blanket fall away, revealing a lower body wholly transformed into a wolf covered in thick white hair. Pavel's mouth dropped open in surprise as Leo appeared to grow taller, broader, and more muscular before his eyes, then covered in white fur.

Pavel stepped fully into the house, his eyes darting to the door handle, signaling his intent. Leo, too, saw this and surged forward, placing a white-furred paw in the doorway as Pavel desperately tried to slam the door closed. The gendarme's heart pounded with panic as he kicked at the paw that prevented the door from closing. Black-clawed fingers slid through the opening so close to Pavel's face that he felt the fur brush his forehead, and he slammed his body against the door in a desperate bid to dislodge the beast and shut the door.

Outside, Pavel heard a rumbling growl joined by an angry-sounding snarl. Suddenly, a tremendous force struck the door, severing it from its hinges and sending Pavel sprawling across the floor. Daylight momentarily streamed into the small house and then was eclipsed by a large shadow. Pavel rolled onto his backside and watched as Leo stepped into the house. That of a large white wolf had replaced the boy's meek face. The beast stood upright like a man and had to dip its head to enter the door; dark lupine eyes gazed into Pavel's terrified face with a flare of anger. Alongside Leo, a second wolf, this one gray and snarling ferociously, entered the house on its hind legs. Terror at the sight of the two beasts gripped Pavel and twisted his stomach into knots. He backpedaled furiously, seeking to distance himself from the two wolf creatures as he fumbled to draw his pistol from its holster.

As the two wolves advanced on Pavel, the tips of their ears nearly brushed the house's ceiling. The white wolf, Leo, came forward more hesitantly while the gray wolf moved more eagerly, clenching and unclenching its feral claws. Its mouth drew back to reveal a mouthful of immense teeth. Pavel collided with a chair, upending it as he scurried backward past the table. The gray wolf grasped the table's edge, flipping it and sending it crashing across the room as effortlessly as with a child's toy.

Pavel's back struck the wall, halting his retreat. Cold sweat ran down his back as he stared at the two monstrosities. His mind struggled to comprehend what he saw as the creatures closed on him. He worked the pistol out of its holster and thrust it out before him, pointing it from wolf to wolf with a trembling hand. Leo reached out, placing a hand on the gray wolf's chest. The gray wolf turned toward Leo, an unspoken understanding passing between the two as it let the white wolf step forward.

The white wolf, Leo, looked from the gun to Pavel's face. Unlike the other wolf, it did not snarl or bare its teeth; it quietly studied the gendarme. Pavel looked into its dark eyes and felt as if he was again looking into Leo's eyes. He saw no malice or aggression in his son's gentle gaze despite the ferocity of his new hulking form. The gray wolf crouched, like a coiled spring set to pounce, as the father and son stared into each other's eyes and souls.

As Pavel looked into his son's eyes, really looked into his son's eyes for the first time in the boy's life, he saw a depth of forgiveness there—forgiveness for a lifetime of wrongs. Pavel felt the gun in his hand dip slightly as the tension in the room seemed to dissipate slowly.

Then, Pavel thought he detected something else in Leo's eyes, a sentiment beyond forgiveness and sadness—pity. Leo, the twisted little boy who spent his life in a chair, looked upon him with pity. The realization galled Pavel, and he felt bile rise in his throat as his anger flared. He saw Leo's eyes widen in surprise at the furious look in Pavel's eyes as he raised the pistol and squeezed the trigger.

The gunshot was deafening in the small house, and Pavel's ears rang from the sound. The report of the shot jarred his teeth and left a metallic taste on his tongue. His aim had been off, his shot wide, and Pavel saw a large splinter of wood fly off the ceiling where the bullet struck. The wolves seemed to be reacting in slow motion as Pavel adjusted and fired a second shot, the white wolf howling in pain as a line of crimson sliced along the side of its head.

The gray wolf sprang forward, roaring in rage, as it threw itself between Pavel and Leo. Pavel aimed the pistol at the creature's center mass, just as they had taught him in the police academy, and fired three shots in quick succession. The beast howled in pain and anger as three dark red holes laced its stomach where the bullets struck. The gray wolf roared, sounding loud even in Pavel's ringing ears, and charged. Behind the creature, the white wolf, too, sprang at Pavel.

He had fired five of his six bullets; Pavel knew three had struck the gray wolf with little noticeable effect other than infuriating the beast. Three bullets in the gut should have stopped any man or beast. Pavel could see the fury in the gray wolf's eyes as it charged, black claws outstretched to tear him to shreds. Over its shoulder, Pavel glimpsed the feral face of the white wolf; he could see its muzzle clearly with lips drawn back over razor-sharp teeth.

Pavel had seen the hunters' bodies, the victims of these monsters. He had seen the torn flesh and ravaged torsos, the final frozen death masks etched in terror and agony on the men's faces and the flies that buzzed upon the reeking carnage of Olga Putina and her brothers' remains. Terror coursed through Pavel Verenich's body and liquefied his bowels in a final stroke of indignity. The very earth seemed to rumble from the charging wolves as Pavel raised the pistol one final time. The tip of the barrel was hot from the rapid expenditure of rounds, and he placed it under his chin and pulled the trigger.

He never heard the shot. The bullet tore through the soft tissue of Pavel's jaw, crashing through the top of his mouth and exploding out the top of his head with a volcanic eruption of blood, brains, and bone. Pavel Verenich was dead before his hand holding the smoking pistol thudded against the floor.

***

"Oh, fuck that hurts," Alexei gritted his teeth and squeezed his eyes shut as he lay sprawled on Leo's bed.

He watched as Leo pressed one of his mother's towels hard against the three bullet holes in his abdomen. Alexei held his breath, trying to stifle a scream, as he arched his back slightly so Leo could loop one of his father's belts around Alexei's waist and cinch it around the crude bandage. Despite his best efforts, Alexei screamed in pain as Leo secured the belt in place.

Leo winced at his friend's pain, "The pressure should help with the bleeding. Are you sure you cannot shift back?"

Alexei shook his head, breathing hard as the pain subsided into a burning ache. After Pavel shot himself, Alexei had collapsed to the floor and shifted back into human form. He tried to return to his wolf body, hoping to speed the healing process, but the wolf would not come. In his mind's eye, Alexei had tried to coax the wolf through the door, but only mournful howls emanated from behind the door. Alexei feared this was a terrible sign, but he did not want to let Leo see his concern.

"We just need to get Oksana and find Bogdan. He'll know what to do." Alexei could see the red blood already saturating the blue towel. He was sure this was bad, even for a werewolf, and likely would have killed an average human already.

Leo nodded and handed Alexei a pair of dark trousers; a thin red line marked the bullet's path across his cheek. "Where is she now?"

"She ran to the church." Alexei grabbed the offered trousers, looked at the short length, and groaned. "Am I never to find my size clothes again?"

Alexei winced, pulling on the trousers with one hand as the other clutched the crude bandage they had placed over his wounds. Leo helped him slide on a dark green shirt, eliciting gasps as the movement jostled his wounds.

"None of the bullets exited your body; Bogdan will have to get them out before infection sets in; if werewolves get infections," concern etched Leo's pale face as he helped Alexei with the shirt.

"Bring something for Oksana to change into when she shifts back from wolf form," Alexei had to concentrate on keeping his mind from dwelling on the pain in his midsection.

"My mother has a dress that would fit her. I'll be right back," Leo waited for Alexei to nod in acknowledgment before running out of the room.

Alexei closed his eyes; his wounds were bad, he knew that. He suspected they were likely too severe for even Bogdan to do anything about. His only chance would be to shift and hope the werewolf's healing abilities would be enough. Yet try as he might, the wolf would not come. *Was the wolf's ethereal body wounded as well?*

He could smell Pavel's blood in the next room, and despite his wounds, Alexei's hunger for human flesh coursed through his veins. Alexei wondered if feeding on Pavel's liver and other vital organs would summon his wolf and speed his recovery. However, he quickly dismissed the idea; watching Alexei ravage his father's corpse was likely more than the sensitive Leo could bear on the day he lost both his parents.

He opened his eyes as he heard Leo approach, and the room spun so severely that Alexei had to brace himself on the bed with his hand. Alexei suspected the blood loss inside and outside his body was occurring at an alarming rate.

"I grabbed her two dresses," Leo patted the small satchel slung over his shoulder.

"That's good, Leo," Alexei rose gingerly to his feet, swaying a bit.

"Here, let me help you," Leo draped Alexei's arm over his shoulder, supporting his friend's weight.

The two friends slowly made their way through the little house that had been Leo's whole world. They slowed and then stopped as they passed by Pavel's body, a cone-shaped splatter of glistening gore adorning the wall behind him. The gendarme officer sat on the floor, eyes open and jaw slack as a trickle of blood continued to run down his mouth and drip from his chin. Alexei felt Leo's body stiffen as he turned to look at his father.

Leo stared silently at the man he had looked up to his entire life, "Selfish coward."

Neither spoke as they left the house. Alexei fought hard to keep the pain at bay and stifle his hunger for Pavel's flesh in a room saturated with the man's blood. However, his hunger did little to stir the wolf inside. Bogdan had warned him that his appetite for human flesh would only grow if he did not fight the urge, and his feeding upon Balkov only served to fuel his hunger for more. He looked down at the wounds in his mid-section; perhaps this was for the best. Sacrificing his life to save his best friend was not such a terrible end. It was undoubtedly better than turning into a flesh-crazed monster, cornered and slaughtered by villagers or the gendarme. Alexei glanced at Leo, but the boy appeared too deep in thought to notice his friend's turmoil.

As they stepped over the ruined front door onto the porch, Alexei thought he caught a fleeting glimpse of rust-brown fur in the trees beyond the house. He inhaled deeply, which caused an agonizing shot of pain to crisscross his midsection like dueling lightning bolts. However, through the pain, Alexei caught a hint of musk in the air and frowned; something within his primal instincts registered the scent as a threat. *Could it be Rostov?*

Alexei ventured into his mind for the wolf, hoping the presence of a threat might stir the creature to return. However, the door was still quiet, with no indication that the wolf beyond stirred or even lived. He let out a deep sigh, and Leo looked at him with eyes etched with worry.

"We'll take the stairs slowly," Leo reassured him.

Alexei gave him a weak smile, "It might be better if you just threw me off the porch and picked me up when you got down."

Leo laughed, then grew serious, "Thank you, Alexei. Those bullets were meant for me. If it weren't for you, I would be the one with a towel holding my insides in."

"What a charming picture you paint of my injuries," Alexei winced as they walked down the first step.

"Do you think the wound on my cheek will leave a scar?" Leo asked as they took another step.

"Worried it's going to ruin your good looks?" Alexei exhaled deeply as another wave of pain rolled through his guts. He could feel that his bandage had drenched with blood and was beginning to soak the top of his trousers. The front of his shirt began to darken with blood, and Alexei grew increasingly concerned he was unlikely to make it to the church, let alone to Galina's cottage, if Bogdan was even there.

"No, I was hoping it would make me look more rugged," Leo smiled broadly, then frowned as he studied his friend's face. "Alexei, you look pale."

Alexei turned to him with mock indignation, "You have looked pale every day of your life, and do I say a word? No. But here's the one day I look a tad whitish, and you treat me like a bruised apple."

They stepped off the last step, and Alexei breathed a sigh of relief. Though the stairs had been rough, he still had a good walk into town to contend with.

"I wish we had Seryy and that wagon," Leo glanced at Alexei. "I never thought I would want to see that damned donkey again, but he sure would come in handy right about now."

The wind carried a fresh musk scent to Alexei's nose, and he glanced sidelong at the woods. He could sense Rostov nearby. If Alexei could not summon the wolf, he doubted Leo would be much of a match for Rostov if he attacked. Despite the pain, an idea formed in his mind and Alexei quickened his step. They just needed to reach town.

"Alexei, wait here for a moment," Leo leaned Alexei against one of the posts supporting the porch.

After walking down the steps, leaning against the post was a welcome reprieve. Alexei gingerly poked at his wounds; they were numb to the touch but still ached terribly though the pain was no longer excruciating. The wolf blood had already healed him of grievous wounds once, so hope remained. However, the bullet wound in the upper right-hand portion of his abdomen was the most concerning. Alexei was sure that his father had told him that was the location of the liver. If so, that would be the one that would prove fatal if his new preternatural healing abilities could not overcome the wound.

He scanned the forest for any sign of Rostov. Alexei could smell and sense the man nearby, but Rostov remained out of sight. Outside, the scent of Pavel's blood and gore within the house was beyond the senses of ordinary humans. Still, to a werewolf, the aroma permeated the air and likely fueled Rostov's hunger as fiercely as Alexei's. If Rostov had shifted, he likely could sense Alexei and Leo and may have been hesitant to take on two werewolves simultaneously. If he was lurking and waiting, there was a significant danger he would attack while Leo and Alexei were separated. With any luck, Rostov was waiting for the boys to leave so he could capitalize on an easy meal.

"Look what I found," Leo grinned as he rounded the corner of the house; behind him trailed the horse Morozov had provided his father.

"Leo, I haven't a clue how to ride that thing, and I know you have never been on one," Alexei laughed and eyed the horse. "We're likely to break both our necks."

"Look, you can't make it into town like that, let alone Galina's cottage," Leo pointed at Alexei's wound, then raised the hand holding the horse's reigns. "You ride on the horse, and I'll lead it."

Alexei had to admit that the logic was sound and likely gave him the best chance of surviving his wounds. Leo guided the horse before him; Pavel had already saddled it, which was good since neither boy knew how.

"We're just going for a little walk, okay?" Alexei stared into the large brown eye of the horse, and it gazed back with disinterest. He noticed the animal's nostrils flare, and Alexei supposed it was trying to determine if the scent of two, maybe three, werewolves posed a threat.

Alexei had seen people mount horses before, and he tried to mimic what he could recall. Leo held the horse's reins and gave him the go-ahead nod as Alexei placed his left hand on the saddle's pommel and turned to face the horse's side. Alexei winced as he put his left foot in the stirrup; the movement sent a wave of pain through his abdomen that felt akin to someone sawing him in half. He took a deep breath, preparing for another searing jolt of pain, then bounced on his right foot and pushed with his left to swing his right leg over the horse. The pain was so severe that Alexei saw flashes of light before his eyes and felt his head spin as he nearly lost consciousness. Leo jumped forward and tried to steady Alexei before he slipped off the horse. Alexei gasped, trying to fill lungs that had constricted from the pain, and gripped the pommel so hard his knuckles were white until the worst of the pain subsided.

As his body slowly returned to its state of aching numbness, Alexei exhaled and opened his eyes. He had not even realized he had clamped his eyelids shut amidst the pain until he had opened them again. Leo's concerned face was the first thing he saw, and he tried to flash his friend a reassuring smile.

"I'm okay," Alexei nodded, Leo's concerned look transforming into a smile. "Let's go."

Leo took the lead, holding the horse's reins and slowly guiding it forward onto the road. The animal offered no resistance and, although the side-to-side motion of the saddle sent tendrils of pain shooting through his abdomen, Alexei admitted it was less painful than walking. He touched the front of his shirt, and his hand came away pink with blood. The seat of his trousers, too, had soaked with blood and squished uncomfortably in the saddle. Alexei scanned the forest for any indications that Rostov still trailed them and noticed that the edges of his vision had darkened. The werewolf blood in his veins fought to heal the grievous wounds. Alexei did not doubt that. But despite even those supernatural efforts, he feared his time was growing short.

"You know, I forgot to ask you. Where did you find your wolf?" Alexei asked.

Leo smiled and shrugged, "I guess when my mother died, it found me."

Alexei nodded, remembering Leo's anguish and transformation in the clearing. He wondered what it would take for his wolf to re-emerge, if at all.

"When I heard about the way you and Oksana connect with your wolf, I tried to picture in my head places where my wolf would be," Leo glanced back as he walked.

"Baba Yaga's hut?" Alexei asked.

Leo smiled and nodded, "That was the first place I thought of, but no, it wasn't there."

"No?" Alexei was genuinely surprised.

"No," Leo shook his head as he guided the horse closer to town. "When I was talking with my father on the porch, an image flashed in my mind of sitting in my chair reading Galina's book. When I opened the book, the wolf leaped out. After that happened, I began to shift again. Now, in my mind, I sit in that chair and can feel the wolf in the book. The cover of the book is warm and pulses with life."

"In a book of fairy tales," Alexei mulled that over for a minute and then decided that was the perfect place for Leo's wolf. "Fitting."

"Alexei, do you think we are in a fairy tale?" Leo had a contemplative look, and Alexei knew his friend meant the question seriously. It would be another one of those times when they had a deep, meaningful conversation about a topic anyone else in the world would consider fanciful.

"No, Leo, I don't," Alexei chided himself for the shortness of his answer, but Leo needed to realize that this was the real world, and they were in danger with Rostov on the loose and stalking them.

"No?" Leo looked as shocked by Alexei's answer as to the brevity of it.

"No."

"Why not?" Leo would not let the topic rest, though Alexei supposed that to Leo, believing they were living in a fairy tale was better than the harsh reality that he had just lost both his parents in the span of a few hours.

"Because fairy tales have happy endings, Leo," Alexei gritted his teeth as the horse navigated a rough patch of road, sending bolts of pain spiraling through his abdomen.

Leo looked back at Alexei, his eyes trailing to the dark wetness steadily spreading across Alexei's shirt, then he turned away. "Oh."

They continued toward town in silence, and Alexei struggled to keep his thoughts from meandering. He thought how carefree the birds in the trees seemed, chirping away in the sunlight as the world below them descended into chaos. Perhaps that was why the birds sang; they delighted in the end of the world of men. Every man that died was one less hunter in the woods, one less thief of their eggs.

Alexei breathed in deeply and noticed the scent of Rostov was not growing fainter, and he suspected the man was following them from within the tree line. He looked down at his bloody waist and realized his blood would be as much a draw for the werewolf as Pavel's. Alexei looked intently at the forest, trying to discern even the slightest movement that might give Rostov away, and he chastised himself for not taking Pavel's gun. By a tree, he thought he had caught sight of something hulking in the darkness but then it was gone.

"Do you smell it too?" Leo said quietly, noticing Alexei's attention to the forest. "Is it another werewolf?

"Yes, I think its Rostov," Alexei responded in a low tone.

"What do we do?" Leo's voice held a note of fear, and Alexei wondered just how much Leo's gentle nature could take of this violent new life.

"We're almost to town," Alexei leaned forward in the saddle. "Leave me at the *Kanti Gans* and go to the church to get Oksana. Take the horse."

"Leave you at the *Kanti Gans?*" Leo began to protest.

"I'll be fine; Rostov won't follow you if he has to pass me at the *Kanti Gans*. Once you get Oksana, Rostov won't dare tangle with three werewolves, even if I am injured." Alexei forced as much confidence into his words as his pain-addled body could muster.

As the road opened into Obrechen, both boys stared in amazement at the empty streets and shuttered homes. There was no familiar cluck of chickens or calls of roosters; not even a stray dog scurrying through the town. Neither boy had ever seen the town so empty.

"It looks like all of Obrechen is hiding from the wolf," Alexei gave a mirthless laugh.

Leo glanced back at Alexei, "Is this because of what happened in the woods last night?"

"I don't think so," Alexei nodded his head. "I doubt news of what happened has reached Obrechen if any of the Romanov's people even survived to spread it. I think everyone hunkered down after word spread of the wolf killing Olga Putina and her brothers at Galina's house."

"Do you think the *Kanti Gans* will be open?" Leo asked as they approached the village tavern.

"I'm sure of it," Alexei smirked. "If one place in Obrechen will be open for business amidst all this shit, it will be the *Kanti Gans*."

***

Oksana opened the church door and ducked her head to enter. She had run through the woods beside Alexei as they raced to Leo's house. Running with a member of her pack filled her with a primal thrill, and she gave herself over to the wolf inside her. The forest had come alive with myriad scents and sounds all around her. She could hear the flap of wings and the beating hearts all about her as she wondered at the breadth of life in the forest, hitherto unknown to her human senses.

Beside her, she was keenly aware of Alexei in a way she had never experienced. She could sense his concern for Leo, and her body intuitively knew when he was changing his pace or direction. No words passed between them, however, she felt a greater understanding of his thoughts, emotions, and intentions than ever before.

They broke out of the cover of the forest halfway between Obrechen and Leo's house. A momentary glimpse of black drew her attention toward town, and Oksana spied the form of Father Grigori, quickly crossing the square toward the church. Returning from paying an evening house call to the wife of one of the hunters in the woods, no doubt.

The hypocrisy of the man who had brought her and her friends so much grief and suffering in the name of his god and righteousness galled her. Memories of all the times she suffered kneeling on that block of wood before the cross came flooding back to her. Images of the priest in the carnal embrace of Vera Morozova flashed through her mind, as did him striking a killing blow against her skull and leaving her for dead in the filth of Obrechen's streets. Oksana stared toward the church, her lips peeled back into a snarl of rage.

The immense gray wolf that was now Alexei paused and looked back at her, the intelligent eyes passing from her to the church. Unspoken communication passed between them, and the wolf dipped its head in acknowledgment before running toward Leo's house. Oksana watched him go, intrigued by this new facet of their relationship, then turned and headed toward the church.

Now, as her rear paws moved silently across the church floor, she felt the eyes of the saints painted upon the walls staring at her, judging the beast for violating the sanctity of their house. Her keen wolf ears could hear Father Grigori moving about in his private chamber. She could smell him, and the scent of a woman was still upon him.

A faint smell of blood tinged the air, and she sniffed, searching for the source of the aroma. Her eyes fell upon the heavy stone candleholder on the small table beside the door to the priest's chamber. A long white candle flickered atop the narrow alabaster neck, but the candleholder's base drew her gaze. The priest had recently washed it, scrubbed it likely; she could smell the strong odor of soap upon it, though that did not hide the underlying scent of blood from her lupine nose.

Oksana smacked the candle away, the flame flickering out as it clattered to the floor. Trembling with rage, she grasped the neck of the candleholder in her clawed hand and turned it over. A dark stain still marred the bottom of the alabaster. The priest had been too lazy to wash clean all the blood from the candleholder—her blood. He had shattered her skull with the offending object, then washed it and returned it to its place as if cleaning off a dirty dish.

The door to the priest's chamber swung open, and Father Grigori stepped out so quickly that he nearly walked into Oksana. His bearded face registered shock and surprise at the unexpected intruder before quickly turning to terror. She had expected a scion of the church to clutch his cross and call down the holy fires of his god upon her, but Grigori only screamed, the sound of a fatted sow gone to slaughter. He tried to flee back into his chambers, however, Oksana was faster. She grabbed the front of the man's cassock and swatted the heavy candleholder at the priest's face. The heavy alabaster base struck Father Grigori on the side of his jaw with a sickening crack that sent a spray of blood and broken teeth spraying across Oksana's chest.

Father Grigori's scream transformed into a frantic gurgle as his jaw hung slack at an impossible angle, one side boneless and malformed. His eyes opened wide, and his pupils were islands in a white sea as Oksana snarled in the priest's face, showing her razor-sharp teeth.

The priest's mouth frothed with spittle and blood as she lifted him from his feet, his ravaged jaw making it impossible to discern whether he prayed or pleaded. A line of urine trailed down the priest's leg and darkened the wooden floor as she carried him across the church, raised high in the air.

Oksana brought him before the wooden statue of the crucifixion and turned him to face the tormented visage of Jesus. His feet dangled above the wood bar he had installed to inflict suffering upon the penitent. How many times had Father Grigori forced her to kneel there for even the slightest infraction? How often had the priest watched in sadistic glee as he made her and Alexei suffer before the wooden crucifix for their sins while he secretly indulged his carnal desires?

She slammed the priest downward, his legs splintering like dried branches as Oksana drove him down onto the wooden bar on the floor. Grigori threw his head back, eyes staring at the ceiling, and screamed through a throat so filled with blood he sounded like he was beneath water. His body shook and convulsed so violently she feared he would lose consciousness. Still gripping the candle holder in her free hand, she swung it at the priest, striking the back of his head.

The candleholder impacted the back of his skull, sounding like an axe handle hitting a tree. His head snapped forward, cutting short his scream, and lolled on his shoulders. Oksana swung the candleholder again and again until fragments of bone and flesh dotted the crucified body of Jesus, and drops of blood ran down the wooden body like red rivers.

Oksana released the candleholder, letting it thud heavily on the floor beside the lifeless body of the priest. She was breathing heavily, her chest rising and falling from the exertion. Her brown fur was dark with blood and gore that glistened in the flickering lights of the church.

She glanced down at the savagery she had done to the priest, and the sight of Father Grigori's mangled skull sickened her. Oksana felt no pity for the priest, but she was horrified by her brutality and what the years of abuse at the hands of the priest, her uncle, and the people of Obrechen had turned her into. The beast within her was Obrechen's creation, not the wolf's. She fell on all fours and wretched, emptying her stomach of all its contents as she shifted back into human form.

With human hands, Oksana wiped the bile from her lips and stood naked and bloody in the church. She walked to Grigori's chambers and cleaned the blood from her skin in his wash basin. Oksana dried her face on the softest towel she had ever touched, looked around at the priest's chambers, and marveled at the extravagance. He had finely sewn clothing, unlike anything she had ever seen, including several dresses that Oksana supposed he intended as gifts for Vera Morozova or other women in town. A green one with an intricately stitched lattice design in the front appeared close to her size, and Oksana slipped it over her head. The fabric was a far cry from the homespun clothes she was used to wearing and even rivaled the finest she had seen in Galina's wardrobe.

The priest had accumulated jewelry, perfumes, spices, and several small boxes of coins and banknotes. Oksana emptied the boxes into a leather satchel ornately decorated with etchings of wild horses until it bulged and weighed heavily on her shoulder. She felt like a thief stealing the coins, but they would need money once they fled Obrechen, and only through unscrupulous means could Father Grigori have accumulated such enormous wealth. As she turned to leave, she spied two beautiful necklaces on the priest's desk, each adorned with a teardrop-shaped alexandrite gemstone, one blue and the other raspberry red. Oksana added the necklaces to the satchel, a gift for her and Galina.

She hurried out of Grigori's chambers, eager to be gone from the church, and avoided looking toward the carnage she had wrought. Light suddenly flooded the church as the door flung open, and Oksana froze, her heart thudding in her chest. With the priest dead and her fleeing in a stolen dress with a pouch of coins and jewels, she would appear a common thief and murderer.

"Oksana?" a voice called as Leo's thin frame stood in the doorway.

"Leo," Oksana was so happy to see the boy she nearly cried with joy. "Is Alexei with you?"

"Alexei's at the *Kanti Gans*. Rostov was following us," Leo's voice cracked. "He's hurt very bad. I think he's dying."

Oksana's heart sank. *No, not Alexei; he cannot die. Not now.*

She rushed toward the door, "Take me to him, quickly."

***

Alexei smiled as he watched Leo run toward the church, his father's horse trailing behind him. If someone had given him three wishes a month ago, Alexei would have used the first to make Leo's body whole. It seemed Bogdan had already granted that one by making the boy a werewolf; he would have to thank the woodsman the next time he saw him. As Leo glanced back, Alexei nodded and gave a slight wave to let the boy know he was still doing fine.

Hurry, Leo. Get Oksana before Rostov shows his face.

Alexei's thoughts trailed to Oksana. He would have used his second wish to make her love him, but that would have been wrong. He was desperate for her heart to be his, but not that way. However, Alexei had to admit that there was a moment when he guided Oksana through the cave opening where he thought he detected a change in how she looked at him. Alexei was probably fooling himself, believing he saw something different in her eyes because that was what his heart desperately wanted. Though maybe not.

A shooting pain in his side snapped him out of his thoughts with a jolt. He needed to stay focused; the blood loss was making it more challenging to keep his thoughts straight. He glanced down the road; Leo's newfound legs quickly got him to the church, which was good. Alexei turned to scan in the other direction and froze, his blood going cold. A dark shape slipped into the woods just to the right of the *Kanti Gans*. He had only seen it for a moment, and had he blinked a second sooner, Alexei would have missed it. However, he was sure he had caught sight of Rostov, much closer than expected.

Alexei grimaced as he slipped a hand inside his shirt and ran it along his bandaged abdomen. The palm brushed against his wounds, sending a fresh wave of pain coursing through his body that made him light-headed and nauseous. His third wish would have been to see his parents again, and it looked like that was coming true, too. Alexei reached into his mind, seeking the wolf, but heard only labored breathing coming from the door.

I will have to do this alone.

The palm and fingers of his hand were red and wet with blood when he slid it out from his shirt. Alexei slapped the hand against the post of the Kanti Gans, leaving a glistening red handprint. Turning, he staggered to the tavern's door and wiped the bloody hand across the door, painting a crimson steak across the worn wood.

That should be easy enough for Rostov to follow. Alexei turned the knob and pushed open the door, not the least surprised to find it unlocked.

As the door swung open, Alexei gasped and reeled as he entered the tavern. The stench of blood and death permeated the stale air of the *Kanti Gans*, overwhelming the ever-present odors of sweat and alcohol. In his mind, he heard the wolf emit a deep growl, and Alexei's heart swelled with hope that the beast would finally be awakening. However, his hope quickly fled as the growl died to a low rumble, replaced by labored breathing.

Alexei staggered into the room and closed the door. A village man ravaged beyond recognition lay spread eagle upon a table. His body had been torn open with such ferocity that the jagged ends of his broken ribs rose from his chest like skeletal fingers. As Alexei approached, he could see the man's internal organs were missing from his torn and hallowed torso. Rostov had been here already.

He glanced around the bar; the tavern was empty except for the aged barkeep, who sat slumped in the corner. Alexei could see that he, too, had been savaged by Rostov; a dark pool of blood puddled the floor around the man. The man's entrails spilled from his body and lay in the deep red puddle like a sea serpent. To Alexei's disgust, the smell of so much blood made his nose twitch and his stomach growl. His eyes glanced down into the cavernous opening in the man's chest; the temptation to have just a taste, maybe a lick of blood, drew him like an addict to the opium pipe.

Alexei took a step toward the man, then caught himself. He would not become a feral beast like Rostov; Alexei would fight the urge to feed on human flesh. The look in Oksana's eyes when she saw what he had done to Balkov would haunt Alexei forever. He would rather die than become a monster in her eyes again.

Crossing the room, Alexei stepped behind the bar and nearly tripped over the body of the red-haired barmaid, Yulia. He recoiled at the sight of the woman sprawled behind the bar, her eyes opened wide and mouth agape in a silent scream. Rostov had torn the clothes from her body. Alexei felt embarrassed for her at seeing the dead woman in such a state of nakedness. Like the others, Rostov had disemboweled her, consuming her internal organs and coating her pale, exposed flesh in blood and gore. However, there was something about the unnatural position of the woman's legs, her knees bent at impossible angles that hinted at a hideous fate before death. Alexei noted bruising around her neck from Rostov's clawed hands and bite marks on her shoulders, neck, and breasts; wounds meant to inflict pain rather than feed or kill.

A rage and shame began to build in Alexei as he stepped over the woman's body and retrieved a dark, stained blanket from the tavern's back room. These deaths were his fault; he had created Rostov and unleashed him upon Obrechen. Yulia had never been kind or even friendly toward him, but the monstrosity of Rostov's actions was something no human should ever experience.

"I'm sorry," Alexei whispered as he covered her body with the blanket, hoping the gesture gave her some final dignity.

He stared down at the distorted contours of the form beneath the blanket; dark, wet spots spread across the stained fabric as it greedily absorbed her blood. Alexei thought of his friends. Bogdan might be able to defeat Rostov, man-to-man, wolf-to-wolf, however, he knew Leo and Oksana would be no match for Rostov. There was a depth to Rostov's evil and cruelness that would overwhelm them. Leo was too gentle a creature for the storm that would assail them, and Oksana was still learning her new wolf form. If he could summon his wolf form to return, they might have a chance against Rostov, but in his present condition, he would only slow them down. The carnage in the *Kanti Gans* would repeat itself with Leo and Oksana as Rostov's next victims. Their blood would be on Alexei's hands.

In his mind, Alexei screamed for the wolf to return. He futilely pounded on the door to stir the beast from its slumber, pleading for it to join him, heal his body, and fight Rostov. Fury rose within Alexei as he channeled all his life's indignities, loss, and hardships into his need to unleash a primal rage upon Rostov, to right his wrong and save his friends. He listened by the door but the wolf's shallow, ragged breathing was his only response.

Turning from Yulia's body, Alexei caught sight of himself in the mirror on the wall behind the bar. The ghostly visage that looked back at him was nearly unrecognizable to him. His skin had gotten deathly pale, and dark circles had formed beneath his eyes. Alexei's lips had taken on a bluish hue that curved up slightly as he smiled at the reflection. Yes, it certainly seemed like he would be seeing his parents again soon.

Alexei gritted his teeth against the pain in his gut and staggered toward the back room of the bar.

Chapter 9

Rostov stepped from the woods beside the *Kanti Gans*, striding upright on rust-brown paws. He caught a glimpse of his shadow on the ground and marveled at the dark outline of his body. The hulking form of the wolf replaced the visage of the short, bald man. Rostov knew he would have towered over his former self as he stared at the muscular arms sprouted from broad shoulders and ending in sharp claws. As far as he was concerned, he would never return to his frail human body again.

I am a fucking god.

He had gorged himself on the nutrient-rich organs of the villagers at the Morozov estate and the *Kanti Gans;* now, the blood coursing through his veins felt charged with energy. The rush that Rostov felt from the fear and pain of the mere mortals he had rent to shreds and satiated his hunger was more intoxicating than any drug. The lips of his lupine muzzle reared back into what passed for a smile, exposing teeth that still dangled thin curtains of human flesh as he recalled satisfying his more carnal desires with the Morozov woman and the buxom bar wench.

I am a fucking god.

Rostov stopped to sniff the air. His nose filled with the scent of blood. He recognized the smell of the three from the *Kanti Gans* and a fourth, whose blood was still warm and fresh—the Jew. Stepping onto the tavern's porch, he dipped his wolf-like head toward the bloody handprint on the post; the blood still glistened in the sunlight. Rostov opened his mouth and ran his tongue over the rough wood, his taste buds tingling with the metallic taste of the blood. He closed his mouth and savored the taste; there was something different about the Jew's blood, human yet feral. Was the Jew like him? Half man, half beast. He had thought he caught the scent of a wolf among the boys.

No. The Jew would be a wolf, not slinking through town leaking blood like a dying goat if he was like me. However, he may be able to call the wolves that attacked my men.

He wanted to make the Jew suffer and die slowly for killing his men, but he would not risk giving the boy the chance to call down the other wolves upon him.

Could the Jew control him, too?

The thought gave him pause; however, he quickly shook off the notion as nonsense. Nonetheless, his attack must be swift. Rostov would not defile his body by consuming the Jews' organs, but how he would relish the pain and screams as he shredded the boy's flesh.

Rostov turned and ran toward the door of the *Kanti Gans*. Splintering the door with a kick from his hind leg, Rostov leaped into the tavern and landed in a low crouch. To his sensitive nose, the room reeked of flesh and blood, immediately heightening his predatory drive. Saliva dripped from Rostov's mouth onto the floor as he scanned the room.

The boy stood behind the bar, though as Rostov studied him with a keen hunter's eye, he could see the boy was leaning against the bar for support. He looked pale and gaunt, a far cry from the healthy, robust boy they had shot and bludgeoned on the road. The boy looked at Rostov with eyes that seemed to struggle to focus as he raised a glass to his lips and downed the contents. Rostov could see the boy struggling to keep his hand from shaking.

"Ahhh, now that's good," Alexei smacked his lips. "Must have been the stuff they kept for the Land Captain and special guests."

Rostov edged closer to the boy, his clawed feet scraping against the floor as he approached. He clenched and unclenched his fists, the thought of tearing into the boy arousing him as he neared his prey.

Alexei cocked his head at Rostov, studying him, then shook his head and laughed weakly, "Rostov, how is it that even as a wolf, you are one ugly fucker?"

Rostov snarled in rage at the boy's impertinence and lack of fear. The boy should be quaking and prostrating before him to beg for his life. He snapped at the air in frustration. Then, a thought occurred to him, and he sniffed the air and scanned the room, looking for signs of danger. Nothing. Just the two of them. He decided the boy was delaying, likely hoping that help would arrive to save him.

Well, it won't.

He decided he wanted to end this now, his hind legs tensing to launch him over the bar, his claws ready to tear out the Jew's throat.

"You know Rostov, the first time we met, you showed me your Jew Hammer; do you remember?" Alexei met his gaze, his glassy eyes unwavering. Then, the boy placed a box on the table.

Rostov paused, studying the unusual object. Then his eyes opened wide in shock and fear.

"Now, I will show you mine," Alexei smiled, a broad grin reaching his eyes as he brought his hand up to the handle of the detonator switch.

Rostov growled in a fury, leaping at the boy as Alexei twisted the trigger mechanism on the blasting machine. The hand-sized box instantly sent an electric current through the long cord behind the bar, through the back room, down the trap door, and to the waiting explosives below. The detonation of the electric cap ignited the mix of mercury fulminate and potassium chlorate, further detonating the dynamite bundles.

The blast of heat and fire disintegrated the laughing boy and the rust-brown wolf as it leaped through the air in the blinking of an eye. The wooden boards of the *Kanti Gans* fed the all-consuming fire and superheated the air as the building exploded.

Outside, the buildings closest to the tavern were flattened and consumed by flames; their unfortunate denizens shattered and burned before they could register what had happened. The burning boards of the *Kanti Gans* rained down upon the thatched roofs of Obrechen, igniting fires that quickly fed upon the dried thatch and spread from house to house. Terrified villagers fled their homes or tried in vain to battle the roaring blazes quickly consuming Obrechen.

On the church's steps, two small figures stumbled backward, buffeted by the wave of hot air that followed the explosion. The horse before them strained against its reins to free itself from the hitching post and run off into the night. A large piece of burning wood spiraled through the night and embedded itself in the church's roof. Immediately, the flames spread across the roof, greedily devouring the dry wooden boards as the two figures stared at the blazing ruins of the *Kanti Gans.*

***

"He got out," Leo looked from the inferno that had once been the *Kanti Gans* to Oksana.

"No, Leo, he didn't," Oksana shook her head as tears streamed down her face.

Leo looked as if he would say more, then turned back to stare at the fire. Oksana knew Alexei had explosives from his father; he had confided it to her once as they sat in the meadow. She did not know how or when Alexei got them to the *Kanti Gans,* but she was sure he had done so. Leo had said he was severely hurt; Oksana guessed he must have lured Rostov to the *Kanti Gans* and detonated the explosives—one last valiant gift from Alexei Kaminer. She shifted the satchel on her shoulder; with Rostov gone, there would be nothing to prevent them all from fleeing Obrechen—all but Alexei.

Oksana looked at the destruction wrought upon Obrechen as the house fires cast dark silhouettes of villagers running frantically about. Alexei would be happy to see this, his final revenge upon Obrechen and the people who had so openly shunned and despised him.

"The church is on fire," Leo turned and stared at the roof.

Oksana followed his gaze and saw the flames spreading to consume the church's roof. One more gift from Alexei: the fire would destroy all traces of what she had done within and consume the hated prayer block Father Grigori forced them to kneel upon so many times.

"What do we do?" Leo looked at her, tears streaking his cheeks.

Oksana wiped a hand across her eyes to dry her tears and then looked at him, "Let's try and calm the horse; we need to get to Bogdan and Galina and tell them what has happened."

"Shouldn't we try to look for Alexei and see if he survived?" Leo looked desperate, but Oksana also saw a more profound understanding that his friend was gone for good this time.

"He's gone, Leo," Oksana raised a hand to her heart. "I can feel it here; he's gone."

Oksana spoke the truth; whether it was their bond of friendship or some connection of their wolf blood, she felt an innate knowing that Alexei was dead. Leo nodded, and from the look on his face, she suspected he felt it, too.

"Get the horse, Leo," Oksana said gently. "Galina showed me how to ride on Seryy; I can get us back to the cottage."

As Obrechen burned, two small figures on horseback rode slowly from town. They were little more than dark silhouettes as they paused briefly before the inferno that had been the *Kanti Gans*. Buffeted by the waves of heat that poured forth from the blaze, they cast forlorn eyes upon the funeral pyre of their friend. As the heat dried the tears streaming down their cheeks, the horse stomped its hooves, eager to escape the burning conflagration. The boy leaned his head upon the girl's back, burying his sadness in her long, dark hair as she guided the horse toward the road leading from Obrechen, departing the town that had been their home and tormentor forever.

***

"Are you okay?" Bogdan glanced sidelong at Galina as they walked the final turn leading to the cottage. "You have not spoken a word since we left the Morozov estate."

"No," Galina shook her head and looked at the woodsman with haunted eyes. "I don't think I will ever be alright again after what I saw there."

"I am sorry you had to see that; Cillian believed the wolf could bring out the worst in us if we let it," He turned away from her, adjusting the worn leather pack on his back, and stared into the woods. "I should have checked the house before letting you enter."

"Bogdan, I am not some delicate flower that needs to be protected; I am as much wolf as you," anger flared in Galina's eyes. "But what I saw in that house, what Rostov did to those women, that was not feral; that was evil— pure evil."

The woodsman nodded, and she could see by the strain on his face and the tightening around his eyes that he, too, was haunted by the carnage they had discovered in the Morozov house. The state of the bodies evidenced acts so sadistic and depraved that Galina's heart broke to think any human should have had to experience that.

The road opened into the clearing where the little cottage and barn stood quietly in the early afternoon sun. Galina glanced at the house that had been her home and quickly looked away, remembering the charnel house it had become when Bogdan slaughtered Olga Putina and her brothers to rescue her. She knew that act of butchery had been necessary, and Bogdan took no pleasure in the killings, but the cottage still stood as a testament to the brutality of her new world. The wolves within them had been their savior in dire circumstances. However, they were also a gateway to the darkest side of humanity within each one of them. Galina knew that Bogdan and Alexei had killed people when they were in wolf form, and she had mortally wounded the Romanov to save Leo. Rostov represented the worst of what their kind could be, but the capacity to be a thing of nightmares lay within all of them.

"I have some supplies stored in the barn," Bogdan gestured toward the old wooden structure. "I'll gather them up, and we'll wait for the others."

"Bogdan, I know you want us to flee this place, but we cannot leave with Rostov still on the loose," Galina's tone made it clear she felt adamant about seeing Rostov destroyed. "Not after what we saw today."

"Galina, after what he did at the Morozovs,' Kalinin will send soldiers and gendarme to comb these woods looking for the beast that committed that savagery. Rostov has given in to the baser side of our kind; he will not stop killing. He will not be able to evade the authorities for long. If we stay, we will only die too. Our presence here will only do more harm. If they killed one of us, the authorities might stop searching, thinking they killed the monster, and that would allow Rostov to escape until he killed again. No, we have done all we can do here."

"Better we all die here and put an end to this curse than let Rostov roam free a second longer than necessary," Galina mustered as much force into her words as she could.

"Galina, this is not a curse," Bogdan began, his expression crestfallen as he looked at her.

"It is a curse, your curse. You brought this upon us and all but created Rostov yourself. All of these deaths are upon you," Galina thrust her finger at him, unleashing a wave of anger born of fear and frustration.

He stepped back as if physically struck by her words, and Galina saw a look of horror in his eyes that was quickly replaced by a depth of sadness she had never seen in the woodsman before. Galina immediately regretted her words and the harshness of her tone. She knew Bogdan had only acted to save them. The Pandora's Box that had opened in Obrechen was as much their fault as it was his.

Galina wanted to tell Bogdan it was just the unspeakable horrors of the last few days, however, the woodsman was no longer looking at her. Bogdan's eyes grew hard, and she could see his body tense as he looked past her.

"Galina, get behind me," Bogdan spoke barely above a whisper, his eyes fixed on the cottage.

Bogdan stepped forward, placing himself between Galina and the cottage. As Galina turned, she saw two men step from the house onto the porch, both with rifles pointed at them. A bearded man in the attire of a Cossack moved quickly down the steps, his rifle trained firmly on Bogdan. Galina recognized the second man from the clearing. Arkady Volkov, the huntsman who accompanied the Romanov to Obrechen. The man Bogdan had lured to the village to avenge his wife.

"Volkov, the woman is not part of this," Bogdan raised his hands and nodded toward Galina. "Let her go; our feud needs to hurt no more innocent people."

"Shut your fucking mouth," the Cossack halted a few paces before Bogdan, leveling his rifle at the woodsman's face.

"Our feud?" Volkov gave a humorless laugh as he dipped his rifle slightly. "I don't even know who you are."

"Who cares who he is," the Cossack growled, flexing and unflexing his finger from the trigger of his rifle. "He killed the Romanov; now he's going to die."

"Calm down, Sergeant Razin," Volkov cautioned.

The Cossack tensed for a moment and started to lower his rifle. Galina exhaled, unaware she had been holding her breath until that moment. Bogdan stared past the Cossack, eyes riveted on Volkov.

However, Galina watched the sergeant's face. She saw the storm of emotions in the man's eyes and the moment he decided.

"Fuck, calming down," Razin's feature went taunt as he suddenly raised his rifle back up to his face.

Galina gasped and jumped at the sound of the gunshot, even as Bogdan crouched and emitted a primal growl. The sergeant's body bucked forward, and the man gave a startled cry as blood plumed from his left shoulder. The force of the blow dislodged the rifle from his hands and sent it tumbling to the ground as the man crumpled, moaning. Behind him, the barrel of Volkov's rifle smoked as the man worked the bolt, loading another bullet into the chamber.

"You'll be fine, Sergeant Razin," Volkov called to the wounded Cossack as he sighted his rifle at Bogdan. "You know you have Sergeant Razin to thank for finding you. I was ready to return to Kalinin, but the good sergeant here reminded me that beasts return to the site of their kills; and here you are. Now, tell me what feud I have with you. What cause have you to slaughter my horse and kill my brother... and Batu?"

Galina noticed how the man's voice cracked as he spoke the name. She looked down; the sergeant's rifle was only a few feet to her left. Unlike other women in the Tsar's court, Galina had taken an interest in martial arms. A young French lieutenant seeking to impress her had taken her riding and shooting several times before he realized that his advances were getting him nowhere with the boyar's daughter and moved on to other potential conquests. Galina could not recall the man's name. However, she remembered everything he had taught her about firing a rifle perfectly.

She did not think she could grab the rifle and hit Volkov under such duress, though maybe she could. Galina had been a good shot, and she felt her chances of hitting Volkov would improve significantly if she had time to aim, even for a few moments.

Nonetheless, the distraction alone might be enough for Bogdan to reach the man. Either way, Volkov would have to choose his target between Galina and the woodsman, and that would give one of them a chance at survival.

The Cossack sergeant groaned on the ground and was clearly out of the fight. Her eyes moved from Volkov to the rifle as the two men continued their tense exchange.

"You killed my wife," Bogdan spoke in a low growl, his body still crouched and his eyes boring into Volkov.

"I have never killed a woman in my life," Volkov spat the words with evident distaste.

"You and your brother, you killed her in Romania," Bogdan narrowed his eyes with contempt. "It meant so little to you that you do not even recall. She was the world to me, and you took her from me."

Volkov appeared to struggle to comprehend what Bogdan was saying, and then a dawning realization crossed his face, "The wolf?"

Bogdan nodded, "You slew her; you and your brother both. I tore the coat he made of her fur from his body."

"You killed him," Volkov hissed the words through clenched teeth.

"I hunted your brother like a wild animal and killed him like a Christmas pig. I knew his death would bring you here," Galina could see the muscles of Bogdan's neck and shoulders tensing as they spoke; he was waiting for his moment to spring, trying to enrage the hunter into an opening he could exploit. "You have been my pawn from the start, Arkady Volkov; even if you shoot me down, I have taken everything from you. The empire will speak of the great hunter who fell to ruin in the tiny shithole of Obrechen."

Volkov shook his head almost imperceptibly, as if trying to ward off the thought, and Galina saw Bogdan's words had struck a nerve with the huntsman. Despite all the perils Volkov faced, despite all the deaths, Galina saw that it was Bogdan's assault upon the man's pride and reputation that Volkov truly feared.

"Change," Volkov ordered through teeth clenched in anger.

"What?" Bogdan looked genuinely shocked by the demand.

"Change into the beast," Volkov ordered again as he sighted his rifle at Bogdan.

Galina watched as Sergeant Razin propped himself onto his good shoulder, eyeing his rifle, and she took a cautious step closer to it. Her heart thundered in her chest and echoed in her ears as she worried that the movement may attract Volkov's attention, but his eyes remained firmly rooted on Bogdan. The woodsman eyed Volkov curiously and then, to Galina's surprise, laughed.

"Change!" Volkov ordered again, his voice shriller.

"No," Bogdan shook his head, and Galina noticed he adjusted his feet slightly. "Shoot me down where I stand, Volkov, but you don't get to run back to your Tsar with the big, bad beast that took everything from you."

Volkov squeezed the trigger, and the rifle boomed and bucked slightly in his hands as he fired a round that sent a small geyser of dirt and rocks into the air inches before Bogdan's feet.

"Show me the beast or the next shot goes in the girl's head," Volkov nodded toward Galina as he worked the bolt to load another round.

Galina watched as Bogdan charged forward, hoping to close the distance between him and Volkov in the seconds it took the man to chamber another round. At the same time, Sergeant Razin lurched toward his fallen rifle; Galina smelled the rush of adrenaline pump through the Cossack's veins seconds before he moved and was already in motion, her knees landing in the dirt, hands outstretched for the gun.

She felt the smooth wood of the weapon's stock slip into her palms just as Razin closed the fingers of his good arm around the muzzle. Razin yanked the rifle, trying to dislodge it from her grip, but her hands held fast. Galina kicked dirt into the Cossack's face, causing the man to cry out as the grit stung his eyes, but it did nothing to loosen the man's iron grip on the rifle.

Galina glanced at Volkov. The man was desperately working to read his next shot. Bogdan was closing ground quickly, but she could see the woodsman would not reach Volkov in time. Suddenly, a loud boom reverberated through the forest, and a plume of red-orange fire mushroomed into the sky from the direction of Obrechen. The explosion drew Volkov's attention for only a few seconds, but Bogdan launched himself toward the hunter in that momentary distraction. Volkov swung the rifle toward Bogdan, and the woodsman managed to bat the barrel out of the hunter's hand just as the shot fired. The weapon clattered against the wooden floorboards of the porch as the shot sailed harmlessly into the trees.

Volkov cried out in shock as Bogdan crashed into him, sending him stumbling back against the house. The hunter recovered quickly and reached for his knife as Bogdan landed firmly on the porch and charged forward. The burly woodsman wrapped his arms around Volkov, pinning the man's arms to his sides. The two men's faces were mere inches apart as Volkov struggled to free himself. Bogdan tightened his grip and let loose a primal scream as he squeezed the man with even greater force. Volkov's eyes grew wide in fear and panic as Bogdan constricted his chest; the man struggled to force air into his lungs and then screamed as his ribs cracked. Blood darkened Volkov's lips in bubbling spurts, running down his chin, as Bogdan let loose a feral growl and continued to crush the man. Volkov's head lolled backward, and he groaned pitifully as the sound of his spine snapping filled the air.

"This is better than you deserve," Bogdan said as Volkov's eyes rolled up in his head.

Bogdan released the man's body, letting it crumple lifelessly to the floor, his breath heaving from the exertion. Galina could see Bogdan's shoulders slump; whether in exhaustion or from the release of the long-sought for revenge, she could not tell. He turned and saw Galina's continuing struggle with Razin, a look of concern crossing his face as he leaped off the porch and charged toward the Cossack. Galina saw the look of alarm cross Razin's face as Bogdan's shadow darkened the ground around him. She tumbled backward as the Cossack released the rifle and rolled on his back, raising his arm defensively as Bogdan loomed over him.

"Enough," Bogdan's voice sounded weary. "Enough killing. Go home and bury your dead. It's over."

Razin appeared to relax, and the tension drained from his face as he slowly lowered his arm. As Bogdan walked past him, Razin sat up, bringing his knees to his chest and dipping his head forward in a gesture Galina took for sheer exhaustion. She exhaled, cradling the rifle in her arms as Bogdan approached.

"Is it really over?" Galina looked up at him.

"Yes, I believe so," Bogdan nodded, but a grim look overtook his countenance, "but I am concerned about that explosion."

"What was that?" Galina turned to look in the direction of Obrechen.

"I don't know," Bogdan shook his head. "I'm worried something has happened to one of the others; I felt a pang of sadness in my heart when it happened. I have only felt such a thing once before, when my wife died."

"I felt it, too," Galina turned back to him. "Like a sudden loss."

Bogdan nodded and then grimaced in pain as a loud crack broke the silence. The woodsman fell to his knees as a dark crimson stain spread across the front of his shirt. Behind him, Razin sat with his uninjured arm outstretched, a small smoking derringer in his outstretched hand. Galina cried out in rage as she brought the rifle up and fired at the Cossack. Razin's body rocked sideways and fell backward as Galina leaped to her feet, pulling the bolt of the rifle back and slamming it forward, chambering a new round as she charged toward Razin.

The man lay on his back, a growing pool of blood spreading from the gaping wound in his side. Galina stood over him and aimed the rifle at his face, tears of rage and sadness streaming down her face. Blood stained the man's teeth, and his eyes wandered wildly.

"Why?" Galina breathed the word as she fought to choke back a sob.

Razin's eyes focused on her momentarily and, with great effort and pain, he struggled to gasp out the words, "He who seeks revenge digs two graves." Then the Cossack's eyes glazed over, and he went still.

Galina let the rifle fall from her fingers and rushed to Bogdan's side. The woodsman was kneeling, his arms slack, as he looked up at the sky. A gruesome hole marked where the bullet had entered his back and exited his chest, soaking his shirt with blood. As Galina knelt by his side, he turned to look at her and collapsed into her arms. He raised a hand to her cheek, the anguish washing from his features to be replaced by a smile.

"Take the others and start a life far from this place of death," Bogdan felt heavy in her arms as he spoke.

"No, Bogdan. We'll all go together. You're going to be okay," Galina said through tears as she took his hand in hers.

"This is not a sad thing, Galina. I will finally be back with my Ana," Bogdan said, looking toward his worn backpack lying on the ground. "In my pack is the coat made of my wife's fur. Burn it with my body so we can finally drift together as smoke on the wind. Will you do that for me?"

"Yes. Yes, of course, Bogdan," Galina nodded as she sobbed. "But please don't leave me."

As a breeze tussled his hair and blew across his face, Bogdan smiled, the warm smile she had seen grace his face in happier times, "Ah, here she is now."

"Bogdan," Galina's voice cracked with emotion as she stared into the woodsman's still, smiling face. When he did not stir, she raised a shaking hand and brushed it across his eyes, closing his eyelids. Then she leaned her head down until their foreheads touched, and Galina let the tears flow unbidden.

Galina was still sitting, cradling his head, the noonday sun was waning as Oksana and Leo approached on a brown mare. They slid from the horse's back, and Leo rushed toward them, halting and staring at Bogdan's body as Oksana trailed behind.

"Bogdan?" the voice that slipped from Leo's lips sounded so young and innocent.

Galina felt the tears begin to flow again as she looked into Leo's heartbroken face and shook her head. Leo dropped to his knees and covered his face with his hands as he began to cry. Oksana approached slowly behind him, her face grief-stricken and soot-covered from the fires that raged in Obrechen.

"Alexei?" Galina asked, her voice trembling.

Oksana slowly shook her head, biting her lip to hold back the tears. Then she rushed forward and collapsed against Galina, burying her face in the young woman's shoulder and sobbing deep, heart-wrenching sobs.

***

They returned to the clearing and retrieved Leo's mother's body from the woods. Crows had begun to feast upon the corpse of Igor Balkov and the other bodies in the clearing; however, Anya Verenicha remained remarkably untouched by fowl or beast. Oksana and Galina wrapped her in a soft, finely woven blanket that had been a gift to Galina in her youth. It was a beautiful shade of red with flocks of colorful birds intricately sewn in a pattern that made them appear to spiral into the air, and Leo remarked with a sigh of sadness that he wished she had the opportunity to wear something so grand in life. They feared taking the roads and encountering any villagers fleeing the conflagration of Obrechen, so Leo carried her to the cottage in a solemn procession through the woods.

Galina suggested burying her in a spot by the garden that received lots of sunlight and was home to a small field of wildflowers in the spring and 1 summer. Leo liked the thought of his mother surrounded by flowers but in the end, he decided it best to burn her body in a pyre alongside Bogdan.

"She would get lonely here by herself. We should let her spirit ride the wind and see all the world; she would have liked that. My mother always dreamed of traveling," Leo swallowed hard, fighting to hold back a rising tide of emotion.

So, as the sun began to dip below the horizon, the three of them stood before two pyres built of hay and wood from the barn. Leo's mother lay atop one pyre shrouded in the red blanket, Bogdan in the other. They had laid the wolf's fur coat on his chest and folded his hands over it.

Oksana and Leo stood on either side of Galina, each holding a burning torch, the firelight glistening off the tears on all their cheeks.

"Should we say some words?" Oksana looked from Galina to Leo.

Leo looked at her with tears brimming in his eyes, then walked forward and placed the intricately carved house Bogdan had given him beside then man's body. Then he turned and slid the torch into the base of his mother's pyre. He silently watched the flames spread across the dry wood, rising toward the timber planks supporting his mother's body as Oksana came forward and slipped her torch into Bogdan's pyre. They walked back to Galina, side by side, as the wood of the burning pyres crackled and popped behind them. The three of them watched as the fires consumed the bodies, their eyes watching the dark tendrils of smoke rise and be carried away by the breeze. Oksana grabbed Leo's hand, holding it tight, as Galina began to sing softly. It was an old Russian folk song that her mother sang to her as a child. Galina's voice was soft and mournful as she sang the tale of a snow girl who dreamed of falling in love and then melted as love finally filled her heart. When she finished, they stood silently watching the blazes consume the pyres, the firelight reflected in their eyes.

"Someone is coming," Oksana said, turning toward the road. The others heard it too and turned, a feeling of dread washing over them at what further terror and heartbreak this day could bring them.

"I don't believe it," Galina stared in disbelief as Seryy walked into the clearing, still trailing the empty wagon behind him.

The donkey stopped by a patch of grass and dipped his head to pull and chew the tender blades as he raised his head to gaze disinterestedly at the three figures before the blazing fires.

"He knew his way home," a sad smile crossed Leo's face as he stared at the donkey. "I'm guessing my father's horse found his way back to the Land Captain's stables."

A smile crossed Galina's face, "I think we just found our way out of here."

***

The pyres had burned down to smoldering embers as they loaded the wagon with the last of Bogdan's supplies by moonlight.

"What should we do with them?" Oksana looked up at Galina, seated on the wagon's bench, and gestured to the bodies of Volkov and Razin.

Galina adjusted the reins in her right hand as she glanced at the bodies, a sour expression marring her beautiful face, "Leave them for the crows and wolves."

Oksana nodded in agreement and climbed up alongside Galina. She took a last look around as Leo approached the wagon. The ghosts of her memories haunted her as she looked at the cottage and old barn, remembering them in happier times: Bogdan sitting on the porch with his broad grin, Alexei sneaking glances at her as he worked in the barn, and the hours of laughing and talking with Galina in the kitchen. Oksana sighed; so much had changed, and so much had been lost. She watched Leo, trapped in a chair his whole life, walking toward the cart and smiled at him, realizing much had also been gained. He awkwardly returned her smile and looked down at his feet.

"Leo, you can ride in the back for now; we can all change spots once my rear falls asleep sitting on this bench," Galina winked.

Leo smiled, and Oksana could swear she saw him blush even in the dim light.

"I," Leo paused, looking down as he shifted his feet before meeting their gaze. "I'm not coming with you to Kalinin."

"What?" Oksana could not contain her surprise.

"Leo," Galina's voice was calm. "You cannot stay here; Obrechen is not safe, especially for us."

"I'm not going to stay in Obrechen. In fact, and please don't take this the wrong way, I don't want to go anywhere where there are people after this. At least, not for a long time." Leo slipped his hands into his pockets to keep from fidgeting.

"I do understand, Leo." Oksana could see from Galina's smile that she genuinely understood. However, Oksana did not.

"Where will you go?" Oksana asked, her brows furrowing in concern. "What will you do?"

"I've spent my whole life sitting on a porch watching people walk by," Leo replied, a wistful smile crossing his face at the memories. "I'm going to spend some time as a wolf; I want to run through the forests, drink from mountain streams, sleep under the stars, and howl at the moon."

"Leo, these woods will be dangerous for a wolf, too," Galina cautioned.

Leo nodded and looked back at the burning embers of the pyres before returning his eyes to the women. "I know. I'm going to head toward Romania. Bogdan told me of his Carpathian Mountains; I want to see them for myself."

"Leo, this is foolish," Oksana began, but Galina touched her shoulder and shook her head slightly.

"Are you sure we can't convince you to come with us?" Galina asked.

"No," Leo shook his head and gave them a broad, genuine smile. "This is what I want."

"Okay, then," Galina nodded and bit her lip to suppress the emotion that comes with sad partings.

"I'm sorry," Leo offered in all sincerity. "I will miss you both terribly."

"There's no need to be sorry, Leo," Galina smiled, although Oksana saw it did not reach her eyes. "We will miss you too."

"Oh, Leo," Oksana tried to be as strong as Galina, but she could not help the tears from flowing. She reached out to him, and he took her hands in his.

"Oksana, it just wouldn't be fair of me to spend all my time with two women and leave all the rest alone in the world," Leo looked up and gave her a gap-toothed grin.

Despite her sadness and tears, Oksana laughed. She wiped the tears from her eyes and smiled at him, "Goodbye, Leo."

"It's not goodbye," Leo grinned. "We'll see each other again, I promise. Now get out of here before we all start crying again."

"Take care of yourself, Leo," Galina nodded as she gently urged Seryy, and the wagon eased forward.

Leo stepped back and waved to them as the wagon began to roll forward. Oksana waved and turned forward with a deep sigh; then, she remembered all the afternoons she and Alexei had sat on Leo's porch and turned back to look at the solitary figure.

"Don't let Baba Yaga get you," Oksana called out to him, waving goodbye one last time.

She heard Leo laugh loudly, and he called back to her, "Just make sure she doesn't get you first!"

Oksana smiled as she turned to face the road. The familiar valediction felt right, and she thought Alexei would approve. When

Oksana turned back again, a large white wolf sat where Leo had stood only moments before. She glanced back one final time as the wagon turned the bend in the road, and the wolf was gone; the cottage and the old barn sat alone in the growing darkness.

Chapter 10

Oksana dipped the hood of her dark cloak forward, hiding her face in the garment's shadows as she navigated the bustling Kalinin market. She grunted as a woman's elbow jolted her in the ribs as the woman attempted to push her way to a merchant selling savory, roasted cuts of meat. There were presently more people in the market than Oksana had ever seen in her life in totality, and the crush of humanity on a girl used to the open spaces of the village was beginning to grate on her nerves. It took all her restraint not to jab her elbow back at the woman or swing a leg out and send the woman sprawling. A week in Kalinin had quickly assuaged Oksana of any notions of life in the city.

In their first days after reaching Kalinin, the sights and sounds of the city overwhelmed Oksana, and she relished the quiet time when they retreated to the privacy of the room they had rented at an inn on the outskirts of the city. While Galina was far more accustomed to Kalinin's hectic pace, she, like Oksana, quickly learned that their heightened wolf senses had a significant drawback. Their sense of smell easily penetrated past the surface aromas of meats, pastries, and flowers from the merchant carts lining the streets. They detected the pungent odors of the city; scents of sweat, filth, and sewage. The rodents that roamed the alleyways of Kalinin did not escape their detection, even in the city's finest establishments. On their first afternoon in Kalinin, they purchased new clothes, the finest Oksana had ever owned, including a matching pair of black hooded cloaks that they would use to conceal their identities as they traversed Kalinin. However, by the end of the day, the barrage of foul underlying scents that assaulted their olfactory senses left them both retching violently.

They slowly mastered balancing smells, as Oksana assumed the wolf could do in a forest full of scents. In the privacy of their room, Oksana would lay on her bed and close her eyes, probing her mind for the wolf. She could feel it there in the forest, pacing like a caged beast, filled with unease. Oksana supposed the city was as unnatural a place for the wolf as it was for her.

Since arriving in Kalinin, Galina had grown steadily distant, preoccupied with thoughts of Mali. On the road to the city, Galina excitedly talked about seeing Mali again. She believed that they would rekindle their love, and Mali would ask her to make her a werewolf so the three of them could flee Kalinin and Count Guriev together and start life anew somewhere no one knew them—Paris or Berlin. Between Galina's money and what Oksana had taken from Father Grigori, they could live comfortably as Bohemian artists.

Oksana thought the notion sounded grand and romantic, and she tried to share Galina's enthusiasm when they spoke. However, Oksana harbored doubts. Unlike Galina, nothing in Oksana's life had made her believe that her story could have happy endings. It did not for Alexei. It did not happen that way for Bogdan; and Oksana doubted it would for her and Galina either. Even if Mali decided to run away with Galina, Oksana doubted that the woman would see a place for a simple village girl in their lives.

However, the immediate problem they faced was how to reach Mali. Aside from the fact that word of Galina's supposed death at the hands of the wolf likely reached the Count and Countess of Kalinin already, Gennady Guriev had made it clear that Galina was a most unwelcome guest, so walking up to the gates of their manor house was not a tenable course of action.

Galina knew Mali often frequented the market, so they spent their days walking among the shops and vendors, hoping to spot her. However, the first days proved fruitless. An overriding sense of tension cast a pall over the market, which was palpable even to Oksana. When Galina inquired of a merchant about the mood, he told her everyone was on edge after *Narodnaya Volya* revolutionaries attacked a small village north of the city. He claimed to have heard that Jews and socialists murdered a distant relative of the Tsar, then burned the village and killed the Land Captain. Count Guriev had already had several of the perpetrators arrested.

"It may be several days before the Count allows Mali to venture out," Galina had told her in hushed tones as they left the merchant.

Galina spent her evenings staring out the window, in the direction of the Count's manor, a large and stately building that sat on a rise in the wealthy quarter of Kalinin. It rose above the rooftops, allowing Count Guriev to look down upon his domain. A protective wall surrounded the manor's extensive gardens, courtyards, and stables. Galina told her the Count's great-grandfather erected the wall after the Decrembrist revolt in 1825. The lights of the manor house blazed at night, a beacon in the darkness, attesting to the life lived within. Oksana imagined it was torturous for Galina to be so close to her love yet held away at a distance.

As Oksana spotted the dark-cloaked figure examining a merchant's bolts of cloth and adjusted her course, she thought Galina's nights of torture might be finally coming to an end.

"Mali is in the market," Oksana whispered as she sidled alongside the hooded figure.

"Where?" Galina turned, her eyes wide with excitement.

"She's by the fruit merchants, in the corner closest to the fishmonger," Oksana replied in a hushed tone.

"We must go quickly before she returns to the estate," Galina said, rushing away.

"Wait," Oksana grabbed her arm and pulled her close. "There's a problem; she's not alone."

"The Count is with her?" Concern flickered across Galina.

Oksana shook her head, "Worse. McMurrough and a few armed men."

"Of course The Count would not let her walk the city alone with so much unrest afoot." Galina looked down at the cobblestone street and bit her bottom lip, a habit Oksana had noticed the woman did when in deep thought. "We have to chance it; come I have an idea."

***

Oksana approached the fruit merchant's cart, walking as Galina had instructed her, with an air of casual indifference to avoid attracting attention. She angled her approach to keep Mali between her and the Count's guardsman standing a few paces behind the Countess, hoping the taller woman would obstruct the guardsman's view.

The merchant, a balding, thick-limbed man, had arranged his four carts of fruit in a rough semicircle, with two positioned front-to-back and one angled off each end. Oksana glanced briefly at the merchant. He was engaged in an animated discussion with a thin, well-dressed man who appeared to be purchasing a large amount of the merchant's produce for a nobleman's birthday celebration. She returned her gaze to the woman, carefully scrutinizing bushels of fresh winter berries.

"I understand the sea buckthorn berries are particularly ripe," Oksana said as she approached the cart across from the woman and pointed to the basket of orange berries.

"Thank you," the woman said politely, barely looking at Oksana.

"Galina said they were your favorite," Oksana said, lowering her voice to a conspiratorial tone.

The woman visibly stiffened, then looked at Oksana, her face tense as she studied the young girl in the dark hooded cloak.

"Excuse me?" Mali asked, the lines of her jaw tightening as she tried to hide her surprise.

"Galina Sekova told me sea buckthorn are your favorite," Oksana locked eyes with Mali.

"Why, yes, they are," Mali feigned a brief smile. "Were you a friend of Galina's?"

"I *am* a friend of Galina's," Oksana corrected, emphasizing the word.

"You must not have heard," Mali placed a hand over her heart, looking grief-stricken. "Galina met with a terrible fate in those troubles in the north."

"Galina is alive; she's here with me," Oksana said, surprised at how sharp her words were. She felt a pang of guilt. This woman had done her no wrong; she was letting her fears of the future jade her against Mali.

"Galina is," Mali paused, shaking her head slightly in disbelief, "alive?"

"Look toward the fishmonger," Oksana gestured with a nod.

Mali turned hesitantly and froze as she saw the hooded woman beside the fishmonger's cart. Oksana heard the woman gasp as Galina pulled open her hood and locked eyes with Mali. Oksana could see a wide grin crossing Galina's face before she secreted herself back within the folds of her hood.

"How?" Mali whirled quickly to face Oksana, the sudden motion attracting the attention of her guardsman escort. The man craned his neck to get a look at Oksana.

"Galina wants to meet with you," Oksana said hurriedly as the guardsman approached.

"Hey, step back from the Countess," the guardsman called as he approached.

Using Mali's title caught the merchant's attention, and the man quickly ended his conversation and began walking toward them. Their time was running short; Oksana looked toward Mali, raising one eyebrow questioningly.

"Tell her to come tonight. I'll send the servants away. Have her use the gardener's gate; it will be unlocked," Mali whispered, then turned to the guardsman. "I am not feeling well. Will you please take me home?"

The man looked from Oksana to Mali and nodded, "Yes, Countess."

"Is there something wrong, Sergeant?" An Irish-accented voice called from behind Oksana, and her blood ran cold as she heard McMurrough's footsteps approach.

Oksana turned to head into the crowd and caught sight of the Irishman approaching in her periphery, flanked by two more of the Count's guards. The man glanced at her, his eyes narrowing as she hastened away.

"Bring me that girl," Oksana heard him order, and one of the guards rushed forward, grabbing her arm.

The man's grip was vice-like, as his fingers closed tightly around her upper arm. In Oksana's mind, she heard the wolf growling from the woods, and a sudden rush of fear coursed through her as she imagined transforming amidst the crowded market. She wanted to glance at Galina, but she feared the movement would also direct McMurrough's attention to her.

"Come here," the guard barked, yanking hard on Oksana's arm.

Oksana gritted her teeth against the sharp pain in her arm and felt her anger rise. She had had enough of men like her uncle and Father Grigori, who thought they could do as they wished because she was a woman. Who had set the world on this path? They were big, and she was small. They were strong, and she was weak. They were men, and she was a woman. So they yanked, and she would have to come. But no more.

With the wolf's preternatural strength in her veins, Oksana yanked her arm free of the man's grip and turned on him with teeth bared in a snarl. The man looked surprised at her ability to escape his hold so easily as behind him, the second guard surged forward. Oksana stepped forward and struck the man hard in the chest with both hands, sending him tumbling backward into his companion, and the two crashed to the ground in a tangled heap.

The crowd around her moved away quickly from the commotion, and suddenly, Oksana heard Galina shout that there were revolutionaries in the market. Shouts of "revolutionaries" and "*Narodnaya Volya*" quickly rippled through the crowd, stoking already simmering fears and moving the crowd into a panic. People began to run in every direction, and Oksana could see McMurrough trying to push his way through the crowd toward her. McMurrough drew his pistol, alarming others in the crowd and adding to the bedlam.

Oksana slipped in among the running merchants and citizens in the chaos as she fled toward safety. As a hand reached out and grabbed her shoulder, she whirled, ready to confront a new attacker.

"Come this way," Galina pulled her toward an alley.

The alley twisted and turned, opening into a series of side streets, the sound of their footfalls on quiet cobblestone streets quickly replacing the din of the market as they ran.

***

Galina glanced up at the night sky. The waxing gibbous moon was nearly a perfect circle, no more than another night or two before it was full. It illuminated their way along the perimeter wall of the Count of Kalinin's manor house without needing lanterns, for which Galina was grateful. Even more critical, in the bright moonlight, the ten-foot-high wall cast a long shadow obscuring the street in darkness. As long as they stayed in the shadows, their dark cloaks would hide her and Oksana from unwanted eyes staring out the manor's upper-floor windows.

"Are you sure this is the right way?" Oksana whispered from behind her.

"Yes, I used to use this entrance to meet with Mali when I lived in Kalinin," Galina responded without looking back.

Something scurried near her foot, and Galina's heightened senses could smell the oiliness of the rodent's fur. Behind her, Oksana gave a disgusted grunt, and Galina knew that she, too, smelled the other creatures using the cover of the shadows to move about the night.

A rectangular shape marred the symmetry of the wall, and Galina smiled as she ran a hand along the iron and reinforced wood of the worn door.

"This is it," Galina whispered as Oksana came alongside her. Even in the dim light, she could see the girl's apprehension and knew Oksana was concerned about how Mali's presence in their small pack would affect their dynamic. She smiled and reassured Oksana, "It's going to be okay."

The smaller girl nodded, her hooded head barely registering the action, as Galina turned back to the gardener's door. Galina took a deep breath, placing her hand on the cold iron ring of the door handle, and steadied herself. If the door remained barred, this would be a very short and disappointing night.

She pushed, and the door eased open. Behind her, Galina could hear Oksana exhale deeply; apparently, she was not the only one holding her breath, which gave Galina an oddly comforting feeling. She was thankful for Oksana's presence tonight; the two had been through a great deal together and, beyond the lupine bond they shared, Galina cherished the girl's genuine friendship.

The heavy wooden door grated and squeaked on its hinges as it swung open, and Galina prayed to whatever god watched over werewolves that none of the Count's guards heard the noise and came to investigate. The door led to a tall hedgerow that traced the inside of the wall. The hedgerow masked the narrow pathway the gardeners used to traverse the grounds, hiding the workers from the sight of the manor's residents and guests as they moved about. The narrow dirt path was shrouded in total darkness as it branched along the wall in either direction from the door. A short cobblestone walk, bulwarked on either side by more of the tall hedge, ran forward from the door for several feet before turning right and opening onto the manor's lawn.

Galina knew all too well that the patio and French doors to Mali's sitting parlor lay only a few dozen feet beyond.

"Once we exit the hedge, we'll be in easy view of anyone looking out a window, so we'll have to move quickly," Galina whispered as Oksana slid the door closed behind them.

"Miss Galina?" a hushed voice asked from the darkness of the gardener's path, and Galina felt the blood in her veins go cold.

Oksana pressed her back against the door as Galina turned to stare into the darkness. She could see the silhouette of a man stooped with age or infirmity standing between the hedge and the wall. As she peered into the gloom, the man shuffled forward into the dim light, and she gasped. It was Jacob, Mali's coachman.

Although the coachman had never dressed in finery, Galina had always found the man's clothing clean and presentable. Now, the man's clothes were dirty and sweat-stained with the pungent smell of manure as if he had been laboring in the stables. However, his face shocked Galina so severely that she brought her hand to her mouth in surprise. His neatly trimmed beard was now scraggly and unkempt, and his left eye socket was puckered and swollen with infection and puss.

"Jacob, what has happened to you?" Galina could see that the man felt self-conscious about her reaction and tried to smooth the wrinkles from his clothes.

"Miss Galina, you should not be here. It's not safe," Jacob stepped forward, his one good eye growing wide with alarm.

"Jacob, who did this to you?" As she looked into the old man's ruined face, Galina felt her features soften with sadness.

He raised a shaking hand to the puckered wound where his left eye had been, then lowered it as his remaining eye brimmed with tears, "I'm sorry, Miss Galina. I did not want to tell him about you and the

Countess. I tried to be strong, but he hurt me. He hurt me so bad, and then he said he would hurt my wife if I did not tell him. So, I told him everything."

"The Count did this to you?" Oksana asked, stepping away from the door.

Jacob seemed startled, noticing Oksana for the first time, and shook his head, "No, it was his Irish dog, McMurrough."

Oksana gave Galina a warning glance at the mention of the Irishman's name and then returned her attention to Jacob. "How did you know we were coming?"

"They sent all the servants home, and the Countess asked that I leave the gardener's door unbarred," a smile briefly crossed his face as he returned his attention to Galina, his voice cracking with emotion. "I thought it might be you, Miss Galina; I waited here to see, to warn you that the Count and McMurrough will hurt you if they find you here."

"It is okay, Jacob. I am here at the Countess' request; Guriev and McMurrough will never see me. Everything is going to be okay," Galina said, touching his arm and then his cheek. "You are a good man, Jacob. It was courageous of you to warn me."

"I am no brave man," a tear ran down Jacob's cheek and disappeared into his grizzled beard. "A brave man would have protected your secret."

"You will always be a brave man to me and a dear friend," Galina gave the man a genuine smile. "My friend and I must go now, Jacob. Take care of yourself."

Galina's heart felt heavy for the pain the broken coachman had endured for her, but she could toil with him no longer. His savaged eye was proof of what McMurrough would be capable of if he found them on the grounds. She could hear Oksana's footsteps behind her, crunching on the short grass as they moved quickly across the lawn to Mali's parlor.

As they approached the two large French doors leading inside, Galina halted, feeling her heart racing. Through the glass panes, she saw Mali seated at a small table with a kerosene lamp, sipping tea. The lamp's flame reflected in Mali's eyes, and Galina felt a growing hunger for the woman building within her. She wondered what it would be like to make love with the wolf blood coursing through her veins. Galina pictured their love as wild and primal. Mali looked beautiful even though her face looked strained with worry, and Galina longed to take her in her arms and kiss all her worries away. Oksana stopped beside her and looked from Mali to Galina.

"Are we going in?" the tone of Oksana's voice suggested she was as equally fine with either answer.

"Yes, of course," Galina breathed and walked forward to lightly rap her knuckles on one of the door's window panes.

Mali's head shot up like a startled cat, her face blanching of color when she saw the two girls at the door. Then she composed herself and stood, wiping away the wrinkles from her dress as she crossed the room to the door. Galina felt butterflies flutter in her stomach at their reunion; however, she felt a tinge of disappointment at Mali's less-than-exuberant reaction to her appearance. She chalked it up to the strain on Mali of meeting her in such close proximity to Gennady.

"Come inside quickly," Mali said as she opened the door, her eyes searching the outside night. "Were you seen?"

"No. By no one, I'm certain," replied Galina, grinning and throwing her arms around Mali's neck. "Oh, how I've missed you, my love!"

"I see you brought your little friend," Mali pulled her head back from Galina's attempted kiss to glare at Oksana.

"This is Oksana Nostrova; she is a good and loyal friend." As Galina turned to introduce her, Oksana dipped her head and curtsied, just as Galina had taught her. "I have so much to tell you, Mali. Something wondrous has happened."

"Let me make sure the servants do not disturb us," Mali stepped back and flashed a quick smile before slipping out the door.

Galina felt flushed. Her heart raced, and her pulse quickened as she watched Mali leave. She could not believe they were finally reunited and would never be parted again after tonight.

"I thought Jacob said the servants were all dismissed for the night," Oksana said, furrowing her eyebrows as she watched the door close.

"Mali is a countess; she has maidservants that are always nearby," Galina smiled as she looked at Oksana and then back to the door, waiting for Mali to re-emerge.

"Is she always so cold?" Oksana asked.

"All of this is very sudden and surprising; after all, she thought I was dead," Galina frowned, annoyed at Oksana's disparaging tone. Then she caught sight of herself in a mirror on the wall, and her hands rushed up to fix her hair. "Look at me; I look a fright!"

"You look pretty good for someone returned from the dead," quipped Oksana as she looked around the room.

"Well, now, that's taken care of," Mali said as she re-entered the room and closed the door. She looked at Oksana and feigned a weak smile before crossing the room and picking up her cup of tea.

Mali took a sip and briefly met Galina's eyes before averting her gaze out the window. Galina felt a pang of hurt and annoyance at Mali's behavior. She did not expect the woman to come rushing to her and fall into her arms. Galina would have loved that, but that was never Mali, especially with someone unfamiliar in the room. However, she expected more than this standoffish welcome. Galina briefly wondered if she should have left Oksana back at the inn.

"So much has happened, Mali," Galina felt flush with excitement. "Some of it will be very hard to believe at first, but the most important thing is that I have found a way for us to be together, far away from this place and Gennady."

"Why couldn't you have just died, Galina?" Mali uttered the words with bitterness as she shook her head and then took another sip of tea.

Galina felt her body suddenly become rigid in shocked; surely she had misheard. However, the look of surprise on Oksana's face confirmed that Galina's ears were correct.

"What?" Galina stammered, her brain not comprehending how Mali could be saying these things.

"Doctor Artyom assured me that if you took that tincture regularly, you would just fade away and die," Mali's eyes were cold and emotionless as she looked at Galina. "Don't look so hurt; you have cancer in your gut; Doctor Artyom is sure of it. The tincture would have taken away your pain and sped your passing. You should see it as a mercy."

"You knew I was sick? Artyom told me they were womanly pains; why would you lie to me?" Galina's hand went reflexively to the place in her side that used to ache terribly before the transformation cured her.

Mali laughed mirthlessly, "Because I know you, Galina. You would have come running to me with some romantic notion of spending your last days together, of dying in my arms as I wept over your body and professed my undying love for you. I told Doctor Artyom to give you something for the pain; he suggested he could add arsenic to the tincture. You would not smell or taste it, but every time the tincture took away your pain, the poison would build in your body until one morning, you simply did not wake again."

"Why would you do that?" Galina was stunned. "I loved you."

"Oh, Galina," Mali scoffed and put the cup of tea on the table beside the kerosene lamp. "Grow up. We had fun as girls in the Tsar's court, but I am a countess—the Countess of Kalinin. I gave you so many chances. You could have married one of the noblemen, and we could have had our dalliances together occasionally, but you were greedy and wanted me all to yourself. You would have ruined everything. Once I learned of your illness, I knew you would have expected me to care for you until the end. I am a noblewoman, Galina, with responsibilities and commitments; I cannot play nursemaid to the dying daughter of some insignificant boyar. The death I offered you was the better option; you have no one to blame now but yourself."

"I loved you," Galina felt breathless, her chest and stomach tightening like a vice.

"Galina!" Oksana's voice warned as the door opened, and two men, McMurrough and Gennady Guriev, entered.

"Good evening, Galina," McMurrough brandished a pistol in one hand. His eyes narrowed, and a cruel smile crossed his lips, turning his mustache up at the corners as he looked at Oksana, "I am happy you brought your little friend; I know some guardsmen who are eager to make your re-acquaintance. Stand over by your whore friend."

As McMurrough herded Oksana across the room with the barrel of his pistol, Guriev leaned against the wall and folded his arms across his chest. He stared at Galina and gave a cruel, mocking laugh.

"You are pathetic," Guriev shook his head. "A stupid little girl who thought she could take something away from me. James, I believe we have captured two of the revolutionaries responsible for the atrocities in Obrechen. I want them thoroughly interrogated, no matter how unpleasant, and then I want them hanged by the neck until dead."

"Count Guriev, I can assure you I will be very thorough," McMurrough flashed a wicked smile, "no matter how unpleasant."

"Mali?" Galina's voice strained as the love of her life turned from her and stared out the French doors.

Galina suddenly felt rooted in place, unable to move, a silent witness to the events unfolding around her. Everyone around her appeared to be moving in slow motion as if their movements were through a water medium. Her eyes shifted to the left as the door to the room opened, and Jacob rushed in, each step taking an innumerable number of heartbeats to occur. His face was twisted in fury as he bellowed McMurrough's name, a double-barreled shotgun in his hands that slowly wheeled to point at the Irishman.

The glass panes of the French doors exploded inwards, a million shards of glass taking a lifetime to fly through the air, showering Mali in a snowfall of glass, each shard glittering and twinkling in the lamplight. Beside her, Oksana screamed and fell to her hands and knees, her scream transforming into a snarl. Galina felt Oksana's wolf approaching, running through the forest in the girl's mind to erupt into this world.

"No, Oksana, not yet," Galina shouted in warning, and she felt Oksana pull back from the transformation. In her mind, Galina felt her wolf battering against the wardrobe door, eager to run with its pack, to tear into the world and reap carnage upon the men threatening them.

Before the French doors, Mali screamed and fell to the floor as an immense white shape leaped through the storm of broken wood and glass. Galina could see it was a wolf, gliding through the air so slowly that it appeared to fly, reminding her of storybook drawings of animals jumping over the moon.

Leo. Oh god its, Leo. Galina's mind screamed amid the chaos.

The wolf roared as it moved through the air and crashed into McMurrough. The Irishman staggered backward, his arm swinging wildly as the pistol discharged. Galina watched the projectile travel across the room and enter Gennady Guriev's forehead, the man's face registering a momentary shock before his head slammed back against the wall, a splash of blood and brain painting the wall in a crimson explosion.

Galina's eyes darted back toward the door as Jacob's shotgun roared, deafening Galina and bathing the room in a bright flash of light. She could see the tight cluster of round lead balls leave the barrel of the shotgun and slowly sail across the room, planets traveling through the solar system in a deadly orbit.

McMurrough struggled to keep his balance as Leo's furious roar transformed into a yelp of pain as Jacob's shotgun pellets completed their deadly journey, slamming into the wolf's midsection. Leo's wolf body contorted around the impact, the force causing his fur to ripple outward from a gaping wound that splashed blood, bone, and gore across his white fur. His body hit the floor heavily, legs bouncing lifelessly.

As if Leo's body striking the floor suddenly jarred time back onto its track, the feeling of slow motion around Galina immediately ceased. The sensation was so jarring that she was momentarily dizzy.

"Leo!" Oksana wailed and reached for the wolf lying prone on the ground, its side moving up and down in a slow, labored breath. She began to crawl across the shards of the glass littering the floor toward him.

"Great shot, old man!" McMurrough stared down at the wolf's body, a smile crossing his face dotted with droplets of Leo's blood.

As he grinned at Jacob, the old man stared in shock at the wolf lying on the floor. Then, as he moved his eyes to McMurrough, his countenance hardened, and he raised the barrel of the shotgun in unsteady hands. McMurrough's smile slowly slipped from his face as his arm whipped up, and the pistol bucked in his hand as it fired. The loud report of the gun made Galina jump as Jacob staggered back, the shotgun falling from his grip as his hands flew to his throat. The coachman gurgled, blood pouring through his fingers in red torrents as he slid down the door, leaving a bloody smear along the white paint.

Enraged, Galina grabbed the kerosene lamp from the table and hurled it at McMurrough. The Irishman, too busy smirking at Jacob seated on the floor choking as his lifeblood gushed from his mortally wounded throat, did not notice the hurtling lamp until it crashed into the side of his head. The glass lamp shattered, dousing McMurrough's head and chest in kerosene oil and splattering the wall behind him. Startled, the man sputtered to spit the liquid from his lips, staring at Galina in wide-eyed disbelief as the oil ignited.

The flames spread, engulfing McMurrough and the oily smell of burning flesh filled the room, mixing with the metallic scent of gunpowder. The man screamed and whirled like a macabre ballerina as he beat at the flames devouring his face. He staggered and fell against the wall, igniting the kerosene streaking the wall. McMurrough's screams died down to a guttural wail as the flesh of his throat blackened and charred to ruin.

Galina walked to where Jacob now lay motionless in a pool of blood, his lone eye staring sightlessly at McMurrough's fiery demise, a silent witness to his tormentor's death. She knelt and retrieved the coachman's shotgun, the stock and trigger now sticky with his blood.

Galina pointed the barrel at the writhing form of McMurrough and paused; the man deserved to die slowly and painfully.

Across the room, Leo had transformed back into human form, and Oksana had draped her cloak over the boy's naked body. The girl was brushing the hair from his face and talking to him softly. Oksana looked back at Galina, and the look in her eyes told Galina all she needed to know about Leo's condition.

The fire spreading up the walls and licking at the ceiling felt hot on Galina's face as she turned to McMurrough. The mewing sound from the hole that had once been a mouth on a face now devoid of flesh and eyes that had since sizzled and popped in the heat evidenced the agony of his death throes. Galina fired the shot, the blast striking McMurrough in the chest and stilling the man, except for the curling of his limbs spasming against the flames as his ligaments contracted from the heat. It was no act of mercy; Galina believed McMurrough did not deserve to outlive Leo, even if his final moments were in torment. Spent, Galina dropped the shotgun and wiped her bloody hands on her cloak.

As Galina walked to where Leo lay and knelt beside Oksana, she could see the flames had extended their reach toward Count Guriev. The man's death mask mirrored the shock of his final moments, his eyes wide and mouth agape as the fire licked at his clothing.

"Leo," Galina's voice was soft as she touched his shoulder.

His eyes moved from Oksana's face to hers, and the boy manifested his gap-toothed grin through lips and teeth were pink with blood, "I told you it was not goodbye."

A cough overcame his smile, and he swallowed hard.

"You did, Leo; you did," Oksana sobbed. "You saved us."

"I always told Alexei I would be the hero of our story one day," Leo's grin returned. "Don't cry, Oksana; it doesn't even hurt. I can't feel a thing. Really."

"Leo, how did you find us?" Galina blinked back tears.

"In the woods, there was a house. She told me to come here. You were in danger. It even had legs like a chicken. I can't wait to tell Alexei," Leo smiled as his eyes took on a far-off gaze, and then he fell silent.

"Leo? Leo?" Oksana shook his body as she sobbed. "Leo, don't go. Don't leave me too."

"Oksana, he's gone," Galina put a consoling arm around her. "We have to go; the fire will bring people if the gunshots have not already."

"We have to take Leo; we can't leave him here," Oksana pleaded.

Galina shook her head, "Let the smoke take him onto the wind with Alexei and his mother."

Oksana looked down at Leo's still body and then back to Galina, nodding, "Yes, he would like that."

They said their goodbyes to Leo, and Oksana bent and kissed him on the forehead before covering his head with the cloak. The room had gotten intensely hot as the flames greedily consumed the walls and ceiling. Sweat ran down Galina's back as they fled toward the shattered French doors.

"Galina," Oksana grabbed her arm and gestured to the still form beside the doors.

Galina looked down at Mali, who appeared to be sleeping on the floor, her arms resting by her side. Her face was so serene that it reminded Galina of how Mali had looked dozing on a pillow beside her on a hundred mornings. Had it not been for the jagged piece of glass that protruded from the side of her neck and the blood that stained her dress and pooled about her head Galina might have thought she was just sleeping.

"It must have happened when Leo leaped through the doors," Oksana observed.

Galina thought she would feel something looking at Mali's body, but her heart felt cold. So many had died so Galina could live—Leo, Alexei, and Bogdan. Yet Mali, who she had loved above all else in this life, was willing to see her killed because she had become an inconvenience. In Mali's eyes, their love was a pale shadow in a life of privilege and comfort.

Galina turned to Oksana, "Let's go."

The two fled across the lawn as the fire spread rapidly across the manor, lighting the night sky. As they passed through the gardener's entrance, people had begun to gather in the streets, and several pairs of eyes studied them curiously as they exited. However, no one hindered their passage as they disappeared into the winding city streets.

***

Seryy slowly pulled the wagon down the road as the morning sun crept over the horizon. Behind them, dark plumes of smoke rose from the smoldering ruin of the Count's manor, though neither turned to look. Galina and Oksana rode alongside each other on the wagon's bench, both silent and numbed by the previous night's events.

A wind blew across their faces, and Oksana stared up at the fluttering branches and smiled. Galina looked at the girl and knew she was thinking of their lost friends traveling in the breeze.

"I miss them—Alexei, Leo, Bogdan," Oksana said as she looked up at the sky. "Do you really think they're up there riding on the wind?"

"I do," Galina nodded and looked up at the sky. "Bogdan is once again with his wife, and Leo and Alexei are probably chasing poor Baba Yaga through the forest."

Oksana laughed at that thought and then grew serious, "Part of me thinks that Alexei was too angry for this world and Leo was too gentle."

"This world did not deserve either of them," Galina leaned over so that her shoulder touched Oksana's.

Galina reined Seryy to a halt as the road before them split three ways. The women stared at the diverging paths as Seryy turned to glance at them with large brown eyes.

"That way leads back to Obrechen," Galina pointed to the road branching to the left. "I don't think we want to go that way."

Oksana shook her head, "Definitely not that way."

"That one leads to Moscow and St. Petersburg," Galina gestured to the right, then pointed to the middle road. "That one eventually goes to Germany."

Oksana stared at each path and then looked sidelong at Galina, asking, "What is beyond Germany?"

Galina thought about it, then responded, "The sea, I believe."

"I've always wanted to see the ocean," Oksana let the slightest hint of a smile cross her lips.

"You know, I have too. North to the sea, it is," Galina nodded and returned the smile as she urged Seryy forward.

As the wagon crossed onto the northward road, both women felt a lightness, as if a great weight was behind them. Galina felt like smiling, and when she glanced at Oksana, she saw that the girl had begun smiling, too.

"You know we're an anomaly in this world. We have no men to try to tame us or break our spirits. The world is ours to explore. We can live where we wish, dress how we like, love who we choose. We can do whatever we want, and we have enough money to last us for a very long time," Galina glanced down at the satchel between them.

Oksana thought about that as she watched the road unfold before them, and she could not help but adding, "And we're fucking werewolves."

Galina smiled and nodded, "And we're fucking werewolves."

Jack Finn is a horror author and active Horror Writers Association member living in the wilds of the Pacific Northwest with his wife and two fiendishly clever dogs. He is a lifelong believer that the Tooth Fairy proves you can trade body parts for cold, hard cash.

Jack's books include THE SEVEN DEATHS OF PRINCE VLAD (Anuci Press 2024), The Wolves of Kalin werewolf duology: PREY UPON THE LAMBS (Anuci Press 2025) and THE DESOLATION OF HUNTERS (Anuci Press 20250, a collection short stories THEY COME WHEN YOU SLEEP (Velox Books 2025), and the forthcoming Book of Alice duology (Edge Weaver Books, 2026)

His short stories have been included in Terrorcore Publishing's DOORS OF DARKNESS, January Ember Press' HORROSCOPE 4, Dark Village Publications' TWELVE MONTHS OF HORROR, Voices From the Mausoleum's HOWLIN' FOR YOU, and Edge Weaver Books upcoming TALES FROM THE CURSED EDGE.

Follow Jack at:

INSTAGRAM: https://www.instagram.com/therealjackfinn/
BLUESKY @therealjackfinn.bsky.social
TWITTER: http://www.twitter.com/therealjackfinn
THREADS: https://www.threads.com/@therealjackfinn
FACEBOOK: https://www.facebook.com/TheRealJackFinn
WEBSITE: www.therealjackfinn.com